For L

with love —

MONKEY TEMPLE

Peter

Monkey Temple

A novel
by

PETER GELFAN

Adelaide Books
New York/Lisbon
2019

MONKEY TEMPLE
A novel
By Peter Gelfan

Copyright © by Peter Gelfan
Cover design © 2019 Adelaide Books

Published by Adelaide Books, New York / Lisbon
adelaidebooks.org
Editor-in-Chief
Stevan V. Nikolic

For any information, please address Adelaide Books
at info@adelaidebooks.org
or write to:
Adelaide Books
244 Fifth Ave. Suite D27
New York, NY, 10001

ISBN-10: 1-949180-98-0
ISBN-13: 978-1-949180-98-5

Printed in the United States of America

To friends, here and gone.

Chapter 1

What the hell was Ralston doing here?

I could see him coming a block away. He moved with the same antsy saunter, scanning the landscape, zigzagging slightly when a woman, a ferret on a chain, a pastry shop, then four kids on one bike caught his interest for a moment. But his legs, whose rubbery flexibility used to give him the bounce of a cartoon sailor, now seemed firmly in the jealous grip of his hips. His hair fell to his shoulders in a fringe, gray and wispy now instead of dark and wild. He'd cut it short for a few years in the early '70s after truckers, construction workers, and clean-cut kids started wearing theirs long, but then he'd let it grow out enough to tie back in a stumpy ponytail.

I stood up from my sidewalk espresso. Ralston caught sight of me. "Jules!" He veered into the café and gave me his usual greeting. "Still mad at me?"

We shook hands and slapped shoulders. His hand felt warm and firm, but the shoulder seemed bonier. I patted it again more gently.

I remembered the ponytail breaking free in the late '70s, downtown on Broadway, across from Trinity Church, when Ralston had spotted another ponytail, this one coifed and conditioned, swaggering behind a Wall Street type in a perfectly fitted suit carrying a hand-tooled leather briefcase into a waiting limo. Without hesitation, Rals had stripped the rubber band from his hair forever, looped it around the tip of his index finger, pulled it back and shot it at the limo. Ponytail, Esq. hadn't blinked as it ricocheted off the tinted window six inches in front of his face.

Now, Ralston looked around. "Where are they holding this ghoulish farce?"

I pointed across the street.

He grabbed my cup and chugged the remains of my coffee. "Break a leg."

Bruno looked better than he had in ages. He'd done it all—read poetry with the beats, meditated with Zen monks in Japan, rode with the Merry Pranksters, studied with Sufis, and, while writing, lived off the land as a hunter-gatherer in the woods of Northern California. The last time I'd seen him, his face had been scarred with fear, loss, disappointment, drugs, disease, and self-excoriation both literal and figurative. Now, many of the lines had smoothed out, and a hint of his once jaunty smile was back. Alone with Bruno for a moment, I laid a hand on his lapel. "See you, old buddy."

Ritz came over and took my arm. "Jules, you okay, sweetie?" No, although this death was hardly unexpected. Now wasn't the time to talk about it. I pressed her hand close to my side. Ralston came up behind us and put one hand on my back, the other around Ritz's waist.

Ritz looked down at Bruno. "Why in God's name did they want an open casket?" It was a macabre ritual, dating back to the funerals of kings and warlords, when the new order wanted to prove to all comers that the old order was indeed dead. Bruno had been as good as dead for years, and everyone knew it.

"To show everybody it wasn't AIDS, I bet," Ralston said. "At least not the ugly kind that wrecks your face." No one knew exactly what had killed Bruno. I'd tried for years to drag him to a doctor, had even offered to pay the bills, but he always refused. After he was found dead in bed in his apartment, the medical examiner's office didn't deem him worthy of a thorough autopsy. Just another lonely old dead guy, spoiled meat in a clean suit.

I glanced over at the new order, Bruno's daughter and two sons, who looked back at me with tight-lipped suspicion and held their children close by. It wasn't personal, it seemed they'd always regarded their father's friends that way, our little crowd anyway. What had Bruno done to deserve such narrow-minded, straitlaced kids? No doubt they wondered what they'd done to deserve a dad like Bruno. Still, their embarrassment as kids and then disdain as adults had torn at him. It came out camouflaged as bitter abstractions in some of his poems—that's how I read them, anyway—or after a couple of glasses of wine on those rare occasions in the last decade when he'd accepted a dinner invitation. I brushed my fingers across his lapel one last time.

From the doorway, the funeral director caught my eye. I walked to a small podium set up in front of the somber rows of chairs. People took their seats quickly, probably energized by the thought that the ordeal would soon be over. Bruno's family circled their wagons in the front row to my left as if this were an acrimonious wedding rather than a ragtag funeral, one their father, in his handwritten will, had insisted they hold as a condition to inheriting his small but steady trickle of royalties. The others, in ones, twos, and threes, scattered themselves throughout the rest of the chairs, occasionally exchanging quiet greetings as they reencountered old friends.

One gray-haired old woman—old, Christ, she was probably ten years younger than me—wept openly, perhaps one of Bruno's ex-lovers. Ralston gathered her in his arms, kissed her forehead, and helped her sit down. Then he settled into a chair next to Ritz at the other end of the front row.

The family would be hoping for a short series of sorrowful platitudes. Too bad. I would do my best to follow the advice I give my clients: have something to say, get to it without a bunch of preliminary bullshit, jump out once you've said it, and avoid clichés.

"We're here to say our goodbyes to our dear friend Bruno," I said. "He lived an artist's life—brief moments of creative triumph paid for by years of struggle, rejection, and loneliness." Bruno's sour spawn sat in stoic pain.

"Like many of our generation," I said, "Bruno was an idealist, and idealists gravitate toward four possible fates. One is self-betrayal. We abandon our ideals, or shrink from their challenges, to take a safer, surer path." Ralston smirked and said something into Ritz's ear, but her eyes stayed on me, her expression almost worried.

"Two, failure. The world we envisioned—peace, enlightenment, beauty, freedom from oppression—seems further away than ever. Impossible. Laughable. One of the embarrassments of youth." A few nods from the other guests.

"Three, delusion. We convince ourselves we've attained what we set out to, and we ignore or explain away the huge pile of evidence to the contrary." Nary a twitch in the serene smile lounging across the face of Bruce Green, now Sri Green Baba, spiritual and culinary leader of an East Village macrobiotic ashram and trendy restaurant named, of course, Green.

"The fourth fate," I said, "is to be consumed by our quest. Addiction, jail, exile, insanity." Bruno's daughter pulled her small son closer.

I paused for a moment to look over at Bruno. "Bruno was among the lucky idealists. He fell into that fourth category, but his consumption was almost symbiotic, for his poetry sustained him even as it ate him alive. Bruno was a great friend…" I almost added that he was a profoundly compassionate human being, but that was only during those short, infrequent moments when he looked outside himself and beyond the notebook and pen that always seemed to eddy among his restless fingers.

"I could go on for hours." A gratifying spasm of horror flashed across a son's face. "But Bruno said it far better." I pointed across the room to a table holding a stack of small paperbacks—slender volumes of verse, in the parlance. "His poems and lyrics. He hoped you'd all take a book home with you."

I looked over at the family and waited for them to relent and speak at their father's funeral. They stared back at me. I wasn't going to fill the sucking silence for them.

Finally, the elder son said, "We've already said our good-byes."

Their good riddances, anyway. After a few moments, I nodded to Rosy, fidgeting near the coffee urn, who hit the button on a CD player. The opening chords of Zits Gone Wild's "Heaven and Hell"—a brief and modest underground hit back in the day, lyrics and piano by Bruno—quavered thinly from the tinny speakers. In unison, Bruno's progeny closed their eyes in excruciation. I smiled.

"See you around, old friend." The bittersweet scene and the music I hadn't heard in years choked me up. "Thank you all for coming." I faked a cough to the crook of my elbow to hide wiping away a tear and stepped away from the podium.

Mourners exchanged kisses, handshakes, and solemn nods. No one seemed inclined to stay long.

Ralston, his jagged leer now longer in the tooth, again had his arm tight around Ritz's waist. "What a load of horseshit."

"What's a funeral without a little horseshit?" I said. He was right of course. I had no idea where Bruno had gone wrong.

His smirk soured. "Who's next? You? Me? I hate these fucking things."

"Why'd you come?" I said. "You couldn't stand Bruno."

"Why's anybody come?"

Ritz pulled my head close to her face, caught my errant tear with a finger, and kissed my neck just below the ear. "Let's get out of here as soon as we decently can." She flicked a glance toward Ralston, who, jaw clenched, was scanning the room through narrowed eyes.

That evening, Ralston strode into our apartment, shoved a bottle of champagne into my arms, kissed Ritz's hand, then turned it over to nuzzle the inside of her slender wrist. Decades ago, I'd told him about that particular erogenous zone of hers, and he'd never forgotten it, had he? He wrapped me in a bear hug. Odd, he didn't used to be much of a hugger. I hugged him back. He felt almost frail.

"Good to see you, man. Why wait?" I peeled the foil from the champagne cork. "How about some glasses, Ritz?"

Instead, Ralston took Ritz's hand and pulled her into the living room. "Hey, Jules, I thought you were the kitchen bitch." Ritz could have grabbed the glasses anyway, but was now sitting across from him, laughing at some whispered joke. At least she'd parried his effort to pull her down next to him on the couch. Her smile and the intensity of her gaze told people they were special to her, a useful trick for anyone to master, but I was sure with her it was genuine. It still made me feel privileged, special among the special. I brought the glasses, sat

6

next to Ralston, and eased the cork out of the bottle with a faint whoosh.

"Still a silent but deadly kind of guy," he said.

"And you just let 'em rip."

"Less than a minute," Ritz said, "and already with the fart jokes."

Ralston's trips from Paris always came without advance notice and ended too soon. I'd started making a list of things I wanted to talk to him about, places to take him, new restaurants to try, secrets to pry out of him. I put on my reading glasses and peered at the label. Vintage Taittinger, higher-priced hooch than he usually sprung for. Something was up.

He poured the champagne, handed out the glasses, and then fixed me with his most compelling smile. "To the best of friends."

Definitely up.

"Best of friends." We all clinked, and I took a sip. "Sorry to hear about your dad."

"He was old. It was his time. *C'est la vie, c'est la mort.*" The who-gives-a-damn spin was no surprise; the lack of a parting shot at the old bastard was.

"*Comment ça va Martine?*" Ritz said.

"Okay."

"Just okay? Something wrong?"

"She's fine. What's Freddy up to?"

"He got a job with a firm downtown," I said.

"Environmental law?"

"Still hopes to." Ralston raised a tousled eyebrow at Ritz. I ducked back into the kitchen.

"Right now they have him on product-liability defense," she said.

"Jesus, what have you two spawned?"

I came back with olives. "A compulsively neat, sweet-natured, hardworking, sexually naïve—"

"We think."

"—drug-free—"

"We hope."

Another raised eyebrow from Ralston. "Hypocrites."

"—vegetarian lawyer."

"So much for genetics," he said.

I nudged his leg with my toe. "So, Martine?"

"We're calling it quits."

As when you walk into a glass office high up in a skyscraper and suddenly find yourself looking a thousand feet straight down, I involuntarily swayed backward, away from Ralston and the apparition of life without Ritz.

She lunged forward and grabbed a handful of his shirt. "What are you talking about?"

"I don't believe it," I said. "All those years."

Ritz tightened her grip. "What did you do to her?"

Like a performer basking in applause, Rals smiled and held up his hands for silence. "Nothing happened. It was just over between us."

"Things aren't just over after what, forty years?" I said. "Not at our age."

What was that word they used in Victorian novels to describe the eyes of a tired old man? Rheumy. Ralston looked at me with rheumy eyes and no smile. "You think getting old guarantees anything besides humiliation and death?"

God, it bloody well better. "Of course not, but still."

"How do Marcel and Françoise feel about it?" Ritz said.

"He's got a fancy-ass job, she's married and pregnant. In other words, they both have enough problems of their own not to worry about their parents."

Ritz sat next to Rals and put a hand on his arm. "How are you?"

He smiled bravely and laid a hand over hers. "I'm fine. We were both in a rut." He worked his thumb around her wrist and softly caressed that spot on the underside. "Change is good."

She pulled her hand away. "Change? What change?"

"I wasn't fooling around, that's not what this was about."

I topped up our champagne. "Which?"

"Which what?"

"You weren't fooling around, or that's not what it was about?"

"Neither. Both." He emptied his glass in one gulp and stood. "Got to go. Just wanted to say hi to you two without a corpse in the room."

"You're not staying with us?" Ritz said. "Where's your suitcase?"

"I brought all my shit with me, so I dumped it with my idiot cousin in Brooklyn."

Typical Ralston, hunkering down when he was low. "For Christ's sakes," I said, "stay with us. Especially now."

He waggled his eyebrows at Ritz. "Especially now, I better not."

"What's your plan?" I said.

A bland smile. "Plan? What plan? There's no big hurry." He squinted at me. "Is there?"

Morning. Ablutions completed, breakfast eaten, no more excuses. The computer monitor beckoned from the desk. More like gave me the finger. I had no idea what to do with the manuscript squatting on the screen like a bloated toad. Actually, I knew exactly what to do with it but hadn't yet found the words—invented the language, chiseled the Rosetta stone—that might convey to the author what needed to be done.

Usually it's the old ones who just don't get it. The young ones get it but don't give a damn, they're out to create a whole new literary paradigm, reinvent the Edsel. The fire, the excitement, the idea that maybe there could be something new under the sun and that they just might be the ones to birth it, all make the quest worthwhile. If only for its own sake. As long as you don't think of it that way. Once you start believing *l'art pour l'art*, you've pretty much given up.

The Old Ones—my age or a little younger. A real cause for worry. Everyone thinks they get it. I think I get it.

Everyone except Adele. I closed the Old One's manuscript and brought up Adele's instead. Adele doesn't bother with getting it. The world's job is to get her, not the other way around. So how come she hired me as her editor? I'd asked her that question. "Todd told me to," she'd said. Todd, her husband, ninth-richest man in the United States. "It wasn't worth a fight. So let's get it over with."

Books. This morning, their premeditated cohesiveness seemed unnatural, oppressive, even perverted. I fled my cramped office for some real life—or, anyway, the living room couch.

A pigeon fluttered down from the window molding, hobbled across the coffee table on its bandaged foot, pecked at the lip of my coffee cup, and took a dump.

"Feeling better now?" I said.

The pigeon stepped back and mistrustfully regarded the clumsy giant before scouting the rest of the table for food. Ritz swooped in from the kitchen with a wet paper towel and leaned over to examine the specimen—round, brown, rather dry with a bright streak of white.

"Good job, Snowshoe." Best avian diagnostic tool, she always said: eyeballing turds. The pigeon scrabbled away from her to the edge of the table. "Don't worry," she said, "I'll release him tomorrow or the day after." She cleaned up the dropping, then flashed her raptor smile. "News item for you."

While letting that sink in, she submissively hunched her shoulders, looked at the floor and sidled toward Snowshoe, who eyed her suspiciously but stayed put. Suddenly her hands darted out and she had him. When I tried that on her patients, I usually ended up with only a feather or two. She smoothed Snowshoe's wings, put him back in his cage, then sat next to me. "I'm retiring."

I jerked upright. "What! When? Why?"

"At the end of the school year."

"Oh. Next year."

"*This* school year. A couple of months. Why are you acting so shocked? We've talked about this for ages."

"I thought they wouldn't let you."

"Two years ago they asked me to stay another year. Then another. I told them not to bother to ask again, and they didn't. Curricula are changing, taxonomy keeps getting reshuffled, I had a good run, and now I'm finished. Not everything has to be complicated." Her calm assertiveness, which she sometimes used to inspire confidence while precluding further discussion, always turned out to mask her trepidation. "You said it yourself, the day will come when we can't afford to stay in the city."

"A *future* day," I said. "Not a *today* day."

"We need to figure out where we'll go." She walked away, as if that was that.

I looked around the room at the scuffed wooden furniture, the faux-Greek plaster reliefs, the paintings and photos by friends, the crammed bookshelves, the African tapestry and masks, the basket of magazines, Ritz's knickknack shelf with its fossil ammonites and dinosaur dung, small Mexican wood sculptures, geodes, feathers, cloisonné vials and vases, and a wind-up plastic nun that shot sparks out of its mouth.

Go? And what was I supposed to do with whatever time I had left?

When I tried to think about it, I had to ask, as a philosopher might, why should there be something rather than nothing?

Chapter 2

The rear of the building, away from the street, faced the block-long garden that lay between our row of brownstones and the backs of those on the next street. Our bedroom, three floors up, had two windows looking out onto the garden. The narrower bedroom next to ours used to be Freddy's but was now mainly a storeroom. We tried to keep it from getting too cluttered because we sometimes entertained on the small terrace it led to.

Ritz was out on the terrace now serving breakfast to her regular guests, those of her ex-patients who stopped by most days for a free meal. When I stepped out to join her, some of them flapped up into the air, while a few bolder ones continued gobbling seeds with barely a glance at me.

I looked at a gray pigeon. "That Lukey?" An abandoned baby who'd been agonizingly shy about finally leaving the apartment to join the local flock.

"A bruiser now." Lukey lunged at another bird who came too close to his food and drove it off with a few vicious pecks, then went back to eating peaceably head-to-head with another bird. "He's got a mate now. Oops, here comes Big Red."

A huge rust-colored pigeon flew in with his mate, chased some smaller birds away from a seed bowl and started chowing down. Ritz had spent a month nursing Big Red back to health after a hawk attack broke a wing, punctured his chest, and tore most of his tail away. When his mate now approached the bowl to eat, he warned her off with a flick of the wing, forcing her to scavenge from the floor instead.

"Aren't they mates?" I asked. "Why'd he do that?"

"He's an asshole."

I went back inside to call Martine before Ritz left for school. Over the years, Martine had sometimes seemed protective or possessive of Ralston, as if I might lure him away from her and back into the vagabond life. Now, over the phone, she sounded happy that I'd called but a little surprised, as if she considered me only his friend and not hers too. I asked her what had happened to their marriage.

"You know Ralston," she said, "things weren't always that smooth. After the news from the doctor, he just—"

"What news?"

"That's just like him, he didn't tell you. I bet he didn't tell me all of it. He'd had a couple of, what do they call them? Episodes."

"Episodes of what?"

Martine sighed. "He wouldn't tell me. Then it was his prostate. They want to take it out."

A familiar lump of dread mushroomed in my chest. "Cancer? How bad?"

"He finally went to the doctor after it started hurting him when we made love. You know Ralston and sex." A cut-off sob. "There was blood once."

I reflexively clutched at my lap. "Why the split-up?"

"He just sort of drifted away. Maybe it was, you know, his mind, too. Old age."

"Martine, we're not that old." I could still picture her, lush and vital, and not so long ago. At least, that's how I remembered her. I don't know whether my recall is getting worse or if I've finally learned just how unreliable memory is at any age. In the last snapshot they'd sent, she was dumpy and gray with a dowager's hump peeking over her shoulder at the camera.

Another sob. "He took too many sleeping pills."

"What!?"

"After he saw the doctor. I couldn't wake him up, I had to call the ambulance."

"Jesus, he tried to kill himself?"

Ritz stepped in and looked at me agog.

"He swore it was an accident," Martine said. "He was drunk and didn't remember he'd already—"

"Pills *and* alcohol?"

Ritz held her head in her hands.

"Not the whole bottle," Martine said. "The doctor said he probably would've been all right anyway."

Ralston didn't usually take halfway measures. "Christ, Martine."

"A few days later he filled out the divorce papers and left."

"Why?"

"I don't know, I don't know, I don't know…"

"Did he…did something happen?"

"No, he was being sweet. Sweet and sad."

"We'll talk to him," I said. "I'm so sorry this happened. He'll be back."

She stopped weeping. "Jules, please understand. I'm fine. I'm not sad for myself. He shouldn't come back if he doesn't want to. I'm just worried about him."

I spent the rest of the morning on Internet medical sites searching for information and any connections amongst prostate cancer, bleeding from the penis, blood in semen, suicide, and abrupt changes in behavior. Conclusion: prostate problems, cancerous or not, can cause bleeding, and God knows what a man will do when he's afraid his dick is about to fall off. Advice: see your doctor—which Ralston had done.

Despite the twinge in my foot—these days, something was always hurting somewhere—I walked to the West Side Brewery, took a window table, and ordered yam fries and two beers. A minute later, Ralston showed up and sat down slowly, gingerly—that was new—as the drinks came to the table.

"Great place," I said. "Make their own beer and the food's all right."

He grabbed a fry and took a bite. "First time you came here, remember who brought you?"

"Bullshit. Want your own plate of fries?"

"I can't eat the greasy shit like I used to." He gave his belly a rueful pat and took another fry. "Food always tastes better off somebody else's plate."

"Rals, what are you doing in New York?"

"Besides bugging you? I'm retired."

"You too? Bad idea."

A beautiful blond walked in with a young man about her age and sat at the table behind Ralston. He raised his eyebrows to me and leered, then sniffed, crinkled his nose and frowned.

"Me, too?"

"Ritz." I told him the news.

"Great, she and I'll keep each other occupied and amused and out of your busy bread-winning hair."

The blond woman's heavy floral scent now reached me. "Seriously, what'll you do?"

"Martine got the apartment, I got the cash. I'm all right."

"But what are you going to *do*?"

He picked up a menu, held it at arm's length, then grabbed the reading glasses from my face and put them on. He ordered a salad. "Let's see. You get too feeble to eat, drink, smoke, and ball your way through life. Instead, maybe a spot of golf? What does Ritz want to do?"

"We talk about moving south. Getting a place with enough space to set up a real wildlife-rehab outfit."

He stared out the window and groped for a fry. "Now, see? Ritz is going to do what she always wanted." He slowly chewed. "If you let her."

"Let her?"

"You think she's going to leave you for her birds? For me, maybe."

"Martine didn't leave you."

Ralston's salad arrived. He took a bite.

"I talked to her this morning," I said. "Why the hell didn't you tell us?" He raised a questioning eyebrow. I leaned forward and whispered, "Prostate."

He waved it away. "No big deal."

"No big deal? Cancer?"

"Who says it's cancer? Anyway, the doctor said you get to a certain age, a slow-growing prostate cancer's not going to kill you, something else'll get you first. I'm not sweating it."

I leaned in to whisper again. "Bleeding from your dick?"

Ms. Perfume's ears seemed to prick up. Rals frowned for a moment as if saddened by Martine's small indiscretion. "I quit smoking, cut way back on booze and grease, I'm taking two prostate pills he gave me, plus saw palmetto." He leered down at his lap. "Ol' Faithful's spouting again just fine." He cocked his head and looked puzzled. "Not quite spouting. Feels just as good but hardly anything comes out." He shrugged. "It's the pill."

"I have a great doctor. We can get you a checkup, blood test for prostate and other stuff, a colonoscopy—"

He laughed. "Forget it."

"Martine talked about episodes."

He gave me a quizzical look. "Episodes?"

I wasn't going to bring up the booze and pills with those scented ears twitching behind him. "So what are you going to do?"

"We had plans, man. Dreams."

The old emptiness clutched at me. I tried to smirk it away. "Sex, drugs, rock and roll?"

He finished his salad and pushed the bowl away. "You know what I'm talking about. You spent half your life chasing after yours. Now, that spring in your step has turned into a limp."

"You wanted to save the world," I said.

"And you wanted to get the hell out of it."

Ralston ate my last fry, drained his beer, stood up and turned to the table behind him. "You're a gorgeous woman, but you've got to lose all that perfume. It's like too much horse-radish in your Bloody Mary, too much Tabasco on your oyster, too much onion with your caviar, too much—how long do I need to keep going before you get the idea of too much?"

She stared at him in horror and grabbed her boyfriend's arm. "Bertie!?"

Rals gave the boy an avuncular smile. "What's the poor lad going to do, beat me up? Bet you've been dying to tell her that yourself." He sauntered out of the restaurant.

I tossed the couple a little wave. "Nice talking to you." I dropped a twenty and a ten on the check, anchored them with a saltshaker, and followed Ralston outside. "Suave." We headed down Amsterdam Avenue. "Why'd you leave Martine?"

"She wanted to grow old in the Paris apartment with her little roof garden and her books and her lady friends."

"Wild Martine? I don't believe it."

"She can't stomach red wine anymore. Her fingers hurt from arthritis. Sex was like, like—oh, man, it was motherly. She wouldn't—"

"You dumped her because she was getting old?"

"Because she was comfortable with growing old, because she was coasting with a glassy-eyed smile on her face, because she'd retired for real. 'Oh, I've had enough excitement for one life.' What kind of shit is that? Does some gland release a chemical that brainwashes you when you hit your sixties? What'd she tell you, that I went nuts or something?"

"That you'd changed."

"Change is bad?"

I grabbed his arm and lowered my voice. "What about the pills?"

He dragged me along a few paces. "Check it out." In the middle of the block, five young men lounged around a parked car that shuddered from oversized speakers blaring rap. A plump woman with big breasts walked past, followed by catcalls and kissing sounds. While I lagged behind, Ralston ambled by the group, throwing them a couple of glances. He stopped just beyond them. They ignored him. "See that?" he shouted to me over the music.

I caught up and pulled him a few steps farther along. "See what?"

"Exactly. We're not on their radar anymore. We're not a threat, we're not competitors. We're not quite human. Can you even remember the last time a woman under fifty checked you out?"

It had been only a couple of days ago, but he didn't need to hear about it. Something about my legs below my shorts had sparked some interest, but by the time her eyes reached my midsection, she was clearly having second thoughts, and my face only got the sparest of glances before she hastily looked away. I tightened my grip. "The pills?"

He pulled his arm away and glanced at his nonexistent wristwatch. "Later, man."

He headed downtown. I followed a few paces behind. "Hang on a sec. What are you going to do?"

An old panhandler was asleep in his beat-up wheelchair, his feet wrapped in rags. Ralston stuffed a couple of bills in the can on the man's lap and looked back at me. "Here's you or me one of these days. I'll call you." He walked away. After a few paces, he glanced over his shoulder. "Hey, Jules." The leer was back. "Don't be Ritz's Martine."

I turned around toward home, again passing the group around the car. Rals was right: no challenging stare, no sneer, not even the quick requisite once-over. They looked right through me. Transparent, air. As if their pheromone receptors and reptilian brains knew something that I hadn't yet quite caught on to.

"Could you get a clean read on him?" Ritz asked. She was undressing, something that still distracted me in a sort of Zen lechery, watching without watching. Down to her underwear.

"When could I ever?" I said. "Something's going on. Something not good."

She took off the panties. "You've never worried about him before." How did she keep an ass like that at her age?

"Before," I said, "whatever else he was up to, he always seemed capable of looking after himself, at least of seeing what kind of mess he was stepping into."

She turned slightly and took off the bra. Did she know this was my best viewing angle? Nice to think it might still matter to her. She lifted her arms over her head in a grand finale, the nightgown slid down over her body, and the show was over. When I took off my undies, she didn't watch at all. Instead, she brushed her hair, which over the years had gradually lightened, and now the infiltrating white strands outnumbered the reddish-brown ones.

"Sweetie," she said, "what are you getting so gnarled up about? We talked about this a hundred times."

"Ralston losing it?"

"Retiring, moving. You can still edit. Write. I'll do my birds."

Ritz, busy-busy to the sound of beating wings and the faintly rancid smell of caged birds who don't bathe often enough. Me in a hushed room, torpid as a November lizard, the monitor long gone to screensaver. The clogged feeling in my brain getting thicker. Time and space, heavy and deadening, pushing me, pushing me, toward a blank wall.

I got into bed. "Right now, I'm worried about Ralston."

"The birds will be outside in a garage or barn or shed, so you get a bird-free house. My pension plus the money we save by not being in the city plus Social Security will more than take up the slack. I'll find a job of some kind, tutoring maybe."

Years ago, the money had plumped up like a comfy green forest on the distant horizon. After scoring big with an initial editing success, which I'd agreed to do on spec against a percentage of royalties, I'd been able to ask for up-front fees, a tradeoff that made for steady income but no windfalls. Then insane costs of Freddy's college and law school had eaten into our retirement accounts, which in turn had incurred tax penalties for early withdrawal, and the price of living in New York hadn't stopped rising.

Pulling up stakes used to mean adventure. Now it seemed more like retreat. "We'd have to have a car," I said. "Maybe two. Insurance and upkeep—think of the hurricanes and mildew."

"Think of our current maintenance payments scheduled to take a big leap in a couple of months, and the assessments for reroofing. We can work all this out, but come this June... Jules, what's the real problem here?"

"What if he *is* suicidal? What if he's...?" I tapped the side of my head.

"Don't change the subject. We need to be out of here. Fast."

Fast. "It's too damn soon for retirement," I said. "I'm not ready. I haven't done..." I turned and stared at the ceiling.

"Done what?"

I lifted my feet under the covers until my toes strained against the sheet. "Squat, baby. I haven't done squat."

"Sure you have, sweetie. You got me, didn't you?"

A morose silence settled.

She slid into bed. "There was your book."

"Twenty years ago. Sank without a trace."

"You help writers. You help bring good books into the world."

I grimaced.

"Boris's book," she said.

"That's one book."

"But it was wonderful. It won prizes and made it to the top of all sorts of bestseller lists."

"Not the *New York Times*."

"Jamie's did."

"Fluff. He was already famous, he just wanted help with his damn commas."

"Adele's book, and you're getting a piece of the action on that one."

"In exchange for a lower down payment. She wants my ass on the line."

She nudged my shoulder with hers. "Who cares? It's sure to be huge no matter what."

"All it's sure to be is a major pain in the ass. Is that what we're talking about—when all is said and done, we balanced the budget?"

"We made a good life," she said. "We made Freddy."

"Anybody can have a kid. A million years of human evolution proves that raising children is idiot-proof. Five thousand years of human history proves that it has to be."

"Still, Freddy. Smart, happy, witty, and apparently well adjusted.

"If that's a good thing."

Ritz picked up her book from the bedside table. "Okay, you've done squat. Neither have I."

"You've taught thousands of kids."

She put the book aside and snuggled closer. "It's so silly for you to feel worthless."

"*I'm* not worthless, I just haven't *done* anything of worth."

"What would be of worth?" she asked. "Cure cancer, bring world peace, discover the secrets of the universe, understand the true nature of reality, write the great American novel? You're getting off to a late start, so maybe you'd better pick just one or two of those things."

I squirmed. Bruno had been somebody. How had he ended up? "Right now," I said, "I don't even know what to do about Rals."

Ritz turned off the light. "It's been a while since I used my pacifier." Her hand snaked under the sheet and found my dick. "So relaxing."

Did she know that her touch was one of the most precious gifts she gave me? A casual pat on the ass, a peck on the cheek, sitting next to me on the couch close enough so our legs pressed against each other. Not that she was generally a touchy-feely person, just with me.

"Ralston feeling you up put you in the mood?" I said. She gave me a gentle yank. And when she died? I'd be far worse off than Rals was without Martine.

Her fingers caressed. "Well, well. Your little guy's up tonight even if you're down."

Of course, I might die first. A selfish hope.

Her pep talk trailed off. I must have dozed for a minute, for next I knew, her hand had slowed to a stop around my semi and her breathing had turned to a whispered snore. The night closed in around us like an echo chamber.

Chapter 3

A teenage girl, the smartest in her class, drops out of school to support her little sister, which their mother can't or won't do. At age fifteen, the little sister runs off and gets married, so big sister joins the navy to see the world but instead gets assigned an office job, where she learns accounting and a million ways to hide the truth about money. After the navy, she goes into business as a financial detective and ends up bringing down a huge corporation that's been ripping off its public, employees, and the U.S. government. When an investment banker tries to buy her out, she won't sell, but she does marry him. Now she investigates charities and makes her husband give millions to the honest and efficient ones. She decides to write a novel based on her life.

"Problem is," I said, "her life's not a story."

Ralston nodded, deadpan. "When I asked you how work was going, I was just making nice."

"Up yours, man." I stood up from the couch and headed for the kitchen.

Drop-bys, another jettisoned artifact of youth. Once you get into your twenties, maybe thirties for the slower, and have an established household, your social events become subject to planning, formats, schedules. Friday, drinks, sevenish? Not even Freddy just dropped by anymore—not since he'd walked in on Ritz and me one afternoon on the living room couch. But Rals had just dropped by. While easily possible that he did it to everyone out of brash inconsiderateness, his unannounced and unceremonious arrival that evening glowed warmly in my heart as a sign of enduring friendship, then slithered into the pit of my stomach as more likely a sign of something else as yet undisclosed.

He followed me into the kitchen. "Everyone's life is a story."

"No, it isn't." I opened the fridge. "Things happen, but that doesn't make it a story."

"But you're talking about Adele. Everybody's interested in her. Ever meet her face to face?"

"Once."

"And?"

I dropped half a dozen baby cucumbers into a colander and ran water over them. "She's okay."

"Don't fuck with me, man. She's mid-forties now? Married for ten, twelve years to Mr. Moneybags, who could have any woman he wants and is long overdue for a trade-up? A guy who's a couple of years younger than her? She's just okay?"

"Good-looking, in great shape, but no movie star." Smart, but no Einstein. Strong, but no Catherine the Great. Exactly what you want as a character in a novel. Without superlatives or melodrama, she could walk into a room or onto a page and take charge. But a royal pain to work with.

"She's a celebrity," he said. "Who cares if her life isn't a story?"

"Because she's trying to write it as a novel. Everybody wants their life to be a story, but it isn't."

"Why not?"

"A story is about something. A particular struggle. With a beginning and an end."

"That's just a cultural artifact," he said. "Right now, in Western literature, people expect a plot. In other cultures, other times—"

I brandished the vegetable peeler. "No, see, that's not true." Here was something I knew more about than Rals. "In all cultures, throughout history, a story is a story—conflict, struggle, resolution. Greek myths, Homer, the Bhagavad-Gita, the Bible, African folktales, classical Chinese parables, Aztec creation stories."

"No shit?" He seemed to be giving it some serious thought. Probably setting a trap.

I glanced over at Ritz, who was shoving blueberries and mealworms down a baby blue jay's throat. "Anyway," I said, "I keep finding myself in the position of having to tell some poor writer who's just poured out her life's blood that she doesn't have a story. Breaks their heart. Makes me feel like a total turd."

"Sure, nobody else gives a shit about their dumb life, nobody ever did, that's why they're writing about it. But the story stuff, that's interesting."

I trod cautiously, eyeing the terrain ahead. "How so?"

"How so? You're the guy with a degree in psych and a minor in lit who spent how many years on your magical mystery tour? You've got a human universal here, if you're not just talking out your ass. Something that helps the beast survive. Why do we need stories?"

"I'm not sure about *need*."

"Mother Nature doesn't invest in frills. You've got how many clients trying to turn their sorry little lives into stories with a meaning? *Need*."

"You could say the same thing about any art form."

"Hey, wow, maybe. But at the moment, I don't have a supposed expert in all art forms with me."

"I'm sure somebody's come up with a theory," I said. "Ersatz, risk-free experience, a form of play that exercises the human specialty of projecting actions and consequences into the future to solve problems related to survival. Or something."

Ralston squinted at the kitchen clock. "Holy shit, that took you seven-point-three seconds. Must be a pretty comprehensive and well-tested theory."

What I wanted was a glass of wine, but with Ralston laying off the sauce—

"And how about some wine, you stingy bastard?"

"I thought you weren't supposed to drink."

"Haven't you heard? Wine is good for your heart."

"What about barbiturates and wine?"

He hawked up a short laugh. "Martine told you about that, too? It was bullshit."

"Bullshit? She couldn't wake you up."

"That's why they're called sleeping pills. She panicked. Or called the ambulance to make a point."

Ritz was now standing at the kitchen door, wiping her hands with a rag while watching and listening. My hands groped the air for words. "So you're saying you didn't try to… to off yourself?"

"Me?"

"Like the Hemlock Society, making your own choices about where, when, and how."

He stared back and forth from Ritz to me, looking truly wounded. Which meant he wasn't wounded at all but harboring some other emotion altogether. "How long have we known each other?"

A sad silence held us in place until I started slicing the baby cucumbers. Ritz led Ralston out of the kitchen and showed him her new patient. I put lime, sea salt, and black pepper on the cucumbers, brought them out to the living room with a bowl of grape tomatoes, and went back to the kitchen for a bottle of red wine. I pulled the cork, as I had at that very spot, with that very corkscrew, at least a thousand times before. I unscrewed the cork from the corkscrew, each twist slower than the one before, and silently laid them down on the wooden counter. I picked up the bottle but felt no urge to move.

In the living room, Ralston was sitting close to Ritz on the couch. He gobbled a cucumber slice then held another up for Ritz to bite from his fingers. She hesitated, and the scene became a Renoiresque tableau with splashes of light and color and pools of shadow, the pretty woman and smilingly aggressive man.

Except it was a scene from an old folks' home. A comfy old folks' home, our own old folks' home, but an old folks' home. The final configuration of a life. A rolling stone come to rest.

East Village, mid-'60s, summer after college, midnight on the second-floor balcony, a strip of tarpaper roof above the dry cleaner. Bob Dylan's latest drifting softly through the window.

> Ain't it just like the night
> To play tricks when you're trying to be so quiet?
> We sit here stranded,
> Though we're all doing our best to deny it.

Whores work the block in front of the boarded-up theater. A lone cop car wails past, headed downtown. A young couple—she's beautiful—crosses the street diagonally in the middle of the block, laughing, smoking. The smell of weed drifts up. As if feeling my gaze, she glances up and tosses me a smile.

> But to live outside the law you must be honest.
> I know you always say that you agree,
> But where are you tonight, sweet Marie?

Where are you tonight, sweet Ritz?

Dawn swoops in on the wings of pigeons. Dozens of them, wheeling, diving, loop-the-looping, barrel rolling, merging into synchronicity then scattering in flight. It looks like play. Why do they do it?

The vision reappears. *An old man with bright eyes approaches, radiating warm wisdom. Spiritual kinship recognized, acknowledged. An invitation to follow him over the mountains to the secret monastery, to enlightenment.*

I've got to get out of here.

Something exploded at my feet. I lurched back against the fridge. Shards of green glass lay scattered on the tile. Red wine dripped from the lower cabinets and pooled on the floor.

Ritz leapt up to help clean up the mess. I waved her away so she wouldn't see my panic. Was it just the startle of the crash? No, it had come earlier. The call to Martine? Ritz's retirement? Bruno dying? All of it at once?

I grabbed a sponge mop and sopped up the mess. When I tried to squat and pick up the larger shards, my knees protested. I stood back up. "Maybe Rals and I should just hit the road. Go find that bird retirement house."

They both stared at me for a few moments. Ralston scowled. "Like you'd do that."

After dinner, he shoved me out onto the terrace. "Find a retirement house and what else?"

"Else?"

"Don't give me that innocent look. This your idea of a mission of mercy or some shit?" He slumped into a chair and stared off across the garden.

I sat down next to him. "When did we last go? That freak show to Oregon?"

"India." He must have been in a self-flagellating mood to bring up India.

"New places," I said. "Clean out our heads. New perspectives. Hey, I'm quoting you. Just when you think you've seen it all, wham, new people, crazier than ever. We used to be scared of the South, remember? KKK out patrolling the streets for hippies? Turned out they were the ones with the long hair and the pot patch out in the cornfield. Look at us, we can pass for respectable now. We'd be doing something useful. Ritz wants that house. I could use a break. You sure look like you need one." Had he ever let me talk that long without butting in?

He looked at me, mouth slightly open, eyes uncertain, then turned his gaze back out over the garden. This was new, Rals not rising to a challenge or co-opting the idea and turning it to his own ends.

The silence stretched out. Finally, with a groan, he slowly stood up. "You're full of shit." He hobbled into the apartment and looked back over his shoulder. "But I got nothing better to do." I stayed outside for a few minutes, and by the time I went back inside, he'd left.

"It's a great idea," Ritz said. We were lying in bed. "Two of you looking, and he knows a lot about houses. He needs something to do."

"He hates the idea."

"He was excited when he left, he was talking about where you guys could go."

"Christ, he's already taking over the project."

Ritz laid her book down on her chest and turned her head on the pillow to face me. "You're probably the second most important person in his life," she said, "and he just divorced the most important."

"For an extravert," I said, "he's the most opaque person I've ever known."

"What does he say about whatever's going on with him?"

"People change, you have to be ready to move on, you can't let life stagnate under your feet, the usual bullshit."

"All of it true."

"Still bullshit," I said. "He talks about himself as little as possible. He doesn't say anything about Françoise and Marcel. Maybe they hate him. Remember that trip with them to the Canaries? Those crazy little projects he'd press-gang the kids into? The fort, the buried treasure?"

"The seashell beach mosaic." She laughed. "Freddy loved it."

"Freddy didn't have to spend his whole childhood with Rals."

She was looking at me the way I probably looked at Ralston when I didn't think he was leveling with me. "Is this really about finding us a house?"

"Hey, I'm not the one suddenly announcing my retirement."

Ritz slowly tapped a single finger against her book. "What do *you* want to do?"

I snorted a laugh. That question always sounded like an offer to live your life over, take back your mistakes, unhurt those you hurt. To accomplish something, anything, and to waste so much less time. At least to be a better, braver person.

It's also the question I always ask my clients when they can't figure out one of their characters: What does the character really, really want?

Can you run out of things to want? Is that what old age is, not really wanting anything anymore except some peace and quiet? For life to just softly, smilingly, approvingly, tiptoe away?

Chapter 4

Ritz faced Ralston and me on the stoop. "I hope you guys aren't just going on a joyride while I'm back here slaving away."

"He could use a joyride," Ralston said.

She looked at us sternly. "What he could use is a place to live." She took my hand. "Find something. At least a good place to start looking." In other words, Rals will see through the trip's pretext if I don't make a sincere effort to track down a house.

He put a hand on her shoulder. "We'll find you a palace."

Ritz didn't break her gaze from me. "Once I finish the term, end of salary. Staying in New York is all wasted time and money after that." So she really did want that damn house, birds and all. She patted my face. "Don't buy anything before I see it."

Rals sneered. "Don't worry, I won't let him."

"I mean it." She was still looking at me. "No down payment, no deposit. We have one shot to do this right." Since when had financial comfort been so important to her?

To us both.

She gently slapped my face. "Jules, promise?"

"Ow."

She squeezed me tight. I held her close. Softly she kissed my lips. The slightest hint of tongue. Ralston watched without blinking.

We were a few hours out of New York, southwest of Philly, in a rented car, me behind the wheel. Ralston pulled a tattered, much-folded scrap of paper from his wallet, took my reading glasses from my shirt pocket, recomposed his face into ostentatious thoughtfulness, and began to read.

"Ten Challenges to Becoming a Real Man. One. Walk into a town without a penny or a friend and thrive." He looked over at me. "I did that in Paris. You?"

"What post-adolescent magazine did you rip that out of?"

"You and I did this list back in college. Or were you too stoned to remember?"

I glanced over at it. "What else did we put on that stupid thing?"

He snatched it away. "All in good time. Yes or no on number one?"

In fact, Rals had had a very good friend in Paris, Martine. But no need to shoot him down. He seemed to be grooving on the ride.

"When I moved from London back to New York," I said, "everybody was gone. I did okay."

"Doesn't count, you had some money."

"Not much. I didn't have Ritz, either."

"Like I had Martine?" He laughed. "I wondered what you were saving that one for. Martine was away when I got to Paris. And pretty pissed off at me. I was on my own. I'd hitched there by myself from India too, pal. Thanks a fat lot."

"That was *my* fault?"

"We do what we have to." He put my glasses back on and looked at his list. "Two. Go one-on-one with the elements—wilderness, small-boat sailor, explorer."

"You still think that list is a good way to measure your life?"

"You got a better one?"

If he was going to play with it, it might as well cheer him up. Here was a neutral topic—weather. "Spain was like that," I said.

"Oh, that was rough. Mediterranean climate, figs and almonds growing on trees, fish for the taking."

"We had to make our own spear guns out of scrap bamboo."

"Or if we didn't, or if it was too cold to swim that day, a buck would buy enough food for both of us. True, we didn't have indoor plumbing, so we had to live cheek-by-jowl with the five primordial elements—earth, air, fire, water, and shit. Can't check that one off yet." He looked at the list again. "Three. Go one-on-one with human violence—foot soldier, cop, criminal, street fighter."

"That's us, all right," I said. "Head bangers, leg breakers."

Ralston hesitated, as if for once considering his words before speaking. The list predated the fistfights the two of us had gotten into with each other, always over a woman—although clownish come-ons aside, never about Ritz. Just as well. Back when casual sexual pilfering was worth bloodshed and the temporarily irrevocable loss of best friendship, I had once gone after Rals with a baseball bat and, in another fight, broken a finger.

"I was in a bar brawl," he said. "In Paris. This guy, he slaps the woman he's with. Some other guy says something to him, and the slapper punches him out. I look at the bartender like, Call the cops, and the guy comes for me. He tries to hit me in the face but I get my arms up. The woman makes a break for the door, the guy takes off after her. I grab a bottle from the bar and swing for the bleachers on his head."

"Jeez. What happened?"

"He went down. And stayed down, thank God. I paid for my drink and split. Left a good tip, too, I didn't want to give the bartender any reason to tell the cops what I looked like. Dead, for all I know. Never went back there."

"Why'd you do it?"

"Seemed like the right thing."

"No, really."

"Really, it seemed like the right thing. And I was drunk." He squinted out at a road sign. "Quarryville, turn here."

"You sure this is a good idea?"

"Yes."

I made the turn. "You killed a guy?"

"That so hard to believe?"

"This was back when you first moved to Paris?"

"No, three or four months ago."

Martine's claim of Ralston's incipient dementia suddenly took tangible form. "Before or after the breakup?"

"During." He seemed almost proud of it. Of course he always acted pleased about everything he did.

"Are the cops looking for you?"

"Not that I know of."

"So he's probably not dead."

"Or nobody gives a shit. Good riddance. French cops have a broader view of that principle than ours do. Some people need killing. Does that run against your neat little set of morals?"

"You meant to kill that guy?"

"There are plenty of people the world would be better off without."

"But the world would be a far worse place if we all thought we had the right to act on that judgment."

He was smiling at me, positively beaming with camaraderie. A sure sign of danger. "We've had this little argument before, haven't we?"

"And I think you lost it," I said. "Cops on your ass, those other bozos in jail. Is that on your little manhood list? Kill some jerk who needs it?"

"Damn, I think we forgot to write that one down. *Our* little list." He mimed adding it to the list. "I can chalk it up as done."

"Why are you going over that dumb list? Why did you save it all those years—jeez, half a century?"

He looked at me for a few moments and laughed. "Man, you're all wigged out. That bar, I was just in the moment, like we used to say. Freaky, how close and easy something like that is. Like the good old days. Here, hang a left."

I pulled into the driveway. We stepped up onto the porch, rang the bell, and waited. An extensive collection of plaster statuary composed a tableau in the side yard. Gnomes, jockeys, toads, Bambi, a unicorn, a couple of children, all arrayed around the central ensemble: Dopey, Sleepy, Grumpy, Bashful, and the whole bunch kneeling in reverence at the feet of the pure and beautiful young woman standing straight and true. Except she wasn't Snow White.

"Holy shit," Rals said. "Get a load of the Virgin Mary and the Seven Dwarfs."

A fat, gray-haired woman opened the door and eyed us suspiciously.

"Hi," I said. "Randy Dillard live here?"

She was looking at Ralston and her face wasn't getting any friendlier.

"Jesus," he said. "Dottie?"

"Watch your mouth in this house. And it's Dorothy." She turned to shout up the stairs. "Randy!" When Ralston stepped in uninvited, I followed like a nervous nanny. Visibly straining not to waddle, Dottie retreated into the kitchen.

Randy had the same squat, milk-truck stature of years ago, but the muscle had turned to flab, and the gravitas to inertia. His smile and extended hand said he was happy to see us; his flickering eyes said he wasn't sure who we were.

Ralston shook his hand and slapped him on the back. "Jules and Ralston." The eyes still seemed uncertain. "I called, day before yesterday."

"Course you did. Great to see you. All those years. Dorothy! How about some Cokes on the porch?"

"You know where they are!"

"I mean you, with us. Hang on a sec, guys." He opened the door, herded us back out onto the porch, then ducked inside.

Ralston raised a disheveled eyebrow. "Cokes? The Randy we used to know, would've been tequila and a fat sloppy joint."

"What's with her?" I asked.

"Little sister." He waggled both eyebrows.

"No."

"Hey, she wasn't fat back then."

Randy shouldered the door open and set three Cokes on the rail. Rals looked askance. "Got a beer?"

"All out." Randy grimaced apologetically then shot a look over his shoulder. "I mean, don't have any. So what are you guys up to?"

"Like I said, looking for a house for Ritz."

"This town's no great shakes."

"Down South," I said.

"Come with us." Ralston's head tilted a fraction of a millimeter toward the kitchen. "Get away for a while. Road trip." He leaned close to Randy. "Beer."

Randy laughed. "Yeah, great."

Rals put a hand on Randy's shoulder and gave him a worried look. "Maybe just for a day or two. We'll put you on a bus home whenever you want."

Randy squinted out off the porch, humming a random tune. Ralston and I exchanged sad glances.

I ripped out a riff on the air guitar. "Still playing? God, you guys were good."

Randy flinched at "God" then opened his left hand to show scarred fingers. "Messed up my hands. We were opening for someone…Donovan?" Donovan: that took a few seconds to sink in.

"I'd just got a new guitar, so I figured, what the heck, might as well send the old one out with a bang." He laughed, then winced as he seemed to remember where this story was headed. "Crashed it on a speaker during the last number. Broke the speaker but the guitar bounced back at me. Almost tore my nose off. How do those guys do it, trick guitars or something? Tried to rip the strings off, and cut the stuffing out of my fingers. Then the blood or something got into the pickups, next thing you know I'm down on the stage flopping like a fish. Electrocuted. Who'd a known, darn thing fought back." He slowly wiggled his fingers. "Cut some tendons or something, couldn't play worth a dead dog after that."

Ralston gently lifted Randy's hand and took a closer look. "Oh, man."

"You paid your dues," I said.

A bright sudden laugh. "That don't always get you into the club, does it?" The puzzled look returned. "So what are you guys up to?"

"Randy!" Dottie shouted from inside.

He jumped at the sound and scuttled inside. His wrinkled shirt, too short for his wide retreating back, threatened to bring tears to my eyes. "This is our future?"

"Tell me it's too soon," Rals said.

"I once got as far as the stoop in my underwear. Don't look at me like that."

He shook his head. "It's part of my routine now—check for pants before opening door." He closed his eyes for a few seconds. "Randy? Who knows, could be the dope."

"Or that electric shock."

"Or Dottie."

I said, "When Jerzy Kosinski started having trouble recognizing people—" I looked away.

"What?"

"Nothing."

"Nothing, bullshit." He yanked his right shoe untied, pulled out the lace and tossed it to me. "Kosinski snuffed himself. You want my belt too? Frisk me for sharp objects?"

"Can the dramatics, would you?"

Randy appeared at the other side of the screen door. "Great to see you boys. Dorothy and me got to go to church. Great to see you."

Ralston slipped his shoe on, then stood up and opened the door. "I'll just pay my respects to Dots." I grabbed his arm but he jerked it away and barged into the house.

Dottie sat at the kitchen table, a Day-Glo-orange handful of Cheez Doodles halfway to her stained lips. Ralston smiled and tipped his nonexistent hat. "Exhilarating to see you again, Dottie."

"Dorothy."

"You'll always be Dottie to me."

"I'll never be anything to you. And likewise. Never were."

He waggled those eyebrows again and seemed to search for a comeback.

I put a hand on his shoulder. "Come on, let's go." He turned to leave.

"Lust," Dottie said, "is one of the seven deadly sins."

Randy's eyes slid around nervously as I tried to usher Ralston out, but instead he turned back and looked at her without expression for a few moments. "So's gluttony," he said.

She sniffed. "I have a glandular problem."

"Me too. Different glands."

Probably in lieu of an undignified attempt to stand, she sat up straight in her chair. "You get out!"

As we walked across the small lawn to the car, Ralston's laceless shoe flip-flopping on his foot, Randy waved from the porch. "So what are you guys up to?"

Chapter 5

We crossed the Maryland state line heading south. I wished I could talk to Ritz about Randy. Somehow, over the years, my circle of confidants had dwindled to the point where she now was the only person I regularly opened my heart to. She, on the other hand, had a group of friends at work. Schedules permitting, they had lunch together and often went out for coffee after school. "We talk about *everything*," she said with a wicked smile. Teasing aside, it was probably true. I'd had girlfriends whose absence was a cool breeze in August, but here I was, barely half a day into this trip, already missing her. Her voice, her touch. Her presence.

I didn't say any of this to Ralston. No doubt he'd point out how it was a weakness of some kind. He'd be right. I missed him, too, when he was away. Which was most of the time. I opened my heart to him when I needed a second opinion. No matter how scathingly incisive his criticism became, or how heated my response, it never threw our friendship or mutual affection into question.

Only his actions could do that.

"You okay, man?" he said. "Don't fall apart on me now."

I had to smile. "I'll live."

"So which of your four fates was Randy's? Betrayal, failure, delusion, or being consumed?"

"You listened?"

"It ranked half a notch above staring at Bruno's wormy corpse. Don't worry, man, you're not going down Randy's road." Had he put a slight inadvertent stress on *you're*, or was that just my own ear?

I looked off to my left at the lengthening shadows. "We better think about where to spend the night."

"Tonight, or the Long Night?" He set down his manly list and pulled out an address book. "Got it covered. Next stop, Marco."

"You kidding me? After how we left it last time, what, almost fifty years ago?"

Summer, East Village. Sketchpads lean against the walls like scraps of shattered plasterboard, litter the floor, and cover the bed. Marco's eerie Munch-like drawings, every line worth a thousand words. "Art is brutal," Marco once said, "no defense against it except closing your eyes."

Marco lies on a mattress in the corner of the room, bare-chested, sweating, eyes closed, coming down from a week of shooting speed and no sleep. Ralston watching Marco while talking about Pedro, our meth connection, "One wigged-out fucker… Crazy crystal freak… Batshit, flipped-out meth head."

Marco jumps up. "Motherfuckers, I can hear you." I calm him down, convince him we're talking about Pedro. He gets back onto the bed, squirms, trying to get comfortable.

About half a gram of crystal meth still lies in its paper wrapper on the table. Ralston quietly folds it up and shoves it between a couple of books on a shelf.

Marco jerks to his feet. "Need another hit." He looks around, paws through the doper debris on the table. "Where's the shit?"

Ralston opens his hands and shakes his head. "All gone, man."

"Fuck." Marco falls back onto the mattress and closes his eyes.

I give Rals a thumbs-up.

Ralston watches Marco. After a minute, I stand up and gesture toward the door. Rals shrugs and shakes his head, like why should he be the one to leave?

Marco's eyes snap open and lock onto Ralston's. Rals doesn't break the stare.

Marco leaps up, shaking, smelling of sour corpse sweat, runs into the kitchen and comes back with a big kitchen knife. "Cocksuckers." Stabs the couch. "I know there's some crystal here." Stabs the couch again. "I know you're talking about me."

"Pedro," I say. "We were talking about Pedro, I swear."

He just stares at us, stabbing the couch over and over. "Where's the meth?"

"No more meth." Ralston stands, then freezes when Marco raises the knife. He stabs a sketchpad, walks around the room slashing all the others.

Throws a few clothes into a bag, heads for the door.

"Marco, wait," I say. "Where will you go?"

Door slams.

Ralston pointed at an overhead sign. "Get onto I-40 east up there."

"You've stayed in touch with him?" I asked.

"Haven't you?"

"Not a word since that night."

"Can you blame him," Rals said, "after that number you ran on his head?"

"*I* ran?"

"Found him on the Internet a few years ago. He's on Maryland's Eastern Shore, right on our way."

Not really. But what the hell. Old home week seemed to have perked Rals up.

He picked up his scrap of paper again. "Four. Be directly responsible for the welfare and success of a group."

"You did that," I said. "A few times. With good groups. Homes for the homeless, cheap loans for working-class students, job training for immigrants." Let's not talk about how those groups fell apart. "I sort of did that too. The London group."

For once, he had no snappy comeback. He stared out the window for a minute or two, slowly rolling up then unfurling his list. Then he looked at it again. "You hire your hippie friends, they think it's a good-karma lark. You hire people who'll actually do the fucking work, they think you're a dipshit who sits in an office all day except when you come out to chew their butts. Over the years, I had a few companies, made two shitloads of money and lost one, but my employees were only there for the bucks. Secretary, salespeople, paper pushers—not much of a group in any real sense. Probably my biggest fuckup in life."

"Don't be so hard on yourself. At least you—"

"I know, I know," he said. "That lecture you once gave me on my people skills."

"Lecture? Once?" Screaming matches, dozens. Ralston had chased any number of people out the East Village pad and a couple of times had almost broken up its core. He did, really, with Marco. I was always the one to run damage control. Now wasn't the time to bring it all up. If ever.

For two days before we'd hit the road, Ralston had spent a lot of time on our phone—the cordless, out on our terrace, with the door shut—with his bulging, tattered address book open in front of him on the table. "Just lining up places for us to stay along the way," he'd said. "Save some money." When I'd asked who he was calling, he shook his head sadly. "Most of these numbers aren't good anymore. Hey, go back to work and leave me alone."

Now, he looked across the car at me. "The London group? They kicked your ass out."

"And why was that?" But the point of this trip was to cheer him up, not refight old battles. "I ran the place for a couple of years. Before that, whenever we didn't make enough money, people would go out and get day jobs. I tried to make sure they didn't have to. We did all right. In that regard. Came up with some interesting stuff."

Ralston pursed his lips, furrowed his brow, and nodded to himself—the face he usually put on before an apocalyptic proclamation. "This could be our last chance."

"For what?" I said. "We're looking for a house."

"And maybe people to live in it."

I was maneuvering the merge onto I-40. "Ritz and I will live in it. You too, man, anytime, of course. What the hell are you talking about?"

"Come on, Jules, think about it. We all had plans—maybe not plans but ideas, crazy fantasies, houseboats in the sky. Things we wanted to do, the way we wanted to live. To make it all…add up to fuckin' something."

He'd never brought up this stuff before, and now here it was for the second time in less than a week. And it was bumming him out. "All kids dream," I said. "It's what makes humans different from all other species. A significant number of us aren't content to do things the way our parents did. So we get chaos and progress."

"Ours was different. Collectively we had a vision, a hazy vision maybe—"

"Smoky."

"It wasn't just the dope," he said. "A vision that went beyond the know-it-all-ism of young assholes everywhere. Anyway, who gives a rat's ass what all kids do? We had a vision of a better world. You sure did, with your pseudo-mysticism or whatever you called it."

"Psycho-Metaphysics," I said. "But we grew up."

"Grew up or gave up?"

"We change. Go on to different things."

"Because we change? You had that mystical quest going, secrets of existence and all that crap. You ran after it like a madman. When did you drop it?"

"Don't give me that," I said. "You know perfectly damn well."

"So it wasn't because you changed, and it sure as hell wasn't because of me. It was because you fucked it up. If you were their fearless leader, why didn't you steer their asses back on track? When you got back to New York, why didn't you pick up some different sack of shit for the gullible?"

"Because I needed to make a buck, for Christ's sakes."

Ralston's triumphant smile. "There's our generation's fifth fate—caught up in life's swirling toilet. We all got knocked off course by three things: fuckups, poverty, and kids. Jesus, look at Bruno's twisted litter. Guess what? Now we got a little money, the kids are old enough to fend for their own damn asses, and we're not quite as stupid as we used to be."

"So what do you want to do?" I said. "Organize more free concerts in the park? March on City Hall again? Another street art show?"

"There's this old joke," he said. "In heaven, the cooks are all French, the lovers are all Italian, the car mechanics are German, the cops are English, and everything's organized by the Swiss. Meanwhile, in hell, the cooks are English, the lovers are Swiss, the car mechanics are French, the cops are German— and everything's organized by the Italians." He shrugged. "I always wanted to be the Swiss guy in heaven, but this is hell and I'm the Italian."

"You? Mess up?" His talk of his failures, something he never used to admit to, sounded too much like a swan song. "Maybe we can still do something with those ideals," I said.

My feeble comment was an empty reassurance, but he sprang back to life, arms outstretched, hands clutching at the future. "Exactly! I knew you'd finally see it. This time we start small-scale, older and wiser and all that shit. Randy's out, but there's others."

"Others for what?" God almighty. "You want to start another goddamn commune."

Chapter 6

Marco's mailbox stood on a perfectly upright post at the mouth of a driveway leading to what was once a farm. Behind the barn, on the other side of a field, in the late afternoon sunshine, the Chesapeake Bay prodded a small inlet.

Ralston whistled. "Fucker must be doing pretty good." Did Rals resent that somebody had outdone him or worry that the artist wasn't about to chuck this spread for a commune? I had to stop playing silent shrink. He was probably just nervous about seeing Marco after so many years.

A screened porch stretched down one side of the house and wrapped around back for a view of the water. A woman stepped from the door, younger than Marco, in her forties. Although trim and pretty, she held herself in a prim, contained, sexless way, body language muzzled, that some women seem to cultivate. Her practiced smile gave away nothing.

"Hi, I'm Elaine, Marco's wife. I'm sorry, who's who?" We introduced ourselves and shook her hand. "Marco's down at the studio. I'll catch up to you there."

"The barn?" I asked.

"The barn's our guesthouse." She pointed around the back. "Root cellar. Can't miss it."

We almost did. At first, the squat stone hut looked too low to house a studio, but half its height was underground. Inside, the north light from the one high window caught an easel and the canvas it held: strange, twisted faces, reminiscent of the young Marco's work but more accomplished. A rangy old man with a salt-and-pepper brush-cut stared at a small TV murmuring on a table otherwise covered with paint tubes and jars of brushes. My brain struggled for a moment to reconcile him with memories of Marco.

As we came down the stairs and through the door, he turned, stood, and eyed us for a few seconds. "Fuck me dead."

Hippies borrowed their attire from three main archetypes: the cowboy, the American Indian, and the Eastern holy man. While most mixed them up—jeans, leather headband, white flowing shirt, bare feet—Marco had been more of a purist, and here he was, the droopy mustache turned gray, snap-button shirt, Levi's, and cowboy boots, which all still fit his lanky build despite the bud of a paunch. He exchanged backslapping hugs with me and a more cautious one with Ralston.

"Man," I said, "it's good to see you again. After that last time."

"Last time?"

"You know, the East Village pad, you just walked out, we didn't know..." I shrugged.

Marco laughed. "Crazy times."

My two-handed gesture took in the studio, the canvases leaning against the walls, the house. "Looks like you're doing great."

Marco fell back into his chair and waved Rals and me onto a stool and a wooden crate. "Pretty good. I paint, teach an art class a couple of days a week, fish. The house and shit, that's Elaine. You got an old lady?"

"Ritz. Married her. She's doing great."

"No shit? When'd you get back with her, before or after you went to London and joined that cult?"

"After." I shook my head. "Not a cult. Psycho-Metaphysics."

"More psycho than metaphysics," Ralston said.

Marco squinted at him. "You should talk, them crazies you hooked up with."

"I figured that out after a couple of months. Took him how many years?"

"At least we weren't blowing anything up," I said.

"Least I wasn't brainwashed by a cult." Ralston held up a hand to halt my comeback. "I know, I know, Tom Wolfe, a cult is a religion without political clout."

"A cult," I said, "is any dedicated group you want to slur with a cheap epithet."

Ralston winked at Marco. "Dedicated."

Marco leaned back. "You fuckers still goin' at it."

I turned away and pretended to groove on Marco's canvases. They were dusty, and the acrylic on his palette looked dry. Was this the best I could do? Defend my failures? Rals was at least game to try his again.

Elaine came down the steps. "Nothing like old friends, is there?" She tossed a glance at the TV. "Soaps?"

"Background noise, helps me concentrate."

She smiled at Ralston and me. "I have to leave in a minute. Come on up to the house, I'll show you your room." She turned to go without waiting for us.

It was on the third floor, a small room with twin beds. "I'll leave you to your unpacking." Again the abrupt departure. We had nothing that needed unpacking, but we sat on the beds until she'd soft-shoed her way back down the stairs.

Ralston eyed the plain wood floor and faded wallpaper. "I bet when her side of the family shows up, they rate their own rooms in the guesthouse."

"I'm in," Marco said. The three of us ambled along the shoreline, poking at driftwood and horseshoe crab shells with our feet. Rals hadn't even finished his pitch.

"Nothing to be in on," I said. "He's building communes in the air, it's just a—"

"Not a commune," Ralston said. "A big house. With a bunch of friends."

"Said I'm in."

I stopped in my tracks. "Into what? Doesn't even make good sense—a commune, at our age?"

"Good sense only works for small decisions," Ralston said. "If people used it for big decisions, nothing would ever happen. No Columbus, no Lewis and Clark."

"No Napoleon," I said. "No Hitler, no Genghis Khan."

Rals smirked. "No marriage, no kids."

Marco skipped a stone across the water. "I said I'm in."

"I'm not talking about an old-school commune," Ralston said, "one that exists just for its own sake. We'd do something useful with it."

The showdown might as well be right now, before this thing got out of hand. I faced Ralston. "Goddamn it, there's no commune."

Ralston pulled into himself like a turtle. His clothes suddenly looked too big for him. His face was dusty pale and his gray hair seemed wispier. He turned away.

I took a breath and forced back my anger. Anger at what? The commune idea would die of its own accord. "I mean, we haven't even found a house yet. Let's not get ahead of ourselves."

No Ralstonian comeback, no "You always gotta stay ahead of yourself."

Our three heads turned in unison to follow a snowy egret as it skimmed the surface of the water a few yards offshore then pulled up, lowered its landing gear, splayed its yellow feet, and settled onto its stilt legs in the shallows to look for dinner. Ralston's neck and limbs reemerged, and he scanned the bay's horizon, spun around to take in the shore, and slapped both palms to his head.

"Look!" As if for kindergartners, he pointed and enunciated clearly and slowly. "Birds. Water. Sunshine. Land. Peace and quiet. Big house. Big barn. Room to build." With a wide smile, he stretched out his arms.

"No, no, no, no, no, no." Marco shook his bowed head. "You don't understand. It wouldn't work here. Any idea what the taxes are on this place? And the people around here, redneck conservative or rich conservative, if they're not slashin' your tires or shootin' your dog, they're callin' their lawyer."

"How's Elaine fit into the picture?" Ralston said.

Marco continued along the water's edge, the heels of his cowboy boots leaving deep pockmarks in the damp sand that slowly filled with water behind him. "This definitely isn't the place." Ralston and I caught up with him and the three of us walked in silence for a couple of minutes.

"Who else is coming in?" Marco asked.

"You're only the second person we talked to," Ralston said. "Randy's in bad shape."

"Daph?"

Ralston and I exchanged glances. "You know where she's at?" he asked.

Marco looked around as if for eavesdroppers. "We keep in touch. Off and on."

East Village. Storefront, condemned building, Avenue C. Flashlights illuminate a rope hanging from the ceiling, a noose at its end, a chair on the floor beneath. A small crowd gathers, some inside, some outside peering through the window.

A figure in a black leotard leaps into the light, vaults from the chair, climbs the rope and swings back and forth, pumping her legs to widen the swing. Twists upside down and puts her head through the noose. Turns slowly as each swing gets shorter. Rights herself, stands on the chair, and with her head still in the noose, lets go of the rope. One foot on the chair's seat, one on its back, playing teeter-totter. Teeter-totter. Teeter-totter.

"Jump!"

"Please, stop!"

"Eek, a rat!" Laughter.

In one motion, jumps up, kicks chair away, grabs rope. Applause.

Sweating now. Leotard's color running down her legs.

Slowly pulls head from noose, lowers herself to the floor.

Not a leotard at all, black body paint on bare skin.

Sauntering sinuously through crowd. Many hands turning black.

Grabs a raincoat from a hook by the door, steps outside and disappears down the dark street.

Back in the apartment, Daph comes out of the shower in robe and flip-flops to join the rest of us. Marco glowers. "Why do you have to get naked?"

"She could have killed herself," Ritz says. "Why don't you ask her about that?"

Marco doesn't take his eyes off Daph. "Why naked?"

Daph unties her robe, lets it slip to the floor, and kicks off her flip-flops.

No one moves or speaks.

Finally, Marco slumps into a chair. "All right, all right." Daph puts the robe back on.

Ralston has the sense to keep his mouth shut.

Dinner was polite but a tad strained. No one brought up the commune scheme to Elaine. Afterwards she was off, "to a meeting."

"Meeting?" Ralston said as soon as she left.

Marco seesawed a spread hand. "She's into the local scene—museum or water quality or some shit." With a remote, he flipped on the large flat TV that hung on the wall.

I picked up our three glasses and the half-full bottle of wine from the table. "Let's sit on the porch, look at the bay." Marco cast a wistful glance at the screen but clicked it off and followed.

As I poured, Ralston disappeared upstairs for a minute and came back with three cigars. "Keeps the bugs away."

Ralston held a wooden match for Marco, who took a luxuriant puff. "Hey, you're right. No bugs." He ran his knuckles along the porch screen, chuckled, and took another puff. I declined a cigar. Ralston shouldn't have been smoking either, but how far could I push the mothering?

"I got some sweet Jamaican shit out in the studio," Marco said. "Elaine isn't much of a doper, but when the cat's away."

I waved off the weed for both of us. Ralston shot me a disgusted look and turned to Marco. "So what's going on here?"

"Going on?"

Ralston leaned back in his rocker, put an ankle across his knee, and dragged on his cigar. I sipped my wine. A moth fluttered against the screen. Marco puffed on his cigar until it lit up the porch, then sucked the glow a good half inch down the shaft and inhaled it slowly like a lover's scent. The words came out husky with smoke. "I'm in a fuck of a rut. Hardly paint at all. Haven't sold a canvas in a turd's age. Watch too much TV. Nobody around I can really talk to. Fuck, I get so bored I even jack off."

The three of us followed a firefly's intermittent twinkle as it zigzagged a path just above the garden.

"They're coming out now." Marco took another lungful. "I used to go for such skuzzy freaks—Daph wasn't skuzzy but jeez, what a freak. Elaine had class, took a shower every day, brushed her teeth after every meal and flossed in between, wore clean clothes, didn't get too fucked up to walk every chance she got, every other word out of her mouth wasn't fuck or shit." He hawked up a fat one and stood to spit it out the door. "She didn't go in for the free-love shit, but that only works great when it isn't your girl in the mix." He looked at Ralston for a few moments, then sat back down. "But these things wear off after a while."

"What'd she see in you?" Ralston said.

Marco rocked forward in his chair and his boots slammed onto the floor. "Fuck you, man. I'm laying out all my shit and you—"

"He's not giving you crap," I said, "he's just—"

"Hey!" Ralston held up his hands, one toward each of us. He looked at me. "I'm not too senile to take care of myself." Then at Marco. "All I'm asking is what it was that cranked her up on you."

After a long moment, Marco's slow trademark smile spread. Although his mustache no longer dangled down below his chin as it had back in his Yosemite Sam days, it was still long enough for him to twist one end of it around a finger. "Probably should have killed you back then when I caught you with Daph."

"You never were much of a runner."

"Elaine. Chemistry I guess. The fucking was primo. For years. And we don't fight, we just stay away from each other if..." Marco looked at his cigar as if having second thoughts about it. "I was something different than those pickle-up-the-ass MBAs she dated." He wiggled his fingers on either side of his face and bugged out his eyes. "The crazy genius artist."

Soft and warm at first but now beefing up, stalking, climbing, striding. The muscles of her thigh as it glides past my face, the veins of my hands. Kicking off the sheet, wrestling now, twisting, prying, gripping, harder and faster, every second a new hold and the perfect counter. The bed tiny and shrinking, like trying to make love on a fencepost. We leap to the floor, throw open the window. Wind and moonlight boom in, mill around the room then settle down like a rowdy ringside crowd. She pounds me against the wall but I see my opening and soon have her backed into a corner until with a trick of the legs she lands us on the canvas. We run outside, phosphorescent and steaming in the moonlight, catching each other in the road up against a stone wall far more fragile than we. Her body no longer flesh but humming, buzzing energy that sparks and crackles as I run my hands over it. We do it all, on the wall, on the ground, in the grass, under a tree, on top of the well, leaning on the house, up against the pen of the farmer's pig who grunts along with us. We drink wine and pour it over our bodies to cool off. We cover each other with dirt, straw, leaves, herbs, flowers, mash ripe figs torn from a tree onto and into our bodies then splash it all off with well water. I take her entire body into my mouth and roll it around on my tongue. I chew her up swallow her then shit her whole again. And she me. We fill and surround each other at once like two snakes eating each other's tails until meeting head to head. We see it all in the greatest of detail, smell and taste it all, feel, finger, fuck and feast on everything in every possible way. The night and the moon give up and go home, but we're growing stronger every minute, we can't get enough, can't get enough, can't get enough.

I zone back into the screen porch. "You still love her?"

"Sure." Too fast. "I'm too fucking comfortable, man." He stepped off the porch and took a leak in a flowerbed. "Keeps the deer away."

We'd had Elaine's homegrown asparagus with dinner, and the sweet skunky smell of Marco's asparagus piss drifted up onto the porch to cut through the cigar smoke.

After breakfast, Ralston and Marco took a walk while I sat at my laptop in the third-floor bedroom to answer my email. Whatever those two were scheming up, I had to keep my real life going. My paying life. I'd told my clients I was taking some time to deal with a family situation, but I still had to touch base often enough so they didn't look for someone more reliable.

I dealt with three or four and saved Adele for last. I'd been trying to convince her that her novel, like most, could use a plot.

"Jules, I want to tell the truth. Everything in my book is true. Why should I make things up?"

I felt like Pilate every time a client said that to me.

Footsteps on the stairs, a knock on the door. "Jules? May I come in?" Elaine. She looked good in shorts. Great, in fact. "I hope you were comfortable up here. We're having some work done on the guesthouse." Her movements were freer now, her smile warmer, and her eyes held a hint of something unsaid.

I took off my glasses. "Very nice of you to put us up, a couple of seedy characters from Marco's murky past."

Great laugh, too. More than my lame comment deserved. She sat on the other bed, our knees almost touching. "Editing—that must be interesting work." Her eyes held mine now, and she shifted her shoulders just enough to bring her breasts into play under the light shirt. Christ, I was swelling just looking at her. Away from Ritz and caught off-guard.

"Sometimes," I said. "Or it can be tedious or painful." I nodded at the screen. "Like this one." Fascinating, her expression said. I outlined the situation.

"Do you think she's confusing fact with truth?" she said.

"Or ego with purpose."

"Always a problem, isn't it?" Her smile hovered between collegial and complicit. "I'm a writer, too. Not published yet, but soon, I hope."

The dropped penny clattered around my brain. "Good luck with it." I took a long final look into those beckoning eyes. "Look, I don't want to give you the wrong idea. I'm a freelance editor, a book doctor. Not an industry insider." The glow in her eyes faltered. "Not by a long shot." And flicked off.

"Still." She stood. "I'd better leave you to your work."

Ralston must have passed her on his way up the stairs. "She count the towels?"

"You remember that old joke," I said, "why do women have pussies?"

Ralston's eyes went wide. "You didn't."

"I didn't."

"I told you that joke. So men will talk to them."

"Why do men become editors?"

Elaine waved a minimalist goodbye from the garden. Marco pushed a fistful of CDs into my hands. "How can you dudes ride without music? Week or two, I'm with you guys. Can't just ditch the students." I glanced at Elaine's tight ass, the big house, the bay fidgeting in the distance. Marco wouldn't toss all this. As if an afterthought, he dug into his pocket and pulled out a slip of paper, which he quickly shoved at Ralston. "Daph's number."

Ten miles down the road, the Grateful Dead still hadn't clicked for either of us. Ralston ejected it mid-track. "Marco still likes this stuff. Is that good, retarded, or just weird?"

"Maybe he wanted to get rid of these CDs."

Jefferson Airplane and even Jimi didn't do it for us either. The Stones finally got us sedately bopping and jiving.

> But what's puzzling you
> is the nature of my game.

"That's just because it's good old honest rock 'n' roll," I said. "Geezer rock. Remember those parties on Formentera?"

DOON ga chika chika chika

DOON ga chika chika chika

Full moon at Australian June's. Candles and hash pipes flicker, congas boom and bongos bop. White-clad freaks balance in a slow moonlit procession atop the stone walls, striking lunatic poses, blouses billowing in the breeze.

An onomatopoeia of drums: dumbeks, tablas, tom-toms, tambourines, African drums, homemade drums, wooden, metal, clay drums. Someone taps a wine bottle with the back of a knife. A flute darts between the beats then soars above, is joined by another. Hands pounded numb, I ride the beat into the night.

DOON chika DOON chik

DOON chika DOON chik

Inside a stone room dimly lit by a few candles and kerosene lamps, thirty drummers pack the floor. Smells chink the sound's surface: incense, smoke, spice, stone, the skins of the drums, and of the drummers, sweat, musk. Tea and smokes slowly circulate. Drummers come and go, but the sound remains unbroken. See it with your ears, a thick snake uncoiling, sliding out the doors and windows into the night.

In a bedroom, John Pujutoki reclines regally, torchlight glinting off his muscle-packed, sweat-misted torso, four half-naked zombie-eyed women crawling all over him. John Pujutoki's story: a ninety-seven-pound, chronically ill, two-bit hustler left Harlem for Mexico to breathe dry desert air and score some dope to sell back in the States. Burned and busted, jailed in the Mexican outback, he fell in with some Yaqui Indians who taught him the secret art of pujutoki, a system of mental and physical discipline that brings about spiritual awareness, physical health, strength, and power over women. The Yaquis cured him, built up his body, and made him what he is today.

Da da DOON ga chika chika

Da da DOON ga chika chika

Outside, not even the olive trees can stand still. The moon rises higher and higher above the writhing green sea. Everything slick with youth and sex and rhythm and flow and the ecstasy of possibility.

Tonight's lesson: John Pujutoki has something going for him the rest of us don't.

In the passenger seat, Ralston twisted around to face me. "Hey, man, where're you going? That was our turn."

I kept driving straight, away from the interchange, past the gas stations, through the commercial strip, and out onto a flatland of cornfields and clumps of forest. Rals stared at me for a few moments then settled back into his seat.

Up ahead, a small side road led off toward a strip of trees. I turned onto it, and the pavement ended. We bumped along the dirt road to the shade of the trees, where I pulled over and turned off the engine. In the stillness, the air felt close. I opened the door, put my feet on the ground, and leaned sideways into the seatback. Ralston did the same, and we sat silently, back to back.

After a while, he turned around toward me. "You okay, man?"

"Just resting."

Fifteen minutes or half an hour later, he said, "I get it."

"Get what?"

"I get it, that's all."

"Well, I don't."

"Like it was all a waste," he said.

I shrugged. That was probably part of it.

"And maybe didn't have to be," he said.

"My brain keeps diving into the past. Instead of the future, like it used to. Is that a sign of dementia?"

"A few years ago, I took Martine to Formentera. To show her a piece of my past. The island we lived on isn't there anymore. Now it's all electricity, plumbing, hotels, boutiques, paved streets, vacation rentals."

I wasn't going to bring up Kathmandu, not now, but it too had mushroomed from the colorful, dirt-road town I had known into a huge tourist circus with ten times the population. We sat silently for a while.

"It all catches up with you," I said. "You always think things can look up, a better day will come. That's true for most of your life. But then the time comes when you realize you won't get better. You won't get younger, stronger, better-looking. Your memory won't bounce back. Your aches and pains will never go away, or if they do, worse ones will take their place. Hot young women will never go to bed with you again. It's too late to turn your life around or start all over. Intellectually, you always knew this day was coming. Then you realize it's already arrived, you're on a slide you can't stop. I'm not talking about depression. This is cold fact."

Ralston sighed but said nothing.

I swung my legs back in. "Might as well push on."

"What else can you do?"

Chapter 7

Back on the interstate, headed south. "No more screwing around," I said. "At least we can find Ritz that house."

Rals slowly nodded. "You know—"

"I don't want to hear any crap about how I'm too goal-oriented to find happiness in a goalless, soulless universe."

"A penetrating observation," he said. "Especially since all I was going to say is we haven't eaten since breakfast."

We stopped for sandwiches and ate them on the road. When Ralston tossed his toothpick out the window and grabbed his scruffy list from the center console, I sighed.

He looked over at me. "You got something better to do, just say the word." He waited a good half-minute before clearing his throat, lifting the list, and peering at it. "Five. Go to bed with a woman you thought far above your reach and knock her socks off."

The list finally rang a bell for me. I'd had Ritz in mind when I contributed point five to the list. In addition to her beauty, her father was a bigwig in the art world, an older brother an entertainment lawyer to the stars, and a big sister photographer and muse to the rock 'n' roll elite. Straight A's at college, president of this and that, at the top of every stud's must-do list. Including Ralston's, but he couldn't get a date with her. I'd fallen in love with her in a lit class.

"Did that," he said.

"Dottie?"

"Oh, the cynicism."

"I do that every day," I said. At least I used to.

"Very true—the above-your-reach part. Better check with Ritz about the socks. Last I saw, they were in no danger of leaving her feet. Me, I ticked off that point at least a dozen times. If you count the ones after my epiphany."

"Can't wait to hear it."

"No one is above my reach," he said.

"Christ, beam down and take me now."

"No one's above anyone's reach. We're both living proof of that."

"I have a theory about that," I said.

"Of course you do."

"Pretty boys don't have to work at it. They think just screwing the lucky girl is gift enough. Besides, lots more are lined up waiting for them, so why knock yourself out for re-peat business? Guys like you and me—"

"Speak for yourself," he said.

"Once we finally get the girl into bed, we have to do a bang-up job on her."

"Well put."

"Make her want more. Hope she tells her friends about what great plumbers we are."

"Lay that pipe."

"Goofy-looking guys try harder."

"That's your motto. Some of us just have the gift." He looked at the list again. "Onward and downward. Six. Marry the woman you want."

I ticked it off in the air with a finger. "Done."

"Close enough," he said. I let it go. "Seven, make and raise children. Check, yawn. But get this. Eight. Face down a hostile group alone."

"Face them down?" I said. "More like turn tail."

He smirked. "Us carpetbaggers may get our chance yet. Okay, nine. Take care of a loved one's death." He looked thoughtful, then morose.

"To hell with that," I said. "Next?"

He sighed. "Ten. Face your own death."

I hawked and spat out the window. But the idea lingered in the space between us for a few moments.

"We've entered the age of dying friends," he said. "Paolo, lung cancer. Trevor, boom, just like that, heart attack. Rob, some kind of medical screw-up during an operation he probably didn't even need—prostate in fact, see what I mean? Now Bruno."

Back in New York, after Ralston had refused my offer to arrange a medical check, I'd gone to lunch with a college friend, not one of our beatnik crowd at the time but a lab partner in a psych course who was now head of psychiatry in a New York hospital just across the park.

"Ralston?" Teddy had said. "You still hang out with that cocksucker?" A dim light flickered feebly from afar in my memory, something about a girlfriend. I described Ralston's physical symptoms to him. Teddy told me it could be this, that, any number of other things, or a combination. "At this age we get like old cars. Things start wearing out, breaking down, falling off." He'd glanced down at his own body. "Faster and faster, one after the other." He had no specific suggestions for Rals, just to get a full checkup. And to talk to a psychiatrist. "Not me," Teddy had said. "Someone who doesn't already know what an asshole he is."

"Like clockwork," Ralston murmured. "One corpse a year for the past few, like machinegun bullets stitching a path toward me. My life has begun to flash before my eyes. Slowly, in little forgotten snippets that suddenly come out of nowhere and take me by surprise. They say that happens just before you die."

"They say all kinds of complete crap." Of course the same thing had been happening to me since Rals came to town.

He waved the tatty sheet around in front of his face. "You know what I love about this list?"

I declined the invitation.

"It's complete bullshit," he said. "Written by two pretentious ass-wipes who didn't have a fucking clue about anything. Anything at all. We did most or all of that shit, so we're real men, right? Look at us now."

He crumpled up the list in both hands, blew his nose into it, and tossed it out the window.

We drove in silence for a dozen or more miles. I'd never before seen him so bleak. I had no idea what to do for him. I kept my mouth shut.

Reading Ouspensky, but Gurdjieff always seems to be laughing at him. Sam knew some people close to Gurdjieff's school who told him that Ouspensky, on his deathbed, said, "There is no system."

Sam himself no longer studies Gurdjieff, has given up strong drugs, says they sap one's psychic energy. Has a tarot deck, does a reading on me, outcome ambiguous. One day I go to visit him. Sam's not there, his wife June is, lying naked in the sun behind the house. Starts to cover herself then changes her mind, says she needs to rid herself of such inhibitions.

A series of solitary acid trips, deliberate risks, a test of drugs as a path. Hours spent sifting through strange perceptions and sensations for something to make sense of it all. Hours of slow-motion dance movements performed naked on a cool stone floor searching for new doors into or out of the body. More hours in cross-legged meditation, straining, then straining not to strain, to pop into a new reality. A long trek across miles of alien rock desert strewn with skulls of the long-dead gleaming white in the light of a harsh uncaring sun, trying to allegorize hallucination as a journey of the soul.

In a dark subterranean cavern, winged beings flap about in confusion, aware of no other existence. Some see a dim light glowing at the end of a narrow shaft and fly up towards it. They find a thick glass window, a view of a world outside full of light, but no exit to that world. Some remain, futilely beating wings and faces against the glass, others give up and flutter downward into darkness. A few turn back down the shaft to the main cavern to begin searching for the true way out.

I decide to figure out what I know, what I truly know with utter certainty. To cast aside all that I have been taught or told, all opinion, anything possibly illusory, and to see what knowledge I am left with.

I know I perceive. I do not know if that which I perceive is reality or illusion, nor the source of what I perceive, if any. But I perceive.

So I know I exist. I don't know the nature of that which I call myself, or even if it's a discrete entity, but I am aware, in this moment, of being.

I find nothing else I can be certain of.

Ralston pulled the crookedly folded map from the glove box. Signs for our next hop-off point had begun to demand our attention. "Good thing I'm bringing you along on this road trip," he said. "I'm going to save your damn ass with it. Again."

Chapter 8

"Sunday in God's Own Town, and everything's jumping but the churches." Ralston was sneering out the car windows at the crowded latte emporia, boutiques, and Thai eateries of Chapel Hill.

"So much for the Athens of the South," I said. True to its name, the town was on a hill, and far too built up for Ritz's bird plans.

But it gave me an excuse to call her anyway. "Looks like Amherst or Northampton," I told her over the cell, "only warm. We're going to head for the coast."

"Forget the coast," she said. "Too expensive, too many people. You want forest, rivers, wetlands."

"Wetlands—swamps?"

Ralston's eyebrows shot up.

"You could have checked all this out on the Internet," she said.

"Where's the fun in that?"

A bearded, beaded, professorial type drove past in a convertible BMW. Could that have been me in an alternate timeline?

"Speaking of fun," she said, "I had my mammogram yesterday."

A spike of fear. "Everything okay?"

"Everything's okay."

"I'll do a more thorough check when you come down here."

"Then hurry up and find something for me to look at."

"I got something for you to look at right now."

"Big talker."

I hung up. Ralston was looking at the map. "Wetlands and swamps? Here we go—Quicksand Junction, Snakebite Creek, Mosquitoville, Chigger Depot."

"We should stop and find someone who knows the area."

"Oh, man. We're just looking for a house. What is it with you, always needing some damn guru before you can take a step?"

"What is it with *me*? Who won't listen to a word of advice from anyone, can't even conceive of the possibility that somebody might know something you don't?" I made a show of slowly cruising the streets, looking up and down each block for a real-estate office.

After a while, he laughed. "You done with the charade? For Christ's sake, it's Sunday."

I hung an abrupt left and hightailed it out of town.

Morning after an all-night party, sharing a pot of tea with John Pujutoki. My hands, swollen like two bunches of bananas from playing a conga for hours on end, can hardly hold a bowl.

He takes a sip, then another, puts down his bowl. "Let me see them hands." Holds my wrists for a few seconds, runs his fingers over and between each of mine. His hands: warm, strong, neither polite nor intrusive, matter-of-fact with an underbuzz of sex. Like he'd fuck me right here if he felt like it.

"I knew this was going to happen," I say. A verbal blink. Stared down by silence. "Kept drumming anyway."

"Why do people do the shit they do?" He pulls me to my feet, runs his hands up my arms and down my back. "Thousands of white boys have made millions pretending to answer that, and I won't charge you a dime to tell you it's a bullshit question." Now down my chest to my hips. "Like that old question, why's a dog lick his balls." Kneads my right hand. "Same thing with a body, it does what it can in the direction that's most natural to it." Now the left hand. "Swells up to protect itself. Got to let it know everything's okay now." One by one, takes each finger by the tip and shakes it. Brisk, certain, neither gentle nor rough. "You got to listen to the body, ease it around, and head it in the right direction. Once you can do that…" Switches to my other hand. "You can do the same with mind. With sex. Spirit."

Chrissie, fresh from bed, in panties and loose shirt, comes outside into the sun, squats on her heels, pours herself some tea. John looks her over, direct, appraising, no leer, no apology. Chrissie, pretending not to notice, takes my hands.

"How are they?" Swelling already going down. She gives John a wide smile. Smiles back. Smiles all around.

I say, "Teach me this stuff."

John looks me up and down. Am I worthy? Jury still out. "Ain't easy."

"Wouldn't want it to be."

"Shit, why not?" John Pujutoki and Chrissie have a good laugh over my spiritual work ethic. Probably part of some test, I later tell Ralston.

"Test of how far he can push some gullible jerk," he says.

Nighttime, a two-lane unlit road. A swampy breeze pushed through the trees. We'd reached the wetlands. Rals and I parked and stepped into the bare-bones roadhouse. Dark wooden bar with high padded stools, mirrored shelves of bottles, a few tables. The jukebox was silent, and the bartender's small radio was playing a ballgame. A faint smell lurked near the restroom door, but the Lysol-to-urine ratio was favorable. We ordered a couple of beers.

The screen door smacked shut. From our table, we contemplated the two women who'd just come in and now bantered with the bartender. One had that supple, wiry look that always seems to promise lack of inhibition, and the other had a sensuous face and a lush body, even if a bit beamy at the hips. Both were pushing fifty if not a bit beyond.

Ralston chewed a peanut and took a sip of beer. "The joys of post-menopausal sex. No pregnancy panics, inhibitions long ago trampled into submission, better staying power."

"Younger women are overrated," I said. "Mature women are less hung up on relationship angst."

"An older woman catches your eye, something sexy, maybe her ass has gone to hell but her tits are still riding high, her face hangs in tatters but the legs are nice. It's enough. It's plenty. Because somehow it doesn't matter as much as it used to, you got nothing left to prove. At least that's what you tell yourself, 'cause the draw is their possible availability to a guy as beat to shit as they are."

The two women did seem to be putting on a bit of a show, nothing obvious, but enough laughter and movement to provide proof of life. Ralston leaned closer. "You always got to ask yourself, are they in great shape, or do they just know how to hide the horrors? Bubble-wrap thighs, mailbag bellies, road-kill boobs? Only one way to find out." As the women turned from the bar, Ralston stood up and pulled out a couple of chairs. "We were hoping you two might appreciate a little civilized company."

Neither missed a beat. The wiry one laughed. "Just so happens that's exactly what we're here for." The bartender handed them their beers, and they moseyed over.

"Civilized?" the lush one said. "He taking a poke at our homey little burg?"

"Not at all," Ralston said. "I was just—"

"'S'all right, honey." Wiry patted his hand. "Poke all you want." The women laughed, Ralston raucously joined in, and I cautiously smiled.

Two well-weathered men stomped into the bar. They stopped for a word with the bartender, then leaned back against the bar and gazed over at our table. One was tall and broad-shouldered, the other wore a tan uniform like a deliveryman's.

"What do you think?" Wiry said softly. "Straight from the cab of an over-powered pickup?"

"With a dead animal in the back," Rals said, not so softly. The women had a thigh-slapping laugh. With a roll of the shoulders and a hitch of the belt, the two men sauntered toward us.

"My, my," Lush said. "Here's that civilized company we came here to meet."

Wiry, in a stage whisper: "Our husbands."

The bigger one flicked the toothpick from the right side of his mouth to the left. "Just couldn't wait till we got here, could you."

A sneer on his lips, Ralston stood up with an insouciant swagger. As the two husbands eyed Ralston almost contemplatively, I managed a quick peek at the arm patch on the shorter one's uniform shirt—Sheriff's Department. And he wore a gun. Ralston wrapped his hand around his empty beer bottle.

I grabbed Ralston's bottle arm and eased to my feet. "I'm sorry, Officer, we had no idea these ladies were with you. We were just asking directions to a motel."

They stared at me, deadpan. The big one tongued his toothpick back to the right side of his mouth. "That didn't come out quite right, did it?" He grabbed a chair from another table.

I took a step back and pushed Ralston behind me. John Pujutoki had taught me some moves, and this one wasn't a cop, or at least hadn't identified himself as such. I bent my knees slightly, and—doing my best not to telegraph it—got ready to leap forward at the man's exposed face or torso under the arc of the chair's downswing.

Toothpick sat down in the chair and waved at the bartender. "Jimmy, where's them beers?" Then he smiled at us, a toothy, predatory grin that stopped just short of malevolence. "Aw, sit back down. I love it when guys try to pick up my wife. It's a sincere compliment to us both." The smile remained ambiguous. Rals, thank Christ, put down the beer bottle and kept his mouth shut. Jimmy arrived with six more beers, giving us all a chance to break eye contact without backing down.

The cop adjusted his holster and sat as well. "You know, I almost believe 'em. About the directions. Must be lost, no other reason to be here."

I rushed out an explanation of our mission to the swamps of the Roanoke River.

Toothpick finished his beer, signaled for another, and pulled out a business card. "You just might get lucky after all. Come by the office tomorrow."

I put on my glasses and looked at the card. Matt Horner, Real Estate.

Chapter 9

The house sat back on a low bluff overlooking the river. "High enough to stay above a flood," Matt said. No toothpick today, no macho swagger, no salesman slick either. Wide stone stairs led down like a ghat to a concrete landing at the water's edge.

He'd showed us a couple of other houses first, either too small or too expensive. "Just to set us up for this wreck," Ralston whispered to me. It was an enormous wreck—at least a dozen rooms on two floors plus basement and attic, big kitchen, roomy shed, a small stable, and a garage, all on six acres, most of it forest.

The long porch was deeper than it had to be, which spoke of a generosity of spirit absent from the abstemiously shallow New England porches I was used to. With Matt out of earshot, Ralston ran his fingers over the intricately turned balusters supporting the porch rail. "Look at this woodwork." The posts holding up the porch roof weren't faux plantation-style columns but slender and turned, with carved struts at the top, some of them broken or missing. The moldings over the door and windows were also carved, with a forest or jungle motif populated by birds and monkeys.

The front door opened directly into a large, high-ceilinged room. The floors were bare wood, the windows tall, and the balustrade of the wide staircase at the room's inner corner even more elaborately turned than the porch rail. Every couple of feet along the molding where wall met ceiling were carvings whose paint had faded or flaked off. I moved in for a closer look: more laughing monkeys in various postures.

Although the house certainly wasn't antebellum, it looked as if it had taken more than a century's worth of hard living and been through its own wars. Paint peeled inside and out, some of the clapboard was rotting, the small back porch listed on its supports, the floorboards were scruffy, the appliances had been yanked from the kitchen without further ado, and some ceilings showed water damage.

And yet, outside and in, it stood like a perfect host with an easy grace, relaxed amid the trees, welcoming in gesture. If this house were haunted, the ghosts would smile and wear old comfortable clothes with an impeccable drape. Outside, in matched colors, the green trim highlighted the soft brown of the shingles against the brushed blue-grays and greens of the trees and Spanish moss, while inside, the off-white walls set off the different woods of the floor, trim, and staircase. When I squinted, the room blurred into an impressionist sketch of a country retreat, its composition sharpened by precisely placed dings and scratches.

I poked a lath at a dusty cloth bundle hanging from the middle of the high ceiling in the big downstairs room. "What's that?"

"Lighting fixtures," Matt said. "Just a bunch of wires and stuff now."

Ralston's frown deepened. "Place is a mess." He'd once run a small Habitat for Humanity sort of operation in Central Africa.

Years ago, I'd asked him, "What happened?"

"One by one, the bastards took off on me."

"What'd you do to them?"

"Fuck you."

"I get the picture."

Ralston, now leading the rest of the inspection, shouted to Matt from the attic. "Needs a new roof!" He then leaned over to whisper to me. "No termites, no dry rot. Plumbing looks good too, what I can see of it. Matt! Where's the septic?"

An hour later, I shook Matt's hand. "Thanks for showing us around. Hope we didn't keep you away from any actual customers."

"Hold your horses," Ralston said. "He hasn't given us a price yet."

"Seller's asking three and a half."

Ralston looked aghast. "Hundred thousand? It'll take that much again to fix it up."

"Maybe at New York prices, not here. River frontage, sound structure—one of them fancy spa-resort companies almost picked it up a month ago. Too far from any airport or interstate, their head office decided."

"Thanks again, Matt," I said.

Rals was still scoping out the joint in that jittery way of his once he got a bug up his ass. "What's the big tree in front, the one that hasn't leafed out?"

"Live oak."

"Thought they were evergreen."

"That one's dead."

"A dead live oak. More money to have it taken down. Mind if Jules and I hang out a bit longer, just to suss out the vibe?"

"Suss all you like. You got my number."

After Matt drove off, we sat on the porch steps. Cicadas whirred, crickets cricked and, once the human sound and motion died down, the birds showed themselves: a mockingbird, a mourning dove, a flicker, then a pileated woodpecker, a male cardinal—or was that flash of red a summer tanager? Even a bluebird. I'd never tried to learn their names, but in hundreds of walks in Central Park with Ritz over the years—

"Tell me she wouldn't love it," Ralston said.

"Sure she would. But it's too damn big. The price, the repairs, out of the question."

"Much too big—for you two. But with our little band of brothers and sisters going in on it with us—hey, hey, let me finish, think about it before you go all AARP on me. There you'll be, if not in this place, somewhere else, far, far from the big city. Ritz will be doing her birds, and what'll you be doing? Okay, maybe some editing. Maybe you'll even get off your ass and write that book."

"What book?"

"But what'll you do the rest of the time? Who'll you talk to? Jim-Bob down the crick? Coon huntin' with Roy Boy when his parole comes through? You remember *8½*, Fellini, that dream, living in one place with a whole lifetime of friends and lovers? Tell me we don't all have that same fantasy."

Eight and a half thousand reasons why not jostled one another in my brain. Logistics. Finances. Healthcare. The erosion wreaked on old friendships by time, distance, and changes. But shoot down Rals's dream? Piss on the flaming wreckage?

Soon. But not this evening. Not while the house's Southern charm still held sway over us, while the woods, the river, the soft breeze and its fragrance welcomed us like new friends who should have been old friends. Not while Rals, happy and excited, was planning a future with his best friends. I gave his shoulder a gentle punch. "How can you tell if Rals thinks he's convinced you?"

"I give up."

"His mouth stops moving."

I leaned back on my elbows and pretended to groove on the moment. Moving here would be the terminus. With New York, the hard part is getting there, and it's easy to see yourself moving elsewhere. This place would be an admission of failure, a surrender. Intellectually, we may believe that we're meaningless and our lives add up to zero, but emotionally? Not even Zen masters believe that. If they did, they wouldn't bother being Zen masters.

"You want to do this," John Pujutoki says, "fall by my crib tomorrow." Walks off, muscles vamping under tight skin and short shorts.

"He's full of shit," Rals says. "There's people who know stuff, and people who pretend to know stuff. How can you fall for his line of crap? Puju-fuck-you doesn't know shit."

"So who knows stuff?"

"Your kind of stuff? Mystical nirvana woo-woo shit?"

"You don't like him because he gets more ass than you do."

"That proves he's enlightened?"

A wandering stud monk? "I have to check it out. Can't just let it pass. He's right here." Fated? Or just my laziness?

Sitting on a hot rock in the glaring sun without food and water for a whole day. My first pujutoki lesson. Staggering home at dusk. Chrissie cooks rice.

"What'd you learn?" John Pujutoki asks me.

"The energy from the sun—"

"Don't give me no hippie horseshit."

That night, sunset to sunrise, sitting on a rock by the sea, wind blowing spray on me.

"What'd you learn?"

"Some patience, maybe. You can force yourself to do stuff. But why?"

"That's a little better," John Pujutoki says.

"Swamp Fox to Amazon Queen, Swamp Fox to Amazon Queen, come in please."

"You think that's funny?"

Rals flipped the cell closed. "No signal. Dead zone."

When we got to town and parked in front of Matt's office, my cell phone managed to scrounge up a ratty connection. "Ritz? How you doing?"

"Nice and quiet for a change. You?"

"We found this place. It's above a river—"

Rals pulled my phone hand to his own face. "Ritz, it's perfect! Don't let him talk you out of it!" Then quietly to me, "I'm going inside to talk to Matt, see how much time we got to shit or get off the pot. Take your time with her. Soft, slow hand, that's what she likes, trust me." He got out of the car.

"How's Ralston?" Ritz asked.

"Half the time just holding up, half the time more like normal—his normal. This house thing has him jazzed, which is a pain in the ass, but a lot better than seeing him so down. He's going to crash when we nix it, it's so damn big."

"Big is good...don't care if...repairs...give you something to do."

I walked around trying to get a sweeter reception spot. "Are you kidding me? He wants to fill it with friends."

"We'll need guests...keep us from driving each other crazy."

"Not guests, residents. He wants to start a damn commune."

"Ralston… How much?"

"They're asking—"

"What?"

"The sellers want—"

"Can't hear you!"

"More than we budgeted. Rals plans to have the others kick in too."

"Sounds…don't commit to…until I see it."

"You're breaking up. When can you come down?"

"End…week. Finals…if that's too long…should have waited until…"

"I don't know, we'll find out."

"Freddy came by…says hello."

"Hello back."

"Wants to buy an apartment."

"He sure he wants to stay in New York?"

"What? Wants help…down payment…loan, he says…co-signer for the mortgage."

"Jeez, with this going on?"

"If we move…nice to…place to stay…the city…" The signal died.

I looked up and down the street. Here? For the rest of my life? A new place always used to be a moment, an episode, at most a phase. You never needed an exit strategy because the door was always wide open.

Inside, I found Ralston and Matt in the midst of an intense conversation. Rals caught sight of me, stood up and shook Matt's hand. "Thanks a lot, buddy. We'll talk soon." He hustled me back outside. "What'd she say?"

"She'll come check it out in a week. Meanwhile we can look—"

"I got Matt to let us stay there."

"What?"

"I don't know anybody down here, who else could I ask? We'll check out of the motel and save a shitload of money, buy sleeping bags, make a fire, crap like that. Cook our own food. Shit in the woods with the possums and armadillos. Live like real men. Like we used to."

Next pujutoki task: walk around the entire island never losing sight of the sea. Two days.

After the first day, what did I learn? The path our consciousness takes through life is the only thing that gives a façade of orderliness to an essentially random universe? Too hippie-dippy. Life only makes sense when it's about me? Sounds too crass, but John Pujutoki might buy it for its contrariness. Enlightenment is about pleasing the master?

Second day. Slap of sandal on stone. Scent of wild rosemary and thyme. Hiss of sea. Sweet serendipity of wild mulberries. Scatter of lizard, stipple of goat. Warm push of shitting in the sunshine, the hot spatter of piss on rock.

The Zen masters talk about—who cares? A woman shouts in the distance, a child answers, a dog barks. A fish leaps, its startled eye fixed on me for an eternal split second before it splashes back into its parallel universe. The moon just rising as I pause for a moment at my starting point before heading inland for home.

At the house, there's Ralston in our bed, Chrissie with hickeys and a just-fucked look.

Ralston struggling into his pants, dick awhirl. "Sorry, man, just happened, caught up in the moment." Chrissie crying. I slam him into the wall and get in a punch to the ribs before he breaks free, feints a counterpunch, and runs out the door. I take off for John Pujutoki's without a word to Chrissie.

John Pujutoki isn't at his house. Probably off balling some chick. I wait, but he doesn't come back, not that day or the next. Another test? I search the usual spots, ask around. No one has seen him.

Anyway, Ralston's probably right about John Pujutoki. But when a door opens…

Back at my house, Chrissie sitting on the doorstep. "Where's John Pujutoki?" I ask. She seems confused. I wait.

She looks down, shakes her head.

"See you 'round," I say.

Starts crying, stuffs her clothes in her duffle. "It wasn't Rals's fault."

"Oh, it was all you?"

"What? God. No. How could you think that?"

Chrissie walking away. I don't spoil the moment by asking her what the hell she meant.

Two days later, Ralston at Klaus's café, massaging his ribs and wincing. I order a café con leche, drink it at the bar. What did I learn? I order another, join Ralston at the table.

"Still mad at me?" he says.

But he won't hang out with me, always has somewhere else to be when we meet by chance or at a friend's. I catch him alone. "What's up with you, man?"

"Just getting around more. There's this chick across the island."

My teacher a bullshit artist. The girl, no Ritz but a good girl, gone rotten. Ralston even more of a dick than usual. I've got to get out of here. Find a real teacher.

Rough it like we used to? Not exactly. This time we had in-flatable mattresses under our sleeping bags. We didn't have to gather wood to cook fresh-caught fish but bought a camp stove to grill our steaks, which we washed down with a bottle of half-decent red. Now we lay in the one-candle glow of the big downstairs room.

"Hear the bugs?" Ralston said.

"No."

"Mice and rats in the walls?"

I lurched up to my hands and knees. "Rats!?"

"Hear any?"

"No. Do you?"

"Nope. Nice, huh?"

I lay back down. "Four-star."

My brain, all on its own, was busily plotting our path away from here. Down the coast? All the way to Key West? Never been there. We could get going now, why wait for morning? The practice run was over, maybe now I was ready for the real thing.

But ever since we'd gotten here, Ralston had been up. "Hear that?" he said. "Owl. Ritz will love it here."

"Go to sleep."

"Right. Big day tomorrow."

"G'night. Wait, what do you mean, big day?"

"Walter's coming."

I twisted up onto an elbow. "Why didn't you tell me?"

"I just did."

"When did you talk to him?"

"While you were on the phone to your ravishing wife. I didn't want to interrupt the tender moment."

"That was hours ago!"

"And now we're back in the cell's dead zone and anyway it's too late for you to call him and tell him not to come."

I pushed myself over onto my back.

After a minute or two, Ralston broke the silence. "Sorry, man. Should have told you."

"That's how you see me? The guy who says no to everything?"

"I didn't know what you'd do. I should have told you. I'm an asshole."

"I'm asking you a question. Is that who I am now?"

When people ask you to be honest with them about themselves, you have to wonder just how honest they mean. Rals sighed deeply, as if pondering this perilous question.

"You've gotten, let's say, a little careful. You never were a cowboy, but in your low-key way, you were out there. You were the first to get into acid, then meditation—the real thing, not this New Age bullshit. You smuggled dope first, you dragged our asses across Asia, you went to gurus and ashrams and monasteries and shit. You wrote a book about it and got it published. You pulled up stakes to go to London and join the meta-psychotics."

"Psycho-Metaphysics."

"And then pulled up stakes again and started editing. You were a pioneer, man. I was just crazy. Now you've gotten conservative. Like you're protecting something, husbanding your resources, hunkering down for the long final winter."

The long final winter. "At this age, maybe you have to consolidate what you have."

"Consolidate shit. There are no guarantees."

"But you can improve the odds. I bet you have a bunch of money socked away."

"I wouldn't devote my life to fondling it," he said, "reading the *Wall Street Journal* and calling my broker twice a day. Squirrel away your extra acorns when you have some, hope they're still there when you need them. Consolidate what?"

Why was I arguing? I didn't disagree with him.

"You think Ritz likes you better all tame and timid?" he said.

As random shots sometimes do, the question knocked me sideways. In fact, she probably did. "Of course not."

"You worry about your accoutrements—your apartment, your nice food and wine, your digital cable with hundreds of movies, which you need because you're so fucking bored, your programmable microwave, your hipster friends or whatever bullshit."

"We did so many stupid things back then," I said.

"We did a ton of stupid shit for smart reasons."

Formentera. Pisces is boring. Enough of the quiet, introspective, waffling life of a Pisces. Aries is exciting, the Ram, roaming the Earth leaping from rock to boulder, a fire sign, a cardinal sign. Besides, I need money to head to Asia. So, a little side trip.

Don't ask Ralston to come, hope he'll insist on it. Cut my hair, shave off my beard, borrow a suit for border crossings. He's still avoiding me but must have heard I'm leaving. A trip alone to a truly foreign place. A necessary challenge, a requisite risk.

They say that if you want to score in Tangier, go see Ahmed the Man.

Fresh off the boat in Tangier. "What do you want, man? Kif? Hash? I got the best stuff, best prices, whatever you want,

just tell me, I get it for you." A dapper man with a car salesman's vibe.

"Ahmed the Man?"

"You know me? I don't know you."

"You're famous. Everybody's heard of Ahmed the Man."

All smiles, waves me along.

The Socco Chico sideshow, streets full of people, lined
with cubbyhole shops and small cafés, cheap hotels. Mostly
foot traffic, the occasional car, small truck, or donkey. Pale
Berbers from the hills. Black men from the south. Children,
dogs. Burros deliver huge fragrant baskets of fresh mint to
the cafés in the quarter. Large glass stuffed with mint leaves
then filled with tea. Old men sipping tea and smoking kif
from long-stemmed pipes with tiny red clay bowls. More true
freaks in the time it takes to finish a glass of mint tea than
you've seen before in your life. Midgets, giants, guys with no
arms or legs, hunchbacks, spastics, twisted wrecks. Horrible
scars, missing eyes, missing noses, misshapen heads, bodies.
Six fingers on a hand, or none. Feet pointing backwards, no
feet. Some beggars, but most working—carrying a load, selling
water, tending a shop.

Women all veiled. Some from the nose down, eyes and
forehead showing. Others in a single garment, a brown or black
tent that covers them from the top of the head to the ground
with only a narrow cloth grid at the eyes, through which their
entire force of presence beams. Never hear them speak.

Check into a small room—bare floor, sagging bed, an old
freestanding wardrobe, window with a rag draped across it as
a curtain. Perfect.

Tiny restaurant, Ahmed and his friend. Ahmed orders.
No idea what I'm eating, tastes great. Wandering around after
the meal, Ahmed and his friend holding hands or with their

arms around each other's shoulders as Arab men sometimes do, implying only friendship. A house, who knows whose. Floor covered with carpets and cushions, more carpets on the walls. Women bring tea, sweets, nuts. Business talk, what Ahmed has, and prices.

Hippies whisper about a burn. The Moroccan dealer tips off the Spanish police, buyer caught at the border and goes to jail, the dope returned to the dealer for resale. Biding my time. Haggling with other dealers. Ahmed the Man thinks I'm playing hard-to-get, lays out his lowest prices. Ahmed's probably no more bent than the other dealers, but I score from a farmer in the hills outside town, each of us frightened of the other.

Stoned off my nut from tasting the product, working my way back to the Socco Chico, the bagful of dope screaming its contents while the streets teem with robbers, spies, stoolies, and cops. Somehow managing to slip past them all.

In my room, chair propped against the doorknob, tightly wrapping candy-bar-size slabs of hash in plastic and tape, airtight, so no slightest smell can escape. Cutting up a T-shirt and fashioning a body vest with pockets in the small of the back, the belly, under the arms. Sew the hash in.

Cruising the Socco Chico, looking for Ahmed the Man. We order tea, bullshit awhile. Letting drop I'm leaving Tangier, taking the noon ferry to Algeciras tomorrow, saying good-bye. I hand him one hit of DMT in a tiny foil ball, tell him to sit down before he smokes it. Gratitude or malice?

Next day at dawn I jump onto the hydrofoil for Gibraltar, then a liner for Italy, won't go near the Spanish border. Cool in my suit, freshly shaven, hair neatly combed, trying to blend in, a smile and a nod. Boom! Boom! Gunshots! Oh, shit. Cops, mafia?

They're shooting skeet off the stern.

Sharing a cabin with a guy about fifty, no luggage, always wears a tuxedo. Travels all the time, needs only one suit of clothes no matter where he goes. When it gets dirty, a while-you-wait cleaner. When the shirt begins to pong, throws it out and buys a new one. Underwear the same. I begin to feel more at home, you find freaks all over.

Napoli. Long line at customs. Sweating—they search every bag. Each person in turn opens his suitcase, the customs inspector scoops out cartons of cigarettes and throws them into a bin behind. Everyone a smuggler. My turn. Opening my bag. No cigarettes. A long hard suspicious look. Then a wave through.

On the road again, traveling by thumb. Dusk, outside Cuneo, trying to get a ride into France before nightfall. Cuneo, on the opium route from Turkey to Marseille, a stupid place to hitch at night. Cops grab me, pull me toward their car. I break away, unzip my suitcase and dump it onto the street. Cops stand around me looking at the pile of dirty underwear and socks, make disgusted noises, walk off. After a night of panicked paranoia huddled in a seedy hotel room, I hitch through France easy as pie and back to Spain.

Guys treat me like I'm The Man. Girls smile at me like some major-league beatnik. The money's good. Even Rals's eyes betray a flicker of respect.

Romance, machismo, making my bones.

Feels good, feels right.

Smells like ego.

"We friends again?" I ask.

"When weren't we?"

"Got pretty weird before I split."

"Bad dope or something."

"We've been here too long," I say. "Let's get off this island and head east."

"Hey, man, that's what I've been telling you all along."

Ralston turned in his sleeping bag. "Fuck the long final winter. How about a long final spring?"

"Long final spring. We have to figure out how to keep Matt from finding out that Walter's staying here too."

"Don't worry," Ralston said, "he won't mind."

Oh, Christ. "How come?"

"I gave him a down payment on the place this afternoon."

I scrambled out of the sleeping bag. "Cocksucker! You promised—" I punched the wall and debris sprinkled down onto my head. "It's all yours, man, it's all fucking yours!" I opened the door, stepped out onto the porch and stared into the night.

Ralston said nothing. For a long time.

I got cold and went back inside. Ralston lay on his back with his arm across his eyes. Shivering now, I slouched back into my sleeping bag.

"You know what the plan was," I said. "Ritz needed to see it. This is about the—forget it." I was going to say it was about the rest of my life but he would see right away what was wrong with that. "If we're going to do this thing together, you gotta— Shit, you know that. Why am I talking?"

Ralston, eyes still covered, looked miserable. Suicidal. It could be an act, although abject contrition would be a drastic departure from his usual repertoire. I had no more heart to rail at him but wasn't going to relent, not this time. I squirmed down into the bag.

Later, in the middle of the night, he got up and went outside. I kept a hidden eye on him from the porch and didn't slip back into my bag until he finished pissing and headed back toward the house.

Chapter 10

Next morning, Ralston was in a state of physical hyperactivity and conversational atrophy, both exacerbated by any attempt to talk turkey as he pried appliance and cabinet debris off the kitchen walls with a tire iron. After last night, it was such a relief to see him engaged, even if manic, that I didn't insist on a showdown or even point out that we didn't own the walls he was demolishing. To show solidarity, I stacked the bigger chunks by the door. Once I caught up with his demolition, I couldn't restrain myself any longer. "How much did Matt want?"

Ralston grunted over a stubborn nail. "Come on, motherfucker."

"How much did you give him?"

"Got you, you little bastard."

"How much?"

"Jesus, hold on, let me catch my breath." But then he lurched up and attacked the next board.

I grabbed his arm. "Look, this whole thing's getting out of control."

"Control, huh?"

"Don't give me that crap. We have to talk about the house—about the goddamn money."

"Absolutely. Just a sec, must be a better pry bar around here somewhere." He ducked outside.

"Rals!" But he was gone. I sat down on the floor. "Crap."

A minute later: "Jules! Jules! Check it out!"

Ralston was standing on a stepladder in the garage, pulling a tarp off something resting on the overhead beams. Dirt, wood dust, cobwebs, and what looked like a granola of dried animal droppings rained down. I ducked back outside. A filthy paddle flew through the door after me, then another. With a soft crumple and a mushroom cloud of powdered shit, the tarp hit the floor.

"Jules! Help me with this!" I took a deep breath, held it, and stepped back into the garage. He was standing on the top of the shaky stepladder, one hand on a beam, the other lifting the end of a long canoe as high as he could. I jumped to steady the ladder. He gave the canoe a shove and canted it over the beam. "Catch it! Don't let it crash."

"I'm trying not to let *you* crash. Don't let go of the beam." I took hold of the canoe's prow. It was lighter than I'd braced myself for. I eased it lower until only the stern's tip still rested on the beam.

"Hold on, hold on." Bowlegged and shaky, he climbed down the ladder and grabbed the middle of the canoe. "Outside, outside." We carried it out. "Hold it up. Higher." With the canoe upside down at arms' length over our heads, he stepped under it and carefully scanned it from stem to stern. "No daylight." We set it down. Hands on his hips, he beamed at it. "We're boat owners. We'll join the yacht club. Or start our own."

"Got to be something wrong with it if they just left it here," I said.

He was tugging at the seats. "Looks good to me. Maybe they moved to the city. Or croaked." He pressed each of the ribs and tried to wiggle them. "Solid. Let's try it out."

"We got to talk, man."

"Just you and me in a canoe, nowhere to run to, nothing to do, you'll have me." No doubt there was a catch, but I picked up my end of the canoe. Before we'd taken two steps, a rumbling came from the drive. "What's that," Rals said, "a fucking tank?"

The biggest SUV I'd ever seen lurched to a stop amid a cloud of dust. The door opened and a short, chubby, balding, gray-bearded man in shorts slid down from the cab and into Ralston's arms.

I shook Walter's hand and slapped him on the back. "You drive all night?"

"Pretty much. Oh, wow." He stepped up onto the porch.

Ralston swung wide the screen door and beckoned Walter inside. "This first room's the Great Hall."

Walter peered through the door. "Cub Scout jamboree?" Instead of going inside, he backed the SUV up to the porch, lifted the rear gate, and unloaded it: chrome-plated tubes, rectangles, and grates; three chests; a propane tank; various boxes and bags. Ralston and I lent some muscle but stood back when Walter started the skilled labor. Tubes joined one another to support a rectangle and form a table, all without a fumble— aha, color-coded joints. The table sprouted an upper shelf and lower satellite tables. On one of them, a metal case opened up to become a two-burner stove, and under it, a small fridge slid into a perfect fit. Walter attached an extension pipe to the propane tank, to which he connected hoses to the stove and a couple of lamps. The third chest, on the other lower table, turned into a fully-stocked nested utensil cabinet. He then ran an electrical cord from a plug under the SUV's hood to the fridge, which whirred into action.

When he was young, Walter had moved slowly, deliberately, like a newcomer to this universe who didn't want to break

anything. Even in his own apartment, he'd fondle a spoon before bringing it to the table, feel the texture of his jacket before
carefully putting it on, get lost in the sound of water running
in the sink. Now, with his stumpy arms and legs and abrupt
manner, he still hadn't attained nimbleness or grace, but almost
made up for them with sheer determination. From the rear of
the SUV, he pulled some canvas chairs, a folding table, and a
frame with mosquito netting, and set them up on the porch.
Hands braced on his lower back, he leaned back, wincing, then
looked around with a satisfied air. "What's for lunch?"

Ralston and I could offer only granola bars. "We haven't
been to town yet today." Walter cooked up a soup from little
packets of freeze-dried vegetables and meat.

After we hauled dishwater up from the river in buckets—
also supplied by Walter—he dragged two duffel bags from the
SUV. With a quick glance around the bivouac in the Great
Hall, he asked, "Which is my room?" Walter set himself up
in one of the bedrooms on the second floor. Battery-operated
inflatable mattress—a thick, wide one, not like ours. Radio,
camp chair and table, laptop. He had work to do.

So did Ralston. "No time to talk now, got to protect my
investment." He went back to demolishing the kitchen. I gave
up trying to force him to talk. Besides, silence itself would
pressure him to spill the beans. At this point, only his neck
was in the noose, and sooner or later he'd have to come to me.

Unless he wanted his neck in a noose.

Walter started to explain his work over dinner—a dinner
he'd brought with him from civilization's last outpost, just in
case—thyme-rich French lamb sausages on sourdough rolls
with mustard mayonnaise, tomatoes, and arugula. Ralston and
I drank wine; Walter swilled blue-green Gatorade that seemed
to glow in the dark.

"I have a… Jules, you'd understand, your whole spiritual thing in London. Something you feel you need to do, a vocation, a, a, a—"

"A calling," Ralston said.

I shook it off. "Mine wasn't a calling, it was curiosity."

"A calling," Ralston said. "It took you all the way to Tibet—took *us*—it nearly killed you, and still pulled you to London. That's a fucking calling. Now shut the hell up and let the man tell his story."

"A calling." Walter seemed to be warming to the term. "I know this sounds crazy, but don't worry, it makes perfect sense."

Ralston made a face. "Famous last words." Rals hadn't visited Walter in the loony bin years ago.

"I saw you on TV," I said. "With Alan Alda, that science program he hosted. Seemed like a nice guy."

"Very quick. Very funny." Walter paused as if to readjust himself internally. "Very demanding."

"Something about plumbing?"

Walter laughed. "My claim to fame. Three patents, tons of money. For a toilet."

"Some calling," Ralston said. "Nature's calling? The Walter closet?" I shot him a warning glance; he should know better than to pick on Walter.

"That's not the calling," Walter said. "When you were kids, didn't you fantasize about having some ability that gave you a huge edge in sports? Like, you were twice as strong or twice as fast a runner as anyone? My fantasy was that I could slow time for myself. The baseball would come at me so slowly that I could always hit it just where I wanted. I could see where the defensive linemen were going so I could always evade the tackle. I could see the punch coming and duck it, and see where the other guy was open and get my punch in. Beat up the bully, get the girl."

Remember past lives, read minds, leave the body, see the truth underlying the illusion we call reality.

"Only it never happens that way," Ralston said.

"Except it did," Walter said, "but not in sports. When I do numbers, everything slows down around me. I solve a calculus problem while the other guy's figuring the tip." Walter used to talk slowly, as if tasting the consequences of every word before letting it venture out into a hostile world. Since then, he'd clearly acquired some social skills. Only time would tell if his newfound equanimity went any deeper.

"Did it pull the chicks like you wanted?" Ralston said.

Walter laughed ruefully. "Like, I was shopping around for a house a few years ago, so I looked up some formulas, and then I updated the current values before I came here. With this location, acreage, square footage, and general condition—"

"Which you figured out in your head?" Ralston asked.

Walter's smile flashed a hint of swagger. "If it goes as usual, they'll ask three forty to three sixty but will accept two seventy to two eighty."

The camp light glimmered off a sheen of sweat on Ralston's forehead. "You talked to our guy?" he asked Walter.

"What guy?"

I looked at Ralston. "You didn't settle on a price, did you?"

"Nothing's final." He turned to Walter. "So?"

"It's more, let's say, relaxing for me to stay away from easy, fast numbers," Walter said, "so I went into fluid dynamics."

"Sounds like some weird New Age underwater yoga." The lame, half-assed joke said Rals was distracted. What had he committed us to?

"The physics of moving fluids—like water in a pipe."

"Toilets."

"Fluid turbulence is one of the least understood subjects in physics, yet it's at the heart of everything from weather systems to Roman aqueducts to squirt guns. Isn't it refreshing that at least one little bit of mundane life can't be neatly wrapped up in a couple of differential equations?"

"A godsend," Ralston said.

Walter seemed to wander off for a moment. Ralston snapped his fingers three or four times. "Right, right," Walter said. "So I was able to design a better toilet. You've probably seen ads for it."

"Can't go wrong," Ralston said, "everybody shits. What's this calling?"

Walter looked away from Ralston, off into the dark distance for a few moments, then stood up. "Couple of things I want to get down while I think of them. See you guys in the morning."

"Watch out for the bat shit," Ralston said.

Once I heard the clomp of Walter's feet on the stairs, I leaned in to whisper at Ralston. "Bat shit? Lay off the crazy jokes."

"All right, Nurse Ratched. Walter and me, two peas in a pod."

My future suddenly opened up before me like a fast-blooming nightmare. Marco would show up, and Randy. I'd babysit my nut-job friends on this funny farm, keep them from killing each other or eating the bird shit or the birds, slap their sweaty paws off my wife.

Upstairs, a window banged open. "Hey, Jules!"

"What?"

"Don't be so damn uptight," Walter called down. "I'm not going to flip out on you. Those days are over."

In Tabriz one evening a man in the street invites us home. Short, muscular, energetic, seems simply hospitable. He speaks no English, we no Turkish or Farsi. A doorway through a high wall into a large compound. Several small one-story flat-roofed buildings, one of them a kitchen full of women. Between buildings, bushes and small trees.

Up a ladder onto the roof of the largest building. Carpets, cushions, a brazier. Stars begin to come out, the breeze gentle, warm. A woman brings tea, sliced melon. The man lights a charcoal fire in the brazier. When the melon is gone he shouts over the side of the house. Two women appear with more food—spiced meat and vegetables wrapped in pastry. More tea.

He pulls out a pipe and opium. We all smoke a little, wrapping ourselves and the world in fuzz. We take a walk to a large modern public building, sit around on marble benches.

Back at his place he indicates that if we need to relieve ourselves to use the bushes, which we do. Then he leads us back up the ladder where we lie down to sleep. He stays with us on the roof. I lie on my back and look up at the stars. In the morning he shakes our hands and shows us out.

Rals lay in his sleeping bag, humming while he read a magazine with my glasses by the light of one of Walter's battery lamps. "Should get yourself some glasses," I said.

"Eyes are fine, just not much light." Ralston kept reading.

"How much did you give Matt?"

He dropped the magazine—a *National Geographic*, which I think he'd grabbed from our apartment—tossed my glasses at me, and stared at me as if wondering where to begin. His lips seemed thin, dry, and his eyes unsteady. He switched off the light. "I'm beat, man. Tomorrow."

"All right, tomorrow. For sure."

"Nothing's for sure."

"Jesus—"

"Okay, okay, tomorrow." He lay his head on his pillow.

Once my eyes got used to the dark, I could see my way around the house by ricocheting moonlight. The French-windowed room at the back, perhaps once a parlor or kids' playroom, invited me to stay awhile. At the corner of my eye, a shape moved outside, but I felt no alarm. Whatever it was scuttled under a bush, a possum or a raccoon—did they have those big rodents here, what were they called, nutrias? The woods were dark but conveyed a sense of quiet benignity, as did the dark shape that flittered overhead, a hungry bat going about its rounds.

I wandered into the kitchen, opened the door to the pantry—a pantry!—and stepped into the narrow darkness. No heebie-jeebies. Pushing my luck, I started down the basement stairs, feeling my way carefully but without foreboding. The floor at the bottom, stone or concrete, was comfortingly solid, and the blackness around me just plain old blackness.

Back upstairs, I felt my way through the rear hallway and climbed the narrow enclosed back stairs to the second floor. My fingers told me these had a round rail attached to the wall with simple square-cut mounts. I avoided lurking outside Walter's door and instead glided down the other corridor to what Matt probably called the master bedroom—Ritz's and my corner room. The bare wood felt almost as soft as a worn Persian runner. From one window I caught a glimpse of the river, and the other looked into the forest, now pale in the moonlight and slightly stirring in the breeze as if breathing in slumber. Our bed would be about here. I lay down on the floor. The hint of wind, the soft shadows, the night sounds of cricket and leaves, the fragrance of wood and woods—a bedroom that caressed the senses, whether to sleep or to excitement.

Better to break the spell than to let it slowly dissipate. I got up and walked quietly back down to the Great Hall. Ralston was snoring. I stripped to underwear and climbed into my bag.

Of course, Walter's cell connection worked. "Booster antenna," he said. "Beta version. Should be on the market in a few months." I was using the computer in his SUV to check my email.

Adele's message was first in line, impatiently tapping its nails. I skipped over it to deal with the others first, and as I answered them, her message gave me the evil eye. I finally opened it.

> I've been working on my protagonist—this "I"
> who isn't really me, as you so kindly pointed out.
> See attachment. Adele

I opened the document. Since one fictional character certainly couldn't stand in for the real-life Adele, she'd divided herself into three characters, each with a brief thumbnail sketch. Della was a hard-driven businesswoman who'd lost her soul somewhere along the way. Leda was an artist who specialized in being a muse for other artists—her true medium was the human psyche, and she'd had a series of tormented lovers whom she made successful and then dumped. Adie was a teenage street kid who earned a living doing dirty jobs for private eyes, madams, and other demimondaines. The three were best friends who couldn't agree on anything.

> Jeez, Adele, this is interesting—fascinating, maybe
> brilliant. More to the point, it could work. So
> what's the story? What do they want, and how do
> they go about getting it? J

The rest of the email was inconsequential—and no new work, which simultaneously took a load off my shoulders and drove a hatpin into my gut.

"Hey, Walt," Ralston shouted, "Jules is wearing out your wanker sites."

Walter peered in through the SUV window. "What's a camping trip without a wank or two?"

"Ah yes," Ralston said. "Your Boy Scout days."

I tried to shoo them off. Ralston, covered with demolition dust, climbed in behind me and snooped over my shoulder. "Suave editorial bullshit. In real life, people want all kinds of things but mostly just keep doing the same old shit day after day."

I closed the email site. "We're talking about a novel, not real life."

"It's all math," Walter said. "Real life minus same old shit equals literature."

Ralston flicked my ear. "Did you know Walt made a bundle with computer dating?"

"I only wrote the program."

"And collected the royalties."

I shut down the laptop. "Aren't there a million dating programs?"

"Mine's a little different. Ever hear of StarLogo?" Head shakes. "SimCity?"

"Sure," I said. "Freddy loved it when he was a kid. You create this city by assigning certain characteristics and parameters, and the thing would build and run itself. Neighborhoods would spring up and change, demographics would shift, traffic jams, slums. Real estate prices." Ralston and I exchanged scowls.

"The point is," Walter said, "you couldn't predict these changes from the start, because all the mutually influencing factors are too numerous and complex to calculate. So instead you simulate them, then speed up the action and see what happens—compress a year into a few seconds, or a few milliseconds. The same idea works on scientific studies, from slime molds to fisheries to highway traffic patterns. My program did the same thing for dating. Certain kinds of men and women, what they want, how they react to certain stimuli, and you can simulate the dating pool and tweak the client's approach to best attract what he or she wants. You tell him or her where and how to meet people, how to dress, what to say, the whole shtick."

"And it works?"

Walter stood up straight and stepped back from the SUV. "Here's a prize package for you. Six-pack abs? I got a keg. A scalp that sheds like a sheepdog, a face that belongs on Sesame Street."

"A bank account that could give a frigid lesbian multiple orgasms," Ralston said.

"I fine-tuned the program for myself."

"So does it work?"

Walter winked. "Wait till you meet her."

East Village, early '70s. Walter's girl Mousy Diane. Pretty features huddled on a frightened face. Wears an eye patch like Moshe Dayan, always in bulky sweaters and baggy sweatpants. Bursts out crying when I suggest boosting the business's income by selling stuff Rals can send from India. "I hate that word—*business.*"

Clifford, the business head, is all for it. Clifford and I, far from friends, but the only vaguely functional members of this little team. Walter into his numbers, doing his numerology readings, Diane stringing her beads, painting her hookahs, sewing her headbands, minding the store.

Mousy Diane never liked the big pad in the East Village either. After Marco fled, Daph wandered off, and Ralston and I left for Europe, with the diaspora nearly complete, Mousy Diane and Walter found their own little apartment with its own little storefront and started their own little head shop.

Now back from Nepal, at loose ends, Ritz long gone, I sleep on the floor of the tiny storeroom. A knock at the door. Diane, sweater and sweats gone, naked, waist you could fit your hands around, long lean legs, high round ass, breasts swaying, kneels by my mattress, shakes my shoulder.

"Jules, help, it's Walter."

Walter curled up on Clifford's mattress in the corner of the bedroom. Clifford snoring in the big bed. Always wondered, never asked. Walter wide-eyed, looking around and slowly reaching out his arms and fingers like a panicked sloth, muttering disjointed snippets of convoluted prophecy.

"He took something," Mousy Diane said. "Acid maybe."

I find the Break-Glass-in-Case-of-Emergency dose of Stelazine and gently persuade him to swallow it. I drag Clifford to his own mattress and help Walter into his bed, Diane lying on one side of him, me on the other. Walter soon subsides into a murmuring daze, manages a smile, and closes his eyes.

Diane and I heave simultaneous sighs of relief and look at each other. Like Adam and Eve, we now see our nakedness. Diane doesn't get under the sheet. She sits up cross-legged on the bed facing me. I creep back to my storeroom, hoping Diane and Clifford won't push Walter back to the crazy ward.

Next day, I hear about Psycho-Metaphysics, a more empirical approach to the Big Questions. A week later, with Walter as compos mentis as he gets these days and still at home unincarcerated, I hop a cheap charter to London.

Chapter 11

When I'd finished my email and Walter had gone back upstairs to his calling, I said to Ralston, "Let's take a walk. Down by the river."

"This isn't the time to nickel-and-dime me to death."

"Come on, goddamn it."

"Or just give me shit on general principle."

"Let's go."

"Drown me like a sack of kittens."

At the concrete landing at the bottom of the steps, I sat down. "What's your plan?"

"Plan?"

"Let's drop the cute stuff. The house, the money."

Ralston squinted out over the river. "Can you swim in this thing?"

"Guess so. What's the plan?"

"Hang on, I'm grosser than a dead dog's butt." He peeled off his clothes and shook some of the demolition dust from them. His dick was still bigger than mine. It had been bigger in the shower room at college and bigger at the swimming cove on Formentera. He jumped in, let out a squeal, and frantically scrubbed himself with his hands for a few seconds while gasping. "Not too bad. Get used to it. Come on in."

It wasn't spoken as a dare, but it was. When was the last time I'd gotten naked in public? Well, there was that time with Lena…those times. I took off my clothes, partially turning my back when I stripped off my undies, but I could hardly back up to the water, and I hesitated an instant before jumping in. Rals wasn't faking, it felt like glacial runoff. I rubbed my scalp, pits, and crotch and was ready to call it a bath. Ralston clambered out and I followed.

"Damn," he said. "Your dick is still bigger than mine. Not as pretty or talented, but a smidgen bigger."

"I thought yours was."

"You were looking? I was only kidding! You looked at my dick?"

"Maybe your own dick always looks smaller. The downward angle foreshortens it or something."

"It's not the angle that foreshortens it, it's your brain." He was drying himself off with his undershirt. "Here's the plan. I put down the earnest. When Ritz—"

"How much?"

"Thirty-one k."

"They usually want ten percent. You settled on three ten?"

"Nothing's settled. The thirty-one keeps it ours until Ritz gets here and the details—"

"Can you get it back if she doesn't like it?"

"She'll love it."

"Can you?"

"Matt's all right, he gets the picture."

"All of it?"

"All of it."

"*All*, all?"

"Minus ten percent and a grand a week."

"Can you afford that, Rals? You can, can't you?"

"Things haven't gone too well the last couple of years. The thirty-one's about all I have."

"Christ."

"If this bombs out on me…" He quickly pulled his clothes on. "I figure we'll get a lot back from the other people who move in."

"You bet everything on this one wild idea? Like it's your last chance?"

"Didn't we always?"

"That's how we liked to think and talk about it," I said. "But we always had something in reserve. Like parents. And being young. Imagine at our age now, showing up at someone's door and asking if you can crash for a night or two."

"Is that what you think I'm doing?"

"You're the one who plunked the money down, remember? Now that you mention it, is that why you didn't stay with us this time, so we wouldn't think you were freeloading?"

"You get a tattoo on your butt or something?"

"What?"

"We got two canoes full of family values staring at your rice-pudding ass."

I snuck a peek over my shoulder. Pop and two small kids in the lead boat pointedly looking away, and behind them, a scowling mom and a teenage girl killing herself laughing. I flipped my shirt over my butt and kept my back turned. "Tell me when they're gone."

"You bailing on me?" Ralston said.

"You hijacked our plan."

"I had a better idea."

"Camping out on a construction site with bankruptcy hanging over our heads isn't exactly how Ritz and I imagined our blissful retirement."

He looked like he was about to throw up. "Retirement."

"You could have asked, we could have planned it together."

He puffed up his face. "And weighed. The pros. And cons. Here was this place, someone had to act, you were under orders not to."

"You were saving me from Ritz?"

"Saving Ritz from you. Look at this place!"

"And who's going to save you if it doesn't work out?"

He looked hurt. "Obviously, no one."

"Come on, Rals. You know that's not what I meant." I looked around to make sure the canoes had passed, then dressed.

"Jules. Just because we're getting old doesn't mean life has to wind down." He looked at me speculatively, as if gauging how much more he could safely say. I waited. "How do people see us geezers? Old. Harmless. Invisible."

"Irrelevant," I said. "Weak. Addle-brained."

"If we've lived this long, we're obviously pussies." He stopped and gazed out over the river. Over the years, I'd learned that nodding thoughtfully was the best way to pump it all out of him. I nodded thoughtfully.

"What if we used these perceptions of us as strengths?" he said. "Way back when, we all tried to look like Che or outlaws or highwaymen, so we were always prime suspects."

"Prime suspects for what?"

"For having done things that needed to be done."

"Like offing the pigs or blowing up recruiting offices?"

"Come on, not the crazy stuff, not anymore."

"Like what then?"

"Demonstrations, where the cops won't dare club or gas us—or if they did, they'd have somebody's croaked granny on their hands to explain away instead of some scary-looking black dude half the country is secretly glad is dead. Eco-sabotage. Even like...okay, for terminally sick people, suicide missions. Like to pollution sites."

"And assassinations?"

He squinted at me.

"Maybe only the necessary ones," I said.

"I wouldn't completely rule it out."

"Jesus, Rals, I was kidding. Kamikaze geezers?"

He smiled. "So you do get it."

"That's your idea for a commune?"

"Stop calling it a commune."

"It's not a bad idea." It really wasn't. Even if your life doesn't count for anything, maybe your death can. "And think of all the Social Security and Medicare that taxpayers would save. Except there's a huge flaw in it. After the first caper, the cops would be all over the dead hero's last known address." I held up my hands and glanced around our little homestead.

He sagged. "I'm working on that part." Translation: he hadn't thought of it. "But forget the whole gray-commando thing for now. First we need a place, whatever we're going to do with it. This place."

"This expensive wreck." Okay, this beautiful expensive wreck.

"I can't do this on my own," he said. "Financially, I mean. You going to pull the plug?"

"All by yourself you get your ass in a jam and suddenly this becomes a cooperative venture?"

Rals clenched his face and fists and seemed about to burst into tears. Instead, he shoved me with both hands to the chest. I stumbled back against the steps and sat down hard. He stood over me. "What's wrong with you, goddamn it? Ritz wants a house, she's trying to do something new with her life. Me too.

What are you doing? What do you want? Just to play it safe? To stand in our way because you don't have the balls to do anything anymore?"

I scrambled to my feet and pushed him back a couple of steps, then a couple more. Ralston, jaw tight, was breathing hard but didn't fight back. I contemplated pushing him into the river, calling him any of a dozen names.

Nor did I have a cogent comeback, much less a better plan.

His eyes weren't angry, but desperate, and again he seemed close to tears. I turned away and headed up the steps toward the house. "This is stupid. It all depends on what Ritz thinks of this place."

Ralston caught up with me in two rickety leaps. "We've got to get everything ready. And think of a better name for this place than This Place."

The local birdwatcher club gave me a lot of what I hoped was seductive material: a list of hundreds of resident and migratory species found locally, a map of the best birding sites, a schedule of visiting speakers and organized walks, and a catalogue of books available in the lending library. The chief birders weren't quite the chatty group of tea-drinking old ladies I'd expected, but a middle-aged married couple. The man was clearly gay, at least to my eye and ear, and the woman attractive but almost comatose with boredom; both looked me up and down with faint interest but little enthusiasm.

The local historical society regretfully informed me that the legendary Revolutionary War guerilla the Swamp Fox had had nothing to do with the local wetlands but had operated in South Carolina and in fact pushed the British troops up into North Carolina, thank you very much. There was always Fort

Branch, which, no, hadn't seen any Civil War action. But Ava Gardner had been born in nearby Grabtown.

Yet it sure was pretty, and the people sure were nice—a claim that despite its desperate, last-ditch ring was also true and would appeal to Ritz. The locals were hardly what I would consider my kind of people, whatever that was, but I liked them and felt comfortable around them.

Ralston found out the local construction industry was in a bit of a slump. "We'll get the work done quick and cheap."

"In theory," I said.

I also retained a local real estate lawyer. We'd need one anyway, if things ever got that far, for title and lien searches or whatever such people did. Ralston looked dubious. "You sure he's not the owner's half-sister's brother-in-law?"

Crickets, owls, and one brief panicked shriek from some small creature down near the river. Veggie burgers for dinner. Ralston raised his eyebrows when Walter first announced his impending culinary contribution but then ate them without complaint, perhaps an acquired point of etiquette of the nouveau pauvre. The porch, glowing a warm yellow in the lantern light, offered more than a safe harbor; it promised happiness and a thousand such evenings with Ritz, Rals, and whoever joined us.

I stood up, kicked a dead live oak branch off the porch, walked to the far end, and stared into the dark woods. This was just a new venue for the same meaningless comfort. I hated myself for being tempted by it.

Should I have hated myself for not being able to accept this gift?

What did hating myself have to do with it?

Ralston wandered off for a piss—another of the house's assets, being able to pee outside—swaggered back and downed the last of his beer. "Walter, what the hell do you do all day up in that padded cell of yours?"

I hustled back over to them in case Walter needed protection. Walter folded his paper napkin, patted his lips with it, nodded, but still paused a little longer, perhaps steeling himself before speaking.

"Writing the next book of the Bible."

"New translation?" I said after a long silence, mostly to cut off Ralston's overdue wisecrack.

"Not translating. New book."

Still crazy after all. I was already babysitting two. Rals gave Walter his narrow-eyed, lips-awry stare; no humoring of the mentally infirm from that quarter.

Walter's smile, on the other hand, was full of good humor for the not-too-bright. "What's the Bible? The laws, fine. Otherwise, it's mostly the history of the Jewish people."

"You mean the Old Testament," Ralston said.

"The Jewish Bible, the Hebrew Scriptures, whatever you want to call it. Historically, you can discount everything before the flood as myth. Anyway, they weren't really Jews back then, were they? But from Abraham and Isaac on, even allowing for tall tales and artistic license—"

"And religious horseshit," Ralston said.

"And religious horseshit, you have the story of the founding of the Jewish people and faith."

Ralston turned to me. "See? Everybody thinks they have a story."

"But it's a great story," Walter said. "Jules gets it. God comes on to these half-starved goat wranglers and says, hey, let's make a deal. Wow, look where it gets them. Wars, murders, betrayals, enslavement, miracles—and with Saul and David, they triumph. But trust a Jew, it can't last. They live high off the hog, the so-called wise King Solomon spends like Rommel has landed at Haifa, and things fall apart. The kingdom splits in two, Israel and Judah, and finally, the Babylonian exile. In terms of plot, the rest is coda. Right, Jules?"

"I'm no Bible scholar."

"But it's a great setup for the next book."

"The sequel," Ralston said. "Bible Two—oops, no, Three."

Walter smiled as if at a cute but unruly child. "The exile was really the start of the Diaspora, a long trek that culminated in the Holocaust. And from that darkest of nights arose the State of Israel—the tribes again united and powerful. In another thousand years or two, if we last that long, there'll probably be another book. But right now, how can anyone even pretend that the Bible is complete without an account of the Diaspora, the Holocaust, and the founding of—"

"Sure, sure," Ralston said, "but all that stuff's been written. What makes the Bible the Bible is that—"

"That God wrote it? Not even rabbis think—"

"No, that it *sounds* like God wrote it. It doesn't read like a history book."

Walter held up an index finger. "You know why? I did a complete statistical breakdown of the language, the characters, the stories. Sure, you have to pick your heroes and your battles and not try to cover everything, but—"

Ralston jerked a thumb at me. "He could have told you that."

"But he couldn't have told me about the mathematical relationships among them, and in the words."

"What are you going to call it?" Ralston said. "The Book of Walter?"

Walter looked at me. "It's not the numbers that drive you nuts. It's that when you're nuts, the numbers offer stability, predictability, beauty without pain, unchanging, eternal beauty."

"The Song of Walter?" Ralston said. "Walteronomy? Don't you need a chapter about the pesky Jesus embarrassment, which continues unabated to this day?"

Walter started picking up the dirty dishes.

Ralston handed him the plates. "Hey, I'm just playing devil's advocate here. It's great you're doing something important. I never did. Because I know what kind of shit you have to take if you try."

"So instead you dish it out," I said.

"Just trying to do my bit."

"Thanks," Walter said. "I appreciate your help. I hadn't thought about a title. Jules just looks at me like I'm crazy."

"Well, you got to wonder," Ralston said. "Why the Bible?"

Walter tried to laugh but it came out more like a sigh. He counted off on his fingers. "Two geriatric beatniks, huddled in the dark, outside a wreck of a house, in the middle of a swamp, in peckerwood territory. And *you're* asking *me* why I'm doing what I'm doing?"

"I never had a calling," Ralston said. Walter carefully put the dishes in a bucket, sat down on the porch and gave us both a reproachful stare. Ralston's upturned palms pleaded innocence. "I mean, like both you guys did. Had a calling."

In the most neutral tone imaginable, Walter said, "I'm bushed. Think I'll turn in." In silence, we moved the camp chairs up onto the porch and killed the gaslights.

Walter had gone upstairs, and Ralston and I were getting into our sleeping bags. "Don't be mean to Walter," I said.

"He doesn't need a protector. Jeez, a calling, at his age."

"You have a calling too. This place."

"Just a pastime," Ralston said. "Providing for our old age."

"Your second childhood."

"Screw childhood. Second adolescence."

"You've been dreaming about it forever. Your calling."

We lapsed into silence. The house's gentle vibe lulled me toward sleep.

A new sound entered the nocturnal aural landscape: music. Then the sound of a vehicle. Kids on a joyride? Was this their hangout spot? There were no telltale signs—beer cans, cigarette butts, broken windows, spent condoms—besides, what kids listened to Lee Morgan's "Sidewinder" at top volume? Ralston and I yanked our pants on and stepped out onto the porch. The music receded for a minute then returned even louder. Lights flickered across the drive then glared at us straight on. A van careened to a stop. The lights and music flicked off.

"Jules! Ralston!" Marco. "You old bastards sure got yourself a hideout here. Almost missed it." The doors opened and the interior light showed two figures sliding out. Marco's cowboy legs and...Elaine decided to come?

The woman launched herself at me, knocking me backwards, and gave me a wet kiss on the mouth even as she supported my weight with both arms until I found my legs again. Then she punched Ralston in the shoulder and grabbed a handful of his ass.

Not Elaine. Straight black hair, Asian eyes, lopsided smile. "Daph!"

Marco was beaming. "Picked her up at the bus station." He looked up at the dark house. "Blow a fuse or something? Where do I plug in my TV?"

Chapter 12

"So we're in bed going at it, and suddenly he looks at his watch and says, Shit, gonna get a ticket, gotta move the car."

Daph looked good in the morning sunshine. Motherhood had filled out her bust and hips while leaving her legs lean and muscular. The lines on her face, neck, and the backs of her hands fit well with her air of experience. People who didn't know her well often mistook her joy for sexual advances; when she was angry, things got broken or turned black and blue.

"Least you guys were still screwing," Ralston said, "after how many years together?"

She stared at him quizzically, slowly scanned the four silent men around the breakfast table, and then looked aghast.

"Without going into detail," Walter said, "Opal and I are doing just fine."

"By all means," Ralston said, "do go into detail." He was talking to Walter but looking at Daph. "New romance, the fountain of youth. Make a woman moan and scream again. Better than Geritol and vitamin E."

Marco watched but didn't say anything. Last night, he'd commandeered an upstairs room for himself and Daph, but she'd unrolled her sleeping bag in the Great Hall with Ralston and me. Finally, Marco had come back downstairs and flung his own bag into a corner.

Daph now refilled her coffee cup from the camp stove on the sunny porch. "Remember that car we once had?"

I laughed. "What a wreck."

"Four-wheeled turd," Ralston said.

"Remember what happened to it?" she asked.

Ralston, Marco, and I looked at one another. "We sell it?"

"I think it got stolen—no, that was my motorcycle."

"Didn't we give it to someone to drive to California?"

"I remember exactly what happened," Walter said. "Some genius couldn't remember where he parked it and none of us could be bothered to go look for it."

"Just a rust stain in some East Village gutter now," Ralston said.

Daph nodded. "So now I'm lying in bed waiting for him to move his stupid car. How upside down everything had gotten. That was that."

"But you'd been together for how long?" I said. She gave me a stupid-question shrug. Could one dumb move drive Ritz away?

The sound of a vehicle came from the driveway. Matt's truck pulled up, and he stepped down from the cab.

"You boys got to get yourself a phone that works. Morning, ma'am."

Daph smiled and waved.

Ralston stood up. "I'll catch this." He walked over to meet Matt.

"Who's that?" Marco asked.

"Real estate agent," I said.

"Yo!" Marco shouted. "When do we get some power?"

Matt looked over from his conversation with Ralston but didn't answer. "Cool it," I told Marco. "We haven't bought the place yet."

Daph shoved her hands into her back pockets, put on a dazzling smile, sauntered over to Matt and shook his hand. His body language said her damage control was working. Marco watched with a flat gaze, slowly twirled the ends of his mustache, then pushed himself to his feet and moseyed over. I followed to defuse the showdown before it came to a fight. Marco, all smiles now, stuck out his hand and introduced himself.

Ralston pulled me aside. "The owner's getting nervous about my foreign check, it'll take a couple of weeks to clear, and they want to show the place in the meantime. Which means we'd all have to split. Can you tide me over? Just until it goes through?"

Unraveling already. "I'll see what I can do."

"What the hell's that mean?" Ralston turned to Matt, who was now chuckling and wisecracking with Marco in full-blown good-ol'-boy mode. "How soon you need it?"

"They're talking about today."

Ralston and Matt looked at me.

"That's all I can say, I'll see what I can do."

"If you need my office for a phone or anything," Matt said.

"Let you know."

Marco slapped Matt on the back. "See you 'round the pool hall, hoss." Daph walked Matt back to the truck and gave his shoulder a light, lingering punch before he climbed into the cab. Marco scowled. After Matt headed out the driveway, I grabbed Ralston's arm and pulled him away from the others.

"You think, just like that, I can lay my hands on thirty-one thousand dollars?"

"Yes."

"You were there when I promised Ritz I wouldn't put down a dime until she checked the place out."

"You made her a much bigger promise. And it's just for a couple of weeks. Let's cut the crap. You going to fork over the cash or throw this place away?"

Rals didn't issue ultimatums unless he was sure of winning. But there was no reason to make it easy for him. "I have to think about it, check over some things."

"You want me to squirm on the hook awhile for having a French bank account? Look, I'll stab myself in the ass with a corkscrew if that'll do the trick. Chop off my left pinky with a rusty axe. But come on, let's not dick around with this place."

I walked away. "Walter! Can I use your Internet connection?"

Ralston caught up and patted me on the back. "Good man."

"All I'm doing is setting it up so I *can* do it. I'm not going to lay out a dime until I talk to Matt."

"Let's go."

"Alone."

Ralston's hurt look seemed too sudden to be contrived. Almost too sudden. "So what do we call this place?" he said. I climbed into Walter's truck. Ralston leaned through the window. "Ralston's Revenge? Ritz's Ritz?"

"Give me some privacy, will you?"

"Those carvings in the Great Hall," Ralston said. "How about the Monkey House, like at the zoo? Or Apeshit in honor of Walter? Oh, hot rats, I got it! Remember the place we were headed for in Kathmandu?"

We? I shook my head. "The Monkey Temple? Too depressing."

"No shit. But a cool name. I'm calling it the Monkey Temple till you come up with something better."

Mashhad, Iran, mid-'60s. A young guy about our age approaches Rals and me in the street. Offers to show us around the city if we'll speak English with him. It's a deal.

At the carpet bazaar, where his father works, Behruz shows us wool carpets and silk carpets, points out the different designs from different areas, explains the number of knots per square inch, the quality of the backing. Little children with their small fingers and close-focusing eyes make the finest carpets of the thinnest strands and tiniest knots, but the art is dying out now since the practice was outlawed because the children go blind. The carpet bazaar is unpaved, unfloored. A beautiful carpet lies spread out on the dirt in one aisle. People walk on it with dirty shoes but I try to edge around it. The man in the stall gestures, walk on it. Behruz says that's how they clean it. The mud soaks up the stains and oils, then they beat it clean.

At the bazaar where craftsmen cut, polish, mount, and sell turquoise—usually a deeper blue and less veiny than our Southwestern variety—Behruz's little old uncle shows us his stones, laughs as he tells smuggling stories, mimes the preferred method with his upright thumb behind his lower back.

Behruz invites us to his apartment, one room up an outside flight of stairs at the back of a house. He cooks eggs and tomatoes over a kerosene stove on the floor.

I ask where we can find Sufis. Behruz says he once had a teacher who was a Sufi.

"What did he teach you?"

"The Koran. A very sad man. He had no children. He's dead now." We sleep on Behruz's floor that night. In the morning, Behruz says, "My cousin knows Sufis."

I leap to my feet. "Let's go talk to him." Ralston looks at me like I'm nuts.

Ralston was trying to organize work crews to clean the place up before Ritz's arrival. Walter had his writing to do and figured his contribution was the camp kitchen and communications. Marco wanted to sketch, but when Daph declined to model for him, he ambled off into the forest without the sketchpad. Which left only Daph, who ransacked Walter's SUV for a broom and pitched in sweeping the porch.

Ralston was clearly torn between trying to convince me to bring him along to see Matt about the money and staying with his crew of one attractive woman who seemed on the outs with her once and presumed future lover. I jumped into the car and drove off alone before Ralston could argue.

At Matt's office, I said, "Fill me in. What figure did the negotiations start at?"

Matt leaned back in his swivel chair. "I'm a little confused. I've been dealing with Ralston."

"Has he put his name to anything?"

"Until the exchange of contracts with the buyer, we usually operate on a handshake." A handshake and thirty-one thousand dollars.

"My wife and I will be the buyers, Ralston's our point man. As I understand it, his down payment got their attention but didn't lock in a price. Did I get that right?"

"Close enough."

"How does this work with two down-payment checks?"

"They'll both go into the same escrow account. I'll write you a refund check when Ralston's clears."

"And if it doesn't clear?"

Matt's eyes narrowed for a moment. "Why wouldn't it?"

I shrugged. "The French."

"If his doesn't clear, we'll scotch the sale if you want, and I'll refund yours, less costs."

"The ten percent and a thousand a week?"

"I told him fifteen and fifteen hundred."

Son of a bitch. "Maybe that's what he said." Matt agreed not to deposit my check until the next day, by which time the transfer of funds I had put in motion should have gone through to my checking account. "Any chance of getting the power and water turned back on? I bet it would help convince my wife."

"Power should be back on soon. Water's from your own well. Once you get power, the pump and water heater will kick in. Ralston says he knows what to do." He stood up to shake hands. "Nice lady, Daph. One of y'all's wife?"

"Somebody's—for now, anyways. None of ours."

"You say hi to her from me. And to Ralston." He seemed to have more to say and walked me outside. "You got me curious. What do you folks have planned out there?"

There are two kinds of real estate agents, those who work for you, and those who work for them. Matt worked for them, the seller, and so was the kind of agent you treat like an IRS auditor: politely, with as little information as possible. "Just looking for a house," I said. "The others are friends passing through."

"Here? Passing through to where?" Matt laughed. "Don't forget to say hi now."

Before I got into the car, and while Ralston wasn't around to hover, I called Ritz. "How are things going?" she said.

"Good. Cleaning things up, getting ready for you."

"I mean with you. Feeling any better?"

"Sure. Guess so. We'll see."

"And Rals?"

"He has two modes, bull in a china shop or basket case. Every time I try to ease him out of one, he flips to the other."

"Bipolar?"

"I don't even know what that really means. Isn't it supposed to be chemical? He seems circumstance-driven. Like he always was, except now he crashes and burns. So I end up either a cop or a nursemaid."

"What are you going to do?"

"Maybe he'll chill out once we get this house thing settled."

"Lots of eggs," she said. "One basket."

A fast stab of anxiety that she would nix the Monkey Temple. "We're doing some work on it, I think you'll like it."

"They're letting you work on it?"

"It's something of a white elephant, so they're bending over backwards. Besides, it's mostly just cleaning up. They know you have to like it before we can buy it. I miss you, baby."

Amazing what a little sweeping can do for a place. Daph had finished the porch and was working on the front path. Ralston carried out some scrap wood, probably from the kitchen. Walter, instead of working on his project, was now picking up dead branches from the front yard and running like a madman to dump them in the woods. "How come no one cuts down this dead tree? It keeps dropping branches."

"If you look that good in your old age," Ralston said, "we won't cut you down."

"Any chance you picked up a rake in town?" Walter asked me. "Sorry."

Walter started kicking the dead leaves away from the house. Ralston dumped his scrap wood by the side of the path. "Not there!" Walter called out. "On the brush pile!"

Rals ignored him. "How'd it go in town?"

"No problem," I said.

"We all set?"

"All set for what? Fifteen percent and fifteen hundred a week?"

"You didn't accept that, did you? I was haggling him down."

I took a deep breath. With Ritz on her way, this wasn't the time or place. I jerked my chin toward Walter. "What's gotten into him?" Walter had grabbed Ralston's wood scraps and was hustling them around back.

"His girlfriend's on her way, must be an ass biter. You give Matt the money? We back on track?"

Marco stepped out of the woods, his hands dirty and the knees of his jeans damp. He stamped the mud off his cowboy boots. "You all right?" I asked.

"I'm cool, little swampy down by the water is all." He wiped his hands on his jeans then looked past us. "Who's that?" A taxi coasted to a stop in the drive and a woman stepped out—willowy, long dark hair with some gray showing, probably early forties, deliberate with her dignity.

"That's what you call a handsome woman," Ralston said. "All the parts look good but the sum of them doesn't add up to a hard-on." He grabbed my arm. "Did you fork it over or not?"

When Walter rushed over to the woman, she leaned down slightly so he could kiss each cheek. Ralston twisted his face into an exaggerated grimace. "Who does she think she is, the Queen of fucking Sheba?" She let Walter lead her over to us. He proudly introduced her as Opal Diamond.

"Opal Diamond." Ralston rolled each syllable over his tongue, basting her name in sarcasm. "Nom de guerre?"

"My parents gave it to me. Ralston—as in dog food?"

Marco laughed. "No such luck."

Ralston looked razor blades at her but had no ready comeback.

For me she had a piercing smile and a strong handshake. "Jules, nice to meet you, at last." At last? I sent Walter a questioning glance but he quickly turned to pay the driver. Opal stretched and surveyed her domain. Her posture was as ramrod as a three-star general's but her movements easy and fluid and her presence supple rather than hard or bristly, confident rather than domineering. As far as I could tell, she wore no makeup or perfume. She sniffed the air and smiled at me again. "I can't wait to get into the tub. Bags, Walter?"

Walter hustled to grab the two suitcases the driver had unloaded from the trunk. "Rals, when are they going to—"

Ralston stopped him with a raised palm, which he then delicately cupped behind one ear. Then I heard it too: an almost subliminal vibration that seemed to emanate from the house.

Walter broke into a grin. "Sixty-cycle hum." He pointed to the porch. The light was on.

Ralston patted him on the back. "Hop to it, boy. Madame wants her bawth. Jules, yes or no, goddamn it."

Opal and Walter stayed closeted in his room all afternoon and, from the whipped-cur look on his face when they emerged, they hadn't been making up for lost nookie. Daph grilled some hotdogs and made a stew from the vegetables I'd brought back from town that morning. Opal declined the dog but accepted a bowl of veggies. "Organic?" Daph shrugged and looked at me, and I shrugged back.

"That a problem?" Ralston asked.

"Of course not. Delicious, Daph. Is that basil?"

"Handful of fresh."

"Nice."

Rals stayed silent the rest of the meal. I volunteered the two of us to do the dishes. In the kitchen, he said, "We need a united front against that biblical plague he's visited upon us. You with me?"

"We don't know anything about her yet. She's Walter's girlfriend, so lay off her. For his sake if nothing else."

"For Walter's sake, I will not lay off. She's a phony, she obviously doesn't like him, treats him like a trained monkey, just after his money. I don't want her here. She pollutes the sanctity of the Monkey Temple."

"It's probably both of them or neither."

"Not if I can help it."

"Christ, Rals. Does it ever occur to you that if you don't like someone, it might just be as simple as that—bad chemistry or whatever you want to call it?"

"Doesn't it ever occur to you that you can tell good from bad, and when you don't like someone, it's because there's something very wrong with them?"

"Of course. Tha t's the fir st thing I think. And then I try to distinguish the subjective from the objective."

"What a bunch of pseudo-intellectual bullshit. Nothing's objective. Anyone halfway smart, from Einstein and quantum physicists to your Zen guys, will tell you that. It's just a copout."

I shook out the dishtowel and hung it on a stray nail above the sink. "Maybe I'm just not so convinced of my own infallibility."

"Or don't have the stones to act on what's right in front of your face."

"Jules?" Opal stood in the doorway, a neutral smile on her face. "Could Walter and I speak to you when you have a few minutes?"

"Sure, we're nearly done." After she left, Ralston and I had a frantic mute conversation: how long had she been there and how much had she heard?

I met them out on the porch. Walter looked sullen but Opal had the serene mien of someone confident in her control of the situation. "We have a favor to ask."

"*She* has a favor," Walter muttered.

"We'd like you to edit Walter's book."

I'd once been sent, years before Katrina hit, a rollicking murder mystery cum ghost story cum courtroom drama cum disaster thriller set in New Orleans during a hurricane, full of local color, characters, and lore, and plenty of sex, violence, and comedy. A regional publisher was ready to snap it up but told the author it first needed editing on his own dime and referred him to me. The task was to pull the main character back from over the top and into the realm of relatability, plug a few holes in the plot, and bring the dialogue, which was straight out of Uncle Remus, up to date. The author agreed to submit to the editing only to get the publishing contract and fought me every syllable of the way. In the end, he didn't pay me, scrapped the editing, self-published his original manuscript, and was never heard of again. I considered myself lucky not to have been sued—the author was a lawyer—and I swore never again to edit against a writer's will.

"But this is different," Opal said. "Walter knows he needs it." Walter chose not to weigh in further on the matter.

"How far along are you?" I asked.

"It's a series of shorter books," Walter said, "like the Bible. I've completed three." There went that excuse to put the whole thing off.

"I guess I could take a look at it."

Chapter 13

"Come on, Daph, just for a little while." Legs crossed, boots up on the rail, Marco held a sketchpad in his lap. The morning was as gentle as a lover's sigh, the breeze warm but not damp, fragrant without bringing a sneeze. I sat down on the porch and let it wash over me.

Daph handed Marco a cup of coffee. He took a sip and went back to his sketching—from what I could see, a jagged version of Daph's face from three-quarters behind, angular, exaggerated, and hypersexual. They'd spent the night downstairs with us again.

Daph gestured with both arms at the woods, the river, the sky.

"I'm sick of trees and animals," Marco said. "I do people."

She went back to examining the posts that supported the porch roof, found one she liked, grasped it with one hand as high as she could and the other at hip level, and with legs together, knees straight, toes pointed, cantilevered herself horizontal for a few seconds. Then she winced, got off the post, grabbed her back, hobbled a few steps like a cripple, then abruptly ended the performance without a lingering trace. "Doesn't your wife pose for you?"

Marco flipped the page and started a new drawing. "Ain't here, is she?"

Ralston stepped out onto the porch. "Marco, you still have a gallery?"

"Sort of. A rep, anyway."

"Decent sales?" I asked.

"Wrong question," Ralston said. "When did he last finish a painting?"

Marco glanced up at him. "When'd you last do anything worth shit?"

Daph clapped her hands once and pointed a threatening finger at both of them.

Walter and Opal came out. Walter poured himself a cup of coffee; Opal, with a box of herbal tea in hand, put a kettle on the camp stove. Rals watched but kept his mouth shut.

"I came here to get back to work," Marco said to Daph. "A little help from you wouldn't hurt too much, would it?"

"Maybe Opal would pose for you," Ralston said.

Opal looked at them both as if reconnoitering hostile terrain. "Pose how?"

"Sketches," Marco said. "Maybe for a painting."

"With my clothes on?"

"Figure studies."

"No, thanks."

"Shy?" Ralston asked.

"The sublime esthetics of the female form—bunch of bull. It's men getting off on looking at naked women and calling it art."

"It's both," Marco said. "What's wrong with that?"

"That's why we're here," Ralston said. "Marco paints. Daph is a performance artist."

Opal touched Daph's arm. "That's so cool. What kind of stuff?"

Daph hopped up onto her toes, fluttered like a ballerina, then crouched into a Butoh-style seizure. Opal laughed.

Marco flipped another page on his sketchpad and started to draw Opal's bare foot. He made the little toe look broken.

"Walter writes," Ralston said. "Jules edits. Opal's here to—what is it you do again?"

"I'm a teacher."

Ralston looked at his naked wrist. "Late for school?"

"Not that kind of teacher. I learn things and then teach others."

Ralston raised an eyebrow. "Things?"

"Massage therapy. Feng Shui. Reflexology. Contact dancing. Tantra."

The last one hung in the air for a moment. Marco punched Walter's arm. "Way to go, dog." Walter blushed.

Ralston smirked. "And people pay you for it?"

"Pay me for what?" She poured hot water over her tea bag.

"Something wrong with my coffee?" Ralston asked.

"There a rule about what we can drink in the morning?"

Daph put her hand over Ralston's mouth. He pushed it away. "If this thing is going to work," he said, "we need to—"

"What's this *thing* you keep talking about?" Marco set down his sketchpad. "All you said was you were getting a big house."

"How many old friends have you lost?" Ralston said. "Not to sex, drugs, and rock 'n' roll but from geezer shit like heart attacks and cancer?"

Daph held up four fingers then a fifth. Marco had three, I four, Walter counted two and Opal held up all the fingers of one hand and two of the other.

"How many of you are feeling your age?" Ralston said.

Opal wiggled her fingers. "Arthritis. Fingers and knees." You had to hand it to her for trying.

"CRAFT syndrome," Marco said. We looked at him blankly. "Can't Remember A Fucking Thing."

Daph stretched her arms over her head and winced.

"Sometimes takes ten minutes to piss," Marco said.

Daph tapped his head with a knuckle. "So that's what you're doing in the woods."

Walter patted his chest. "My doctor's talking bypass."

"Can't eat like I used to," I said. "Guts can't take it." And lack energy and make stupid mistakes I never used to. And not talk about it.

Rals sighed. "Tell me about it. My farts don't even smell like mine anymore. Not many of us left. If we don't all come together pretty damn quick, we'll all die alone."

No one had a comeback for that.

"But that's the stick," Ralston said. "The carrot is that maybe, for the first time in our lives, we can do whatever the fuck we want, with whoever we want. If we play our cards right."

"You mean our money," Daph said.

"I mean pooling resources."

Daph held out two empty hands.

"But we want you here at the Monkey Temple," Ralston said. "So we work something out."

Marco leaned back, propped his cowboy boots against a porch post and looked at Daph. "Maybe first we better figure out if we like it here."

Walter turned to Ralston. "You have a plan? Numbers?"

"When we're all ready, we can talk turkey. Ritz isn't even here yet." Ralston's face held that desperate-for-money look I hadn't seen for so long, but it still scared me.

Kabul, the Noor Hotel, hippie outpost. I'm close to tears. Where's Rals?

Six weeks ago, Rals planning a Russian-roulette hash run, a short flight from Kabul to Tashkent then a train via Moscow to Stockholm. A walk in the park for a pile of bread unless the Soviets catch you and then you're never heard from again. "While you get this Sufi bullshit out of your system." Should have been back by now.

The hippie variation on the do-you-know namedropping game:

"Hey, man, good to see you again. Where was it last time—Beirut, '65?"

"Torremolinos, '64."

"I was in Singapore in '64. Istanbul, two summers ago?"

"I was in India. Marrakesh last year?"

"That's it—no, wait, that was two years ago. Paris?"

And what they did there. "These three chicks had a farm-house out in the Turkish boonies and grew this dynamite shit."

"I stayed with some dervish cats for the winter."

I stay out of the game. My own dervish cats would praise my self-restraint, but I'm grooving on my aloof cool.

Forty days in a tiny room with nothing but a mat. Food every other day. Praying as best I can from a tattered English Koran. Trying to conquer my *nafs*, my carnal self. Which seems too easy with all temptation removed. The Sheikh speaks English, asks me about dreams, visions. Invites me out to join the group. Lectures, which an eager young Pakistani translates into my ear in fragmented whispers. Remembering God, surrendering to God, ripping out wrong desires, bad habits, illusions and false teachings, to climb the levels of attainment toward becoming a complete soul.

Contemplation. To what end? Purity. Yes, but then what? Love. Our own love, God's love. I dare tell the Sheikh, "Sounds like Christianity."

He impales me with a ferocious glare. Seconds pass, maybe a minute. Finally, he laughs. "Maybe the Christianity of Jesus."

Ralston, where the hell are you?

Forty days. Now in a rundown hotel garden listening to hippie war-and-peace stories. A French cat saying, "This Zen monk showed me how this is all…" Sweeps his hand around to take in the world, the past, the future, laughs at the absurdity of it all.

A Belgian girl. "The mountains east of Marrakesh? Witches. They can do stuff, cure people, kill people. Amazing women, they can see right into you."

I don't ask, "Then what are you doing here with us?"

"Stockholm, last week. Oh, man, those Swedish chicks." Ralston! In new threads and kicks. Grabs my shoulders. "Hey, still mad at me?"

I pulled Rals down to the river ostensibly to check the bank for erosion. We sat on the steps. How to approach the matter with some finesse, ease him off without slapping him down.

"Now I remember what I hated the most back in the day," Ralston said. "Ever try to get three hippies to do the same thing at the same damn time besides get stoned, eat, or fuck?"

"I thought that was the point of all this," I said. "Not to have to do what everyone else is doing or what anyone else wants you to do."

"But not to make a goddamn religion out of it. That wasn't the point."

"What was?"

"That there *was* a point to it," he said. "To go beyond just-for-the-fuck-of-it. Push through it, get past it."

"Only to discover that there really *wasn't* a point to anything."

"That was the point, that it wasn't just a slogan. Once you discover true pointlessness—"

"Then you can get to the point."

"Exactly," he said.

"What if *your* point isn't *their* point?"

"Then you're the Italian guy in hell."

"But you don't want to be the Swiss guy," I said, "neat little houses and cuckoo-clock banks. You like people who'd get tossed out of Switzerland for disorderly conduct."

He seemed to think about that awhile. "You still got to have some, some…something."

"Boss?" I said. "Leader? Guru?"

"Unity of purpose."

"Of whose purpose?"

Suddenly he was up and snarling. "Don't pull your Premenstrual-Mystic crap on me, I know what you're saying with your condescending Socratic bullshit, I'm a little Hitler trying to—" And then, like nothing I'd ever seen from him before, he slumped back down. "Fuck. Maybe you're right."

Now was the chance to press ahead and get his agreement to live and let live. But it would be like kicking him when he was down. It would also never stick, even if for a while he tried. I gently bounced my fist twice on his knee.

"You know," he said after a silence, "the only group I ever got along with—operationally, I mean—were those crazy blow-shit-up motherfuckers. Planning was straight ahead, capers went like clockwork. Maybe it was because I wasn't trying to be in charge. Yet." He sighed. "Unity of purpose."

Maybe this was just bleak despair, but possibly an epiphany that would lead to change. I let up for now.

A hundred yards away, behind Ralston's back, Marco walked along the water's edge then turned and stepped into the woods.

Walter's manuscript wasn't bad—the writing, anyway. I had to read it on-screen, which was all right except that he and Opal hovered. I didn't ask them to leave me alone, which would convey I was taking it more seriously than I wanted to commit to. I read a few pages to get a feel for it. "How come it's in English, not Hebrew?"

"This isn't a ceremonial thing, I want people to read it. Anyhow, my Hebrew is pretty rudimentary."

Walter was using modern English—no *thee* or *thou*, no *cometh*, *goeth* or *shalt*—but had affected a dignified, semi-poetic tone that only occasionally prolapsed into pomposity. Walter usually managed to become competent at whatever he set out to do. The underlying rationale was another matter.

I scanned through the chapters and outline to see how Walter was organizing his material. "Looks like each chapter follows one character instead of narrating a chunk of history."

"That's what the more engrossing sections of the Bible do."

"Smart. Are these historical figures?"

"Some are actual people—Hillel, bar Yohai, ibn Daud, de Léon, Zevi, Maimonides obviously. Others are historically correct composites—the wandering Jew, the Holocaust survivor. Sort of like Jesus."

"He's in your book?"

"No, I mean a historical composite."

"Jesus was a real person," Opal said. "But that doesn't affect this."

"You Christian?" I asked her.

"No. And not Jewish." I let it lie. Her presence distracted me. Close by, she emanated an aura, perhaps chemical or magnetic or electric, that set my nerve endings abuzz. Sort of like a strange smell you're not sure whether you like or not.

"What angle do you want me to take on this?" I said. "I'm not a Bible scholar, so I can't comment on content. Your approach seems sound. Stylistically, the writing is appropriate—which is quite a feat, mind you—though it needs a tweak here and there."

"It's a first draft." Walter was scowling. "Not much more than an outline."

It was a lot more than that, but even discounting the weirdness of a modern-day addition to the Bible, something was wonky in its premise that I couldn't yet put my finger on. Walter had always been able to come up with an impeccable chain of reasoning, but you could never be sure of his jumping-off point. I stood up. "Then it's a promising start, what more can I say? I'll leave you to it."

"I'm worried about characterization," Opal said. "And subplotting."

"That's just not the damn point," Walter said. "There are mathematical rhythms that run throughout the Bible—frequency of mention of God, of rulers as opposed to prophets, of certain key words, but most amazing"—his face suddenly glowed with fervor—"are the rhythms of the mentions of numbers themselves, and what those numbers are. Forty days and forty nights, twelve tribes—"

"The Beast 666 and all that, I get it, but—"

"No, that's New Testament gobbledygook, throwing numbers around for effect. Believe me, I studied it, years ago in the hospital when I had nothing better to do." Walter grabbed a worn English-language Bible and scrabbled through it. "I'm talking about the older stuff, like here, eight hundred and fifteen years, five pillars and five sockets, five curtains, then six curtains and fifty loops, and so many twos—two branches, two rings, oh, check this out, two young pigeons, sometimes with two turtledoves but once with two turtles…hmm, could be a translation error. Three sons, ten loaves, ten—"

"None of which I can help you with at all," I said.

Opal grabbed his shoulders. "It's more than just numbers." This sounded like a rerun of earlier arguments they'd had. "Look at your own personal hero, Pythagoras. He thought the whole universe could be boiled down to whole numbers and the ratios between them. He even started a religion about it. Then he discovered these weird numbers that can't be expressed as ratios of whole numbers, and—"

"Irrational numbers," Walter said. "Like pi. They're not weird."

"Remember what he did?" She pointed a finger at Walter as if he'd been there in a past life. "Interrupt me if I'm factually wrong, but otherwise let me finish. He made all his followers swear never to tell anyone that his religion had a hole in it big enough to drop the Parthenon through."

"Except they hadn't built it yet," Walter said.

"You got me. And when one of them blabbed, they killed him."

I made it to the door. "I can't help you with the numbers business, that's between you two."

Opal laid a hand on my arm. "You've been a big help."

I looked over at Walter, who had turned his back to us.

"We'll let you know when we're ready for more," she said.

It was fully dark outside now. Downstairs on the porch, I found Ralston, Daph, and Marco passing around a joint. "Where'd that come from?" I asked.

Marco held it out to me. "Brought a little with me." I smiled and shook my head, but when Marco's arm stayed put, I shrugged, took a hit, then passed it to Daph.

"She give you a lesson in that tantra stuff?" Marco asked.

Opal glided out onto the porch in a sari. "Would you like one?"

"No one ever accused me of needing lessons before," Marco said.

Daph exhaled a rush of smoke with a laugh and offered the joint to Opal. "It's always a trip, isn't it, pitting a man's ego against his id? Must be getting old, Marky, to let your ego win so easily."

Opal smiled and shook her head at the joint. "I was asking Jules. In exchange for the editing."

My mind was already zooming out from telephoto to wide angle, casting about laterally instead of progressing linearly. Synchronicity: Marco had nailed it. The buzz Opal gave me came from her mention of tantra. A challenge. A sex expert. Sexpert. Words, huh! What are they good for? Absolutely nothing. "Whoa, Marco, what is this stuff, it's kick-ass strong." Why was Opal looking at me? "Oh! Thanks anyway. My wife might not like the idea."

"She'd love it," Ralston said.

They all laughed, even Opal, who had the grace to drop it. Thank Christ Rals was feeling better. Maybe the grass would keep him mellow.

"This is why I hardly ever smoke anymore," I said. "These days, I have a tough enough time focusing." A manuscript or book reminded me of something else, and I'd be off searching the web, ruminating, or daydreaming. I could try to put a good spin on it, the widening perspective and richer interconnectedness of maturity, but it was probably just the jiggling, loosening slack of a date-expired brain. It was one thing to crack geezer jokes, but quite another to give your friends—or your wife—reasons to write you off.

"Contrary to our youthful delusions," Ralston said, "pot doesn't make you think like a wise man. It makes you think like an old man."

Opal set up a small incense burner near the edge of the porch, a small bowl with a mesh bottom suspended over a votive candle. She lit the candle and sprinkled a pinch of incense into the bowl. The smoke, its fragrance, her sari and smile, the talk of tantra, Marco's killer weed, the ghat to the river…

A smoky market square in Benares. Threading among the crowd towards the river and the ghats, half the people yogis, sadhus, monks, or hippies. Some cover their faces or entire bodies with mud or ashes. Others painted solid colors, or with patterns and symbols. A man propped up inside a tripod, having vowed never to get off his feet. Some cross-legged with eyes closed, another glaring at everyone who passes. Three sadhus laughing together long and loud. Another standing on one leg.

Rals grooving on it. "The Haight, the East Village—amateurs, man. These cats got their freak chops down solid."

They know tradition, ritual, dogma, and maybe the surface striations of their own psyches, but anything else?

"A teacher?" Rals says. "You shitting me? These are street guys, look at 'em, scheming and scamming, shooting the shit."

I stop to question one especially serene looking man. Has a lot to say to me, smiling, insistent, seems to be giving advice. Can't understand a word.

Thousands of people descend the ghats to bathe in the Ganges then climb back up again. Smoke from burning funeral pyres drifts across the river.

The next morning, hands on hips like a drill sergeant, Ralston stood in the doorway surveying the Great Hall. "Looks like a Civil War campground." Four sleeping bags gaped from the floor. Limp air mattresses lay exhausted after the night shift. Daph's underwear hung drying from random nails and splinters. Men's socks sprouted from the floor like forest fungi. Backpacks, toiletry kits, shoes, coffee cups, a couple of books, a jar of peanuts. "Ritz'll puke and go home. Hey!" Rals turned to lean outside. "Enough with the breakfast. We got to get this pigpen cleaned up before Ritz gets here."

Marco and Daph put down their cups and slowly bestirred themselves. Walter the Neat smugly stayed put, but Opal nudged his shoe with a bare toe and got to her feet.

"For starters," Ralston said, "no more campouts. Grab a bedroom. Not the big one in the back corner."

Marco put his arm around Daph's shoulders. "Let's go get ourselves a nice quiet one."

She mimed horror-movie fright.

He sighed and closed his eyes. "What's the problem?"

"I don't know your wife well enough yet to cheat on her."

Once I'd hauled my own gear up to the bedroom, I went downstairs to the Great Hall, which was now clear except for a few candy wrappers on the floor.

"I'll sweep it out," Opal said.

"Hold on a sec." I looked up at the cloth cocoon hanging from the ceiling.

Rals joined me. "Looks like shit, doesn't it?"

"No getting around it." I headed for the door. "Isn't there a bigger ladder in one of the sheds?"

Once up the stepladder, with Opal and Walter bracing its rickety legs and Rals kibitzing from below, I untied the sheet and let it fall to the floor. Matt was right, there was a tangle of wires. But in the midst of it, encrusted with grime, verdigris, and cobwebs, and missing all its prisms, hung an ornate brass chandelier engraved with geometric and floral patterns.

The four of us gaped at it for a few moments. Ralston slapped his forehead. "Fuck a duck, that's what those things are." He trotted upstairs as I climbed back down the ladder, and he returned a minute later lugging a small but heavy cardboard box. "In the attic." Inside, the chandelier's prisms lay in rows, each layer separated by tissue paper. "Will that thing support their weight?" Rals said. "Wait, how the fuck would you know? Hold this chingadero."

With Walter and me steadying the ladder, Ralston clambered up and yanked and twisted the chandelier's main stem. "No sweat. And the little hooks for the danglies are still attached." When he flexed the wires, rotten insulation crumbled to the floor. "Needs rewiring. Meanwhile." He climbed back down, put a hand on his back, and winced. "Walter, got any Brasso?"

"Nope."

"Well, what are you waiting for? And lamp wire—twenty feet. Connectors and tape."

"I've got work to do."

Opal tugged his arm. "Come on. This is fun."

"Hey, hold up!" Ralston hobbled out for parting words to Walter before they drove away.

Upstairs, I pumped up the air mattress, spread out the sleeping bag in a semblance of a made bed, and arranged my clothes and backpack as neatly as I could. Then I scrubbed the bathroom. As a final touch, I picked some wildflowers, stuck them in a Cheerwine soda bottle I'd found out back, gave them some water, and set them on the windowsill.

Ralston was up on the ladder in the Great Hall. I didn't invite him to go with me to pick up Ritz. Maybe the chandelier project would keep him occupied, upbeat, and out of trouble.

Chapter 14

How long had it been since we'd been apart for more than twenty-four hours? I caressed her hair, her face. That writer's conference in Ohio I'd spoken at last winter, but that had been only three days. She clung to me a little harder than a simply affectionate greeting demanded. Slender, compact, firm. "You lose weight?" I asked.

"Pining for you? But thanks anyway."

The moment soured. Just how dependent had I become? Ritz looked different somehow. Her easy self-assurance, which I'd always admired: could it simply be a mannerism she'd cultivated? After all, I'd always lacked self-confidence but had learned to muster up a jaunty air when needed, which after a while became habitual when with strangers who mattered. Maybe self-confidence isn't so much inner strength as a convincing way of acting— convincing for oneself as well as others—that eventually becomes automatic.

But still. I hugged her again then drove home from the small regional airport at a leisurely pace. Home—I'd even begun to think of the place that way. She usually accused me of driving too fast, and I didn't want to piss her off. Her first sight of the place ought to filter through a nice day and a good mood. Along the way, the birds cooperated too: two mocking-birds and a bluebird presented themselves, and even an osprey put in a brief, high appearance.

"The place sounds so big," Ritz said. "Can we afford it?"

"In a word, no."

"Then why did I spend the money to get here?"

"You should see it. Rals has some ideas."

"Oh, terrific. Rals, our financial manager."

"He got so attached to the place, and it's pretty nice." But she'd nailed it right there, hadn't she? I stepped on the gas, squealing the tires around a turn.

She gave me a questioning glance.

"This goddamn trip was doomed from the start," I said. "I can't make you happy while taking care of him." I screeched around the next curve then eased off. This wasn't her fault. "You'll have a look, we'll make nice, then, if you want, you can go home. I'll chase everyone off and bring Rals back to New York. If he's still talking to me."

She silently stared out the window for a few minutes, then ran a soft hand from my shoulder to my hip.

Rals must have whipped the troops into spit-and-polish mode. The front yard was free of debris, only the camp chairs remained on the porch, and the vehicles were now neatly parked in or near the garage. Walter, Daph and Marco had big hugs for Ritz. Ralston's quick kiss to her lips implied a deeper intimacy or a closer bond with the presumptive future owners. I stayed outside the circle of warmth.

Opal smiled at Ritz and shook her hand. "I love birds, the way they live so in the present. Makes us feel close to nature."

Ritz glanced at me. "Not everybody wants to feel so close to nature."

"Which is why we have civilization," said Rals, the expansive host. "And speaking of which, welcome to the Monkey Temple. Come on in."

"Monkey Temple?" Ritz shied away from the front steps and instead rambled around outside the house, looking more into the woods and over the river than at the house.

"Come see inside," Ralston said, then slapped his hands to his sides when instead Ritz made a beeline for the shed. He got there first and pulled the door open for her. "See, still fits its frame, sign of a stable structure." She looked around, sniffed the air. I caught it too, a faint hint of ammonia. "Probably once a chicken coop," Ralston said.

Marco wandered in behind us, cowboy boots clomping on the thick plank floor. "Fuckin' A, look at this light." Long ago, someone had hacked a rectangle out of the wall facing the river and installed a wide window, whose years of dust, rain tracks, tree droppings, and cobwebs filtered sunlight into the pale gold of white wine. Marco eyed Ritz as she swam through the viscous light. "Hey, Ritz, model for me?"

I leaned against the doorframe, keeping my distance. She was still beautiful, but she'd always looked that way to me. She'd kept her shape. Her legs in those shorts—none of that hanging, jiggling, turkey-wattle fat that some women get and a few don't bother to hide, which could almost be a deal breaker—but maybe not, you get used to things. As she, I hoped, got used to my slow metamorphosis to repulsive old fart.

In London, Lena had started putting on weight, and I'd still had sex with her, but with less visual pleasure. Ritz's legs looked lean and strong, but would someone else see them as old-lady scrawny? That spidery purple vein behind one knee: if I'd been twenty, or even thirty, would it be a turnoff? Back then, the idea of lusting after a retirement-age woman… Those tiny vertical wrinkles she'd developed along the edges of her lips the way older women do. Did Marco find her attractive? Elaine was a decent piece of ass herself and younger than Ritz by at least twenty years. Did Marco see Ritz as a shining example of womanly grace and beauty, or did he just need a willing body to draw? Even worse, was he headed back toward his earlier Goya-esque grotesques? The Preening Crone. Christ, strip down for Marco? Sheer masochism.

She might do it—as a test. A test of herself or of me. She'd liked tests even before she'd become a schoolteacher; must drive the kids crazy. Now she was blocking out spaces with her hands. "Small cages here, operating table."

Tests, the taskmaster of science but the ogre of mystical pursuits. Proof? We don't need that kind of mechanistic vibe. Even Psycho-Metaphysics, with its principles and resets supposedly based on observation and reason, sniffed shifty-eyed at proof. Spiritual advance is about your own perceptions of yourself and the world. Well, of course. From there it's but a short giddy step across the abyss to accepting telepathy, astral projection, past lives, alien visitation, and the Word of God Almighty Himself, all based on My Teacher Says and the elation of having joined the spiritual elite.

"Rals," she said, "think we could cut another hole in the side over there for a flight cage?"

"Sure, no problem." He took her arm and headed for the door. "This is nothing, wait'll you see the house." He brushed past me. "Out of the way, sourpuss. What do you see in this guy anyway?"

But the stable was her next stop. "We could do something with this, we can figure out what later." Then down to the river. "Maybe a swim pen for ducks." Even the garage got the once-over.

Finally, Ritz stepped up onto the porch. With a deep bow, Ralston swept open the door. Ritz sat down in one of the camp chairs outside.

Rals slowly closed the door. "Would Madame care for a martini?"

"Some water would be nice. Not to mention a way to pay for a place like this."

Ralston snapped his fingers at me but Walter was already off and running for the kitchen. "We've been figuring out the money," Ralston said. "I have some, and—"

Ritz put a finger to her lips and shook her head, then shaded her eyes and looked up and down the dead live oak. "Look at all the woodpecker holes."

"They wanted to chop it down," Rals said, "but I knew you'd like it, so I wouldn't let them." Walter came back with the water. After a few sips and a mop of the brow, Ritz stood up, opened the door for herself, and walked into the house. I followed, then Ralston, who flipped the light switch next to the door. "Ta-da!"

A shower of radiance sprang forth from the ceiling. They'd polished the chandelier to a deep bronze, screwed in the couple dozen small bulbs Walter and Opal must have picked up, and hung the prisms.

Ritz laughed with delight. "Our ballroom." With her "our," Ralston flashed me a thumbs-up behind Ritz's back and waltzed her around the room.

Marco or maybe Daph had tacked some of his sketches to the walls: Daph's face, Opal's writhing foot, but also the live oak looking deader than ever, a panicked bird, a jubilantly vindictive squirrel, the river that seemed to flow like spilled blood across the page, the house squatting like a laughing Buddha among the brooding trees. So that's what Marco had been doing in the woods. But without his pad?

149

Ritz wrinkled her nose. "What's that smell?" A faint acrid odor, half-organic, half-chemical, somehow familiar.

Ralston dove for the light switch and flipped off the chandelier. "A work in progress. Come see the kitchen." I stayed behind to make sure the burnt odor dissipated rather than thickened.

"What kitchen?" Ritz said. "You plan to cook on camping equipment like a bunch of geriatric Cub Scouts?"

"Once it's ours," Ralston said, "we'll buy a fridge and a stove."

"That's not the half of it—not the tenth of it, not the thousandth of it. What about the floor? The walls? Cabinets?" She sniffed loudly. "The wiring. The plumbing? Counters and surfaces?"

"No big deal."

"No big deal? You're talking ten, twenty thousand just for your kitchen." How fast "our" turned into "your." Why was Ritz delivering the bad news to Rals when I'd said I'd do the dirty work?

The rest of the tour went quickly and with little conversation—a cursory glance around the upstairs, a look-see into our bedroom. We ended up in the second-floor hallway.

Rals gave her a big smile. "So, Ritz."

"I don't want a sales pitch."

"No, I just—"

"I'm not kidding. I need to think about this. And talk to Jules. It's a lot of money."

"Sure," he said, "let's talk."

"With Jules. Just the two of us."

Hard to tell for sure, but Rals looked stung as he headed down the stairs. "Hey," I called after him. "Better switch off the breaker to the chandelier."

"Breaker? You're lucky we even have fuses here, but it's the same one as the light in the kitchen. I'll tape the switch."

Ritz and I went into our bedroom, where she lay down on the makeshift bed. "I'm bushed." I lay next to her. She was right to call off the whole thing now before Rals got in too deep. A soft breeze blew in through the window; a mockingbird sang nearby. Though I wouldn't have minded staying a bit longer.

I used to live for change. Or so I'd thought. I didn't leave them sprawled around on display in the living room, but I glanced through the AARP magazine each month. You've got it made, so relax, enjoy yourself, you're still young enough to have fun but mature enough not to have to worry. Husband your resources, spend time with your family, help your community. Hey, be creative even.

I closed my eyes and tried to meditate away the dread. Comfort's a loser's solace. Maybe risk was what I needed—though risk for its own sake was kid stuff. Something to keep life rolling forward rather than slowly juddering to a halt.

"I didn't come sooner," she said, "because yesterday I had a meeting with Freddy and the guy at his bank. He wants to borrow fifty thousand from us over five years."

"Fifty! He's the damn lawyer in the family, why's he need our money?"

"He went over the whole thing with me, I'll let him explain it to you. The point is, do we do it or not? Plus cosign on another half mil."

"Half a mil! What are they—"

"Jules. Focus. That's the place they want, the deal they can get, and the help they need. Either we take it or leave it. He's our kid, are we going to say no?" I sat up into a slouch on the edge of the mattress and stared at the floor between my knees. She said, "So how can we possibly manage buying this place?"

"Exactly."

She slapped the pillow. "I'm not saying we can't, I'm asking how."

I turned and stared at her. "You've changed your mind?"

"I haven't made up my mind. Could we make it happen if we wanted to?"

"Financially, it would leave us a long way out on a very slender limb." Unlike Walter, I knew the answer didn't lie in the numbers. It all depended on what Ritz and I truly wanted. And maybe Walter? "Let me think about a few angles," I said.

Chapter 15

A knock on the door woke us up the next morning. Ralston, with two cups of coffee. He handed one to Ritz. "Jules and I have a surprise for you." He took a gulp from the second cup then handed it to me. "Let her see for herself, don't tell her."

What now? "Wouldn't dream of it."

After a fast breakfast, Ralston led us down to the river. Bobbing in the stream, the canoe gently tugged at the line tying it to a cleat on the landing. "Hop in."

"My bird book!" Ritz ran back up the steps and toward the house.

"You nuts?" I said to Ralston. "We don't know it's safe."

He dragged me to the edge of the landing. "Look. You see any water in that canoe? I put it out an hour ago. Watch." He scrambled aboard, took a few steps fore and aft, stood with feet apart, hands on his hips, and rocked the canoe from side to side. "Solid as a rock. Hand me the backpack."

"What about lifejackets?"

"What do you think this is, white-water rafting? Worse comes to worst, we can all swim."

"There alligators in there?"

"They can eat you out of a lifejacket, yummy little pig in a blanket. Don't be such a mommy. The river can close the deal for Ritz."

She came back with her bird book. I got in next, rocked the boat a few times, then helped her in while Ralston steadied the canoe against the landing. He handed me a paddle. "You're the muscle, you paddle from the rear. Ritz, you stay right there, passenger in the middle like Cleopatra on the Nile. I'm the guide, in the front like Columbus on the *Santa Maria*."

"More like the *Andrea Doria*," I said. "You don't know anything about this river."

He pulled a wad of folded paper from the backpack and waved it. "I'm a freakin' expert, Walter downloaded these maps off the Internet."

We headed upstream. Ritz spotted egrets, a kingfisher, and what she thought might be an anhinga. Turtles sunned themselves on logs and rocks along the banks. The inside of the canoe stayed dry. Ralston pointed his paddle toward a small winding tributary that headed off into the deep woods. "Hang a left, Popeye."

"What's this, a bayou?" I said.

"This ain't Louisiana. Shut up and paddle, leave the guiding to me."

"What is it then?"

He slipped a pair of my glasses onto his face and peered at his papers. "A creek. They got rivers, creeks, and swamps here. No bayous." In contrast to the open river, here we could often see bottom and had to navigate around rocks, logs, and tangles of downed branches and trees. Fish meandered in the shallows. Every minute or two, as we paddled against the gentle current, we'd hear a splash from the bank.

"Frog," Ritz said the first time. Another time it was a furry rodent. "River rat?"

"Woodchuck?"

"They don't swim."

"Beaver?"

"Too small."

"Nutria?" No one knew.

"Oh, my God." Ritz stared into a particularly dark section of the woods. On a big black tree stump, amid a stand of drowned trees, sat a huge bird with a black head and neck perched above a fluffy white body. Against the forest's dark grays and browns, her breast feathers seemed to glow with a bluish light. We slowly paddled closer. The plump bird looked at us but didn't even stand up, much less fly off.

"A goose," Ritz said, "Canada, I think. She must be on eggs." The regal bird plucked at her wing feathers a couple of times, settled in more comfortably, then glanced at us as if to say, You still here? We backed off and continued upstream.

The creek opened out into a wide expanse of water, more like a large pond than a stream. The current was imperceptible; one stroke of a paddle would send the canoe along a slow straight path in whatever direction it was pointed. Ralston turned us toward the water's farthest point. "That way." Our breathing and the sound of the dripping paddles were the loudest sounds in this quiet world. The occasional small bird flitted amongst the trees but didn't call out.

A great blue heron eyed us from next to the bank. We stopped paddling but the canoe's momentum brought us closer. With a few beats of its huge wings and a series of hoarse, snarling honks, it skimmed the water to the other end, where it daintily alit in the shallows to continue fishing. When we approached the far end, the heron again cursed us out and flew off. We paddled a little farther and found we hadn't reached the end of the swamp but rather a right turn in the creek, beyond which it widened. As I paddled, Ralston started softly singing. "Sita Ram, Sita Ram, Sita Ram." I laughed.

Crossing the Ganges in a taxi-boat with about twenty other people. They sing about the divine lovers Rama and Sita. Ralston and I soon learn the chorus and join in. "Sita Ram, Sita Ram, Sita Ram, Sita Ram."

We land a bit upstream of Benares, where the river is a little cleaner, and the passengers get off. I ask the boatman, who doesn't speak English but understands the key word of my question, "Mataji?" Beckons us back into the boat, shouts something to the people waiting to get on, and for a few minutes motors upstream, where he ever so gently pulls up next to an old houseboat. Two young Indian guys and a European sitting cross-legged on the deck ignore us.

Mataji. A name I keep hearing. A teacher who sizes you up quickly, teaches you a lot in a short time, and then keeps you or sends you on.

A shout from ashore. A wiry brown woman lugs a cloth bag up the gangplank. Mataji has a servant? The boatman smiles, puts his palms together under his chin and bows to her. She waves us aboard. The boatman refuses payment for the side trip and putts off down the river.

Mataji. By my tiny knowledge of Hindi, great or holy mother. She looks me in the eye long and hard but sympathetically, then welcomes me. Rals gets a quick smile. Probably about fifty, strong, positive, bossy. She cooks a potato stew and we all eat.

Later she takes us all to a village festival. Parade, music, fireworks, elephants. Streets unpaved, lined on both sides with tiny stalls selling sweets, incense, bells, food, tea, herbs, religious pictures and sculptures, unidentifiables. Everyone both spectator and participant. Most people seem to know her, greet her respectfully. One Sadhu pointedly snubs her, fear in his eyes. She neither ignores nor acknowledges him.

The next day, Mataji lends me a loincloth, a long narrow white strip. I wrap it around my waist and between my legs. Ralston shakes his head. "Man, you have any idea what goes into this river?" Over the side of the houseboat into the river, off with the loincloth. I am naked in the Ganges.

The river flows noticeably but gently. The water doesn't feel like normal water, but thicker, heavier. It's muddy, but not a uniform brown; dirt and minerals swirl, tiny flecks glint in the sunlight.

To truly bathe in the Ganges, one must immerse oneself totally. I go under and swim downward. Surface sounds become faint and far away. Waterborne particles massage my scalp, face and eyeballs. The river glows earth-brown in the sunlight, tastes of glacial ice and mountain rock rather than organic waste. Basking in the water, I feel clean and peaceful with a sense of accomplishment but not of journey's end. Back on deck, the sun dries the water off, leaving a perceptible crust of holy Ganges on the skin.

Ralston clasps his hands together and bows. "Bless me, O Sainted One."

Slap!

Ralston jerked upright from his slouch. "Gunshot?" We stopped paddling. I pointed forward. A hundred yards away, ripples spread. He and I scanned the banks on both sides.

Ritz squinted directly ahead. "The ripples are in a circle, but there's a straight line, too."

"Two straight lines," I said.

"Come on, paddle," Ralston said.

As we got closer, we could make out a distinct wake with a roundish object at its apex. "A turtle?" I said.

Slap! A new circle of ripples spread from the wake's apex. "A beaver!" Ritz said. "It's warning us off."

We slowed. The beaver slapped its tail at us again then veered toward the bank and a low mound of branches and sticks. We passed close by the lodge, saw nothing moving, then paddled on toward what seemed to be the creek's continuation, only this time we found a wall of forest. Ralston pointed in one direction and I in another, both toward narrow streams disappearing deeper into the woods. "Or there," Ritz said. A third stream.

Ralston looked at his map. "It doesn't say—hey, Ritz, there goes your heron again."

"That's not a—oh, my God." The huge bird tried to land on a branch too thin to bear its weight, fell to a lower branch, scrabbled for a footing and righted itself, then looked around suavely as if there'd never been an awkward moment. "Oh my God, oh my God." Ritz pawed through her bird book. "It's a bald eagle."

"Its head isn't white," Ralston said. "I can see that much."

"It's a juvenile, probably recently fledged, that's why it's still a little dorky. It takes a couple of years to get the white head. It's late in the spring for it to be here, I think. If this map is right." She was looking at the bird rather than the map. Without any apparent effort, like a hang-glider stepping off a cliff, the eagle spread its wings, leaned from the branch, drifted across the water, and flapped twice to swoop up and over the trees. "Wow." Ritz looked post-orgasmic. "Wow." She scribbled the date and place next to the adolescent bald eagle in her book. "Wow, wow!"

Rals winked at me and smiled.

Ralston's stream was too shallow for paddling. I got next choice, and at first mine looked more promising but soon petered out. Ritz's turned out to be a network of narrow but navigable streams, which we zigzagged up, often skidding the canoe on the creek's bottom or across a sunken branch.

Ralston pointed up across a clearing to a tall dead tree. Something lay spread-eagle on a horizontal branch. Something hairy.

"A bear cub?" I said. We looked around nervously.

"Too small," Ritz said. "Is it alive?"

A rear paw came up to scratch a pointy face. "Raccoon," Ralston said.

"Sunbathing," I said. "I've seen squirrels do that on parked cars in the city."

Ritz nodded. "Birds do it too. Drives out the mites and lice." She looked around. "Do you think anyone's ever been here before?" Close to the river, we'd seen the occasional cigarette pack, beer can, or plastic bag, but since we'd entered the maze, not a speck of trash.

"That way," Ralston said. The tack meant paddling over a submerged log, which we got hung up on for a few moments. Five minutes past it, we ran out of creek.

Ritz lifted her sneakered feet—they were wet. "We'd better turn around anyway." An inch of water sloshed around the bottom of the canoe.

"Just runoff from the paddles," Ralston said. Neither paddle was dripping into the canoe. There was no argument about turning back.

This time we found a way around the submerged log. Once on the other side, I tried to head in one direction, Rals in another. "Which way's downstream?" I asked. There was no visible current.

Rals pulled a leaf from a bush and dropped it in the water. It slowly headed toward the opening he'd originally aimed for. "See?"

"That's the wind," I said. "Try something that'll stay under the surface, a wet dead leaf or something." He fished one from the bottom and let it go. It drifted straight down.

"While you two geniuses were playing Lewis and Clark," Ritz said, "I was watching for landmarks. That way."

"Aye, aye, Sacajawea. Except there's no river there."

"Go." The stream soon came into view. "Faster. It's up to my ankles." She started bailing with her hands.

When we got back to open creek, we paddled as fast as we could. Suddenly Rals back-paddled and veered the canoe to the left. "Ease me in to that log." I slowly paddled toward it as Ralston stretched out his oar toward a beer can lodged in the mud. Suddenly he lurched backwards and sprawled at Ritz's feet. "Back! Back!"

I flailed the water with the paddle. Ritz put a hand to her mouth and gasped. Now I saw it too, a huge snake coiled just beyond the log. "Cottonmouth," she said.

We found another beer can soon enough, although we wasted a skittish minute before putting our hands outside the canoe. Over and over, while Rals and I paddled, Ritz dunked the can into the three inches of water in the canoe then held it over the side to gurgle out. "It's getting deeper," she said. "More cans." Soon she had four, two filling under her shoes while she emptied the other pair.

The water continued to rise, although we offered differing opinions as to how fast, how much time we had, and whether, as in a high school algebra problem, it would make more sense for two to bail and only one to paddle. "Where's Walter and his toilet mathematics when you need him?"

Ralston's strokes became longer and slower. "Paddle faster," he said, and I did, while if anything, he slowed. But we had a rhythm going and were making progress.

"No fair," Ritz said. "Now I've got lots of birds but can't look them up."

A cloud passed over the sun, and all at once, the forest and river turned dark, chilly, forbidding. Without speaking a word, we picked up the pace.

An unearthly howl pierced the gloom. I froze. "What the hell was that?"

"Keep paddling," Ralston said, but he'd stopped too. Another long, drawn out howl. I looked around. The two cans in Ritz's hands were empty but she didn't reach for the full ones under her feet.

Crack!

"The beaver again?" Ritz said. It didn't sound the same.

Crack! Crack! "Those *are* gunshots," Ralston said. "Keep paddling, damn it. And bailing."

A crashing came from the woods, as if something large was forcing its way towards us through the trees and underbrush. Rals turned to look back and stopped paddling. "What the fuck?"

Maybe a hundred feet behind, two dark forms swam toward us. "Just beavers," Ritz said. They were much bigger than beavers. Rals and I now paddled like maniacs. Ritz pointed to the far bank. A deer ran alongside the water. Then two more broke from the trees and followed the first. Two howls now, closer. I looked back. The two forms in the water veered to the bank and climbed out, tongues lolling. Two more hounds bounded from the woods and waded out into the water for a drink. Then with a couple of howls, all four took off after the deer again.

Ralston peered back the way we'd come. "Probably why that raccoon was up a tree." His face looked pale.

"We going to have hunters shooting at us now?" I said.

"That's not how you hunt deer," he said. "Not how you're supposed to, anyway. And it's not deer season. Must be swamp hillbillies hunting for food. Hope they don't mind three witnesses."

"No wisecrack about *Deliverance*?" I said.

Two hounds splashed into the water again. Ralston, breathing heavily, stopped paddling and glanced back at them. "Any luck, they'll get lost and eaten by gators."

"Gators?" Ritz scanned the stream, then leaned over to peer into the depths—and tilted the gunwale the last few inches to the surface. Brown water poured in. Rals and I tried to compensate for the list but too late and too far. The opposite gunwale dipped under and slowly, inexorably, the canoe sank.

Ritz gasped. "Oh, that's cold!" And it was. "My Sibley's!" She grabbed her bird book as Ralston fished for his maps then stuffed them all into the backpack, which he held above the water. I lunged for a paddle before it could drift away. "Sorry," Ritz said.

"You all right?" I asked her. "It's not your fault."

She was treading water like mad. "Cold." I couldn't touch bottom.

With both arms across the bottom of the canoe, Ralston seemed to be catching his breath. Then he lifted one end of the canoe. "Jules. Lift. Empty this thing." It wasn't hard to let most of the water slide out of the upside-down canoe, but when all three of us tried to lift it high enough to get the rest out, we just went under. "Put it right side up," he said. We managed to float the canoe with only a couple inches of water in the bottom. He threw the pack onto a seat, then the paddles.

Ritz's teeth were chattering. "How do we get in?"

"We'll hold it steady and you climb in," I said.

When she tried, her weight pushed us under and the canoe tipped over and swamped. We emptied then righted it. "Push it to shore." The bottom was too muddy to give us a place to stand. Now we were all shivering. "Further in," I said. "We have no choice." Finally, in mud nearly up to our hips, Ralston and I got enough purchase to hold the canoe steady so Ritz could clamber in.

From her higher vantage, she pointed ahead. "Big log." When Rals and I started to push the canoe, she grabbed a paddle. "You swim," she said through clenched teeth. "Faster. Exercise. Warmer." With a deep stroke, she propelled the canoe ahead. I swam frantically after her while Ralston took his time. The feverish activity did feel good. The water wasn't all that cold once you got used to it, and swimming washed the mud off.

Ritz pulled up alongside the log. "Snakes?" Ralston gasped.

Ritz jerked back, then relaxed. "Shut up." But she tapped the log with the paddle and had a good look around before snugging the canoe up against it.

The bottom was still too muddy for me to hoist myself into the canoe. I slithered like a moccasin up onto the log then rolled into the canoe. Ralston hung onto the log. "Come on," I said.

"Just letting…" Gasp. "You guys…" Gasp. "Settle in."

I reached out a hand. "Need some help, man?"

"Fuck, no." He took a deep breath, hauled himself up onto the log, then flopped into the canoe.

The sun was behind clouds, the wind had picked up, and the canoe was leaking faster than before. I tore off my shoes and handed them to Ritz. "Bail with these, it'll be faster."

And then, like figures in a sped-up old-time movie, shivering madly, we paddled and bailed as fast as we could. Every minute or so Ralston would stop paddling and look around, acting the part of the brave captain or something while he caught his breath. I wanted to tell him to give his paddle to Ritz and try bailing awhile, but that would only have spurred him to paddle faster. At least his color was coming back.

It was late afternoon when, with the river again within two inches of the gunwales, we gingerly slid up to the landing. After tossing our stuff onto the concrete, Rals and I held on to the dock while Ritz got out, and then we crawled out. Ritz grabbed her bird book and took off toward the house. Ralston tried to pull the swamped canoe up onto the landing. "Just leave it there for now," I said, but he wouldn't. I grabbed the prow. "Let me do it." Together, we tipped the canoe over in the river then pulled it out.

He leaned forward at the waist as if to puke, and when he'd half caught his breath, straightened up to give the canoe a hard kick. "Piece of shit."

I put my sneakers back on and, shivering violently now, lurched up the first few stairs. Ralston sat down heavily on the landing. I came back down. "You okay?"

His teeth were chattering. "She hates the place now."

"Can't blame her."

He kicked out at the canoe again, halfheartedly. "How was I supposed to know?" He crossed his arms over his chest and huddled. "You gotta calm her down, man. Stroke her smooth. Just an accident. Talk about that bald eagle, lots more where it came from." He didn't sound like he believed it.

I grabbed him under his shoulders and tugged him to his feet. "Come on, let's go, I'm freezing my ass and so are you."

"Sissy." We made our way to the house, me running a few steps then jumping up and down and slapping my body while Rals, plodding, caught up. "We're fucked, aren't we?"

Wrapped in a bathrobe, her wet clothes on the floor, Ritz was separating the pages of her bird book and trying to dry it with a hair dryer.

I pulled off my clothes. "You okay?"

"Now that I'm dry. What about Ralston?"

"Exhausted. I don't know. He seems okay."

She looked up at me. "Seems?"

"Physically. The rest? After our little voyage to disaster, he's beginning to accept the inevitable. I'll let the real estate guy know."

"Jules, the river is so wonderful. The rest of it was our stupidity, and still the place was gentle with us." She kissed me, a real kiss. "Thank you for my surprise."

I held her at arm's length and searched her face for sarcasm. "Glad you liked it." I dashed for the warm shower.

When I returned, she said, "We're back to how can we afford it. Or if."

"You're serious? You want this place? Middle of nowhere, pretty much a wreck?" And as comfortable as a favorite old shoe.

She looked at the stained ceiling, the discolored wallpaper. "A lot of money and a lot of work."

"More money than we have, that's for sure," I said. "If we want a nest egg too."

"The improvements would raise its value."

"Which only counts if you sell it."

"How could we do it?" she said.

"Rals still thinks we can get other people to buy in or pay to live here. This crowd, pay?" Wasn't I too old for another life-shattering learning experience? "Dumb idea. The whole thing."

She looked at me wide-eyed. "Are you kidding? I love this place, it's perfect."

Chapter 16

That night, we all gathered on the porch, and Ralston called the meeting to order. "We've got to come to a decision on the Monkey Temple. First, who's in? Besides me and Ritz. And Jules."

Walter raised his hand and waited to be called on, but Opal did the talking. "We love it here, it's perfect for writing Walter's book. Say at least six months for us, then we'll see."

Daph mimed a big hug for the place and us.

"I'm in," Marco said.

"What about...?" Ralston hooked a thumb in Elaine's general distant direction.

Marco lifted his chin. "What about it?" Years ago, hair billowing in the breeze around his turquoise-banded cowboy hat, Marco had said exactly the same thing—God knows about what—to a pissed-off biker with three buddies. And stood his ground.

"Good enough," Ralston said. "So next we come to money. To fix it up, to run it, to live on, but right now, to buy it."

All eyes drifted toward Walter. "Of course we'll pay rent," he said, "or however you want to work it—in advance, if that'll help, for the first six months. After that?" He shrugged. "We'll see how it goes." Opal played the innocent bystander. Rals glared at her as if daring her to speak.

"My stuff has sold before," Marco said, "it'll sell again. I got some irons in the fire. But right now my cash stash is like, I could come up with enough to maybe get us a big TV and a dish or something, but forget about me buying in, at least for a while."

Ralston hooked his thumb northward again. "Gotta ask. What about her cash stash?"

Marco closed his eyes for a few seconds then glowered at Ralston. "No fuckin' chance."

"What if—"

"Just drop it."

"I always make money," Daph said. "Teach aerial and dance, wait on tables, I always find something. I've a couple of friends I could call. Except they're broke too. I'll pay my way, but I can't help you buy the place."

"Maybe we could offer classes here," Opal said. "Dance, art, yoga, birding, writing, massage."

Marco sucked his teeth and slid his eyes toward me. "What about Ritz's daddy?"

Ritz looked up at the dark sky. "He's gone, years ago."

"Cut her off when she hooked up again with lover boy here," Ralston said.

They looked at me with newfound respect in their eyes. All of them except Ritz.

"Maybe we can rent out a couple of rooms as an artist's retreat," Opal said, keeping her eyes away from Ralston. He snickered.

"We need to put some numbers on all this," I said. "We have to buy the place and then crack a monthly nut."

Walter raised a hand. "What would rent be for us? A thousand or two a month, maybe for a bedroom and an office? I can do that."

"That's a start." For the nut but not the purchase. "Who else?"

Daph shrugged. "I'll see what I can make."

"Same here," Marco said. "Meanwhile." He pulled a joint from behind his ear, fired it up, and passed it to Ralston.

"Any other ideas for who could come and help pay the way?" I asked. "Anything?" Nothing.

Rals took a drink of Ritz's water. "I'm the business head here." He glanced at Walter, who looked down at his hands and kept his mouth shut. "So I'll let you all know what I come up with once I run the numbers."

When we got up to our bedroom, Ritz threw her sandals into the corner. "Three hot seconds from business to lighting up. Just like the bad old days. Nothing gets settled. We still have no idea how to pay for this place. We're not just going to wing it."

Back in the old days, good and bad, I used to sneer at people who wanted a certain future. Like Freddy, the straight-arrows had it all mapped out through the same territory their forebears had trod for a hundred generations. No eye, or a fearful one, for all the paths not taken nor even considered. Now those old untaken paths were so well trod the entire landscape looked like Yasgur's farm the morning after. Where are the new less-traveled paths? Poverty and physical hardship, which back then seemed like worthy companions for freedom and adventure, now seemed like enemies—and to Ritz, always had. But she loved this place, didn't she?

"I should go home," she said. "You should look for something else. Or come home too."

Retreat? "What about Rals?"

"Rals and this house aren't inseparable," she said.

"Tell *him* that."

By the time I came back from brushing my teeth, Ritz was asleep.

After breakfast the next morning, Ralston and I, stiff and creaky from yesterday's voyage, sat at the far end of the porch with a legal pad and a calculator. He had gotten property-tax figures from Matt and general estimates on electricity and gas charges. Like the water, the septic system was our own, both bringing all the liabilities of ownership—burnt-out pump, dry well, overflows, clogs, contamination. Gas came in tanks rather than through pipes. Ralston hit the TOTAL button and laughed. "This is so much cheaper than New York. Or Paris. We can crack this nut no problem."

"Food's not in there. We'll need cars, medical insurance—"

"That's all personal stuff. I'm talking about the house."

"You're leaving out the biggest expense, maintaining this wreck."

"That's too unpredictable to give a number."

"Exactly, a financial loose cannon—a financial loose nuke."

"Not if we first find all the shit we know is wrong with it." Rals stood up to point at the roof, the rotting porch support, the flaking paint. "And take care of it to begin with."

"Which leaves nothing left to pay upfront toward the house. You know how big that would make my mortgage? We should do repairs and improvements bit by bit, as we need to and can afford to, from what we make."

"You can't expect renters to pay for capital improvements."

"You can't expect the owner to foot the bill for maintenance."

"Listen to us, couple of fucking capitalists."

I took a deep breath. "We need another investor."

"You mean Walter. But that bitch is standing in the way. If she weren't here, it'd be easy to bring Walter in."

"Probably."

"So how do we get rid of her?" he asked.

I thought for a while. "Wrong question. You see how he acts around her. How can we get rid of her without alienating Walter and without her taking him with her?"

Rals opened his mouth to speak, then closed it again.

"Besides," I said, "he'd be devastated. The more doable question is how to get Opal to convince Walter to come in with us."

"You want me to kiss that bitch's ass? She wouldn't believe it from me anyway."

"Step number one is you have to lay off her. Stop giving her all that crap, especially in front of Walter."

He began to put on his affronted-innocence face then dropped it and shrugged. "Okay, okay. I'll try."

"Then, we get Ritz to buddy up with her. The woman-to-woman connection. New best friends."

Ralston smiled for the first time since the canoe capsized. "Not bad, maestro. Let's run this past Ritz."

When we went to find Ritz, Daph perfectly mimed Marco sketching, right down to the expression on his face, then posed like a model and pointed toward the shed. The door was closed as we approached. A hoe and a rake stood propped against the side of the shed.

"Gardening?" Rals asked.

I opened the door and stepped in. Marco was sitting on a bucket with a sketchpad and pencil in hand. I froze.

Ritz stood in profile by the window, naked. The diffuse light coming through the weathered glass made her body look almost immaterial, a wavering golden glow. A few strands of hair at the back of her neck slowly swayed in the sunlight, her silvering bush reached out its tendrils like some shy undersea creature, and in the cool morning air, her nipple stood erect.

Rals stared at her over my shoulder. "I didn't need to see that."

"Then stop looking."

"Take it outside," Ritz said. "We're working." But when neither of us budged, Ritz broke pose to turn and face us, fists on hips. As if the artist had reached out with an eraser and rubbed it smooth and clean, the left side of her chest was featureless but for a fine, neat, horizontal incision scar that ran all the way across it. "I'm not kidding, you guys. Take a hike."

"I *really* didn't need to see that," Rals murmured, and backed out the door.

I forced a smile, gave the artist and his model a little salute, and followed Ralston.

After lunch, Ralston and I walked Ritz down to the river to present our strategy.

"Before you start," Ritz said, "I called Artie Wong. He says we can't go into retirement carrying two mortgages—three, if Freddy has problems. The only possible way to make it work would be to sell the apartment, roll over the capital gains into this place, use our retirement accounts to stay afloat, and then, hell or high water, make some income. Unless someone else kicks in a bundle."

Ralston spread his hands, palms up and empty. "You already got what I had."

"Call Martine," I said. "If she sold the Paris apartment and came over, you two could go halfsies with us."

Ritz's head snapped up and she scowled at me. She was right. What a turd I was being.

Ralston smiled sadly. He knew it too. "I already called her on Walter's phone. She'll never sell that place. Anyway, she's sure I'm demented. Probably thinks I'm down here engineering a mass suicide." He held my gaze until I looked away.

"Then it's all or nothing," Ritz said. "There's no going back."

I explained to Ritz the plan about Walter and Opal.

"You're right," she said. "Walter's your best bet, and to get him, you need Opal. I like her, and I'll see what I can do, but when? She's closeted with him all day except when we're all together for meals, and I can't exactly have an intimate girly conversation with her then. And I have to go back to close out the paperwork for the school year." She took a breath. "And my career." She looked at me. "So it has to be you. Anyway, you're more on her...esoteric wavelength and the one who's going to see the most of them by far because of the editing."

"Which Walter hates."

"Then make him like it."

We sat in silence awhile. I tried to figure out how to bring Opal into the editing process but couldn't yet see how to make it either workable or convincing.

Rals gave us his sly smile. "I think I have an idea."

Ritz frowned. I said, "Come on, we can't screw this up with some crazy stunt."

"Don't worry," Rals said. "Let me think about it some more and I'll run it by you tonight."

He took off to town to talk to Matt. Walter and Opal were at work upstairs, and Marco was on one of his strolls. Daph was doing exercises on the porch, using the rail for a barre. Ritz, damp Sibley's in hand, went on a birding expedition along the river. Since the mastectomy and chemo, she'd devoted more and more time to birds and had even become birdlike in her movements—quick, unhesitant, in the moment. Once we got settled in, would every day be like this one? Everybody peaceably doing their own thing then hanging out together at night? Not bad.

But once the novelty wore off? Ritz would have her birds and Walter his calling. Who'd get bored first? Marco, who had the least excuse but had, once before, more or less given up art? Daph, without an audience and the city's constant diversion? Opal, without students or initiates or followers or clients or whatever she called them? Probably Rals. His great quest was to set up a commune, not to spend the rest of his life piddling around in one. But he'd probably stick to it the longest rather than admit failure.

And me? Would this all turn out to be just a final aimless adventure? A fast end I don't see coming would be a blessing, salvation from pointlessly hanging on. I wandered back down to the river.

Mataji's houseboat on the Ganges. Rals trying to act offhand, not meeting my eyes. "I'm not into this shit. Stay if you want." Choked up? Splits in the crowded taxi-boat.

Mataji's face close to mine, peering into my eyes. "No lying. How you feel, your friend gone?"

"Sad he won't stay and learn from you too."

"No lying! How you feel?"

"Relieved. Freer."

"And?"

"Guilty that I feel that way."

"No more lying. No stealing. No alcohol or ganja. No sex. No killing."

"No killing? That's a rough one." She doesn't laugh. Waits. "All right."

"No talking. You have questions, ask me. No chat-chit with the others."

Sitting cross-legged, hands in my lap, breathing. Concentrating on two things at once: the ebb and flow of air through my nostrils, the swelling and shrinking of my belly. Thoughts come, but instead of struggling to banish them and empty my mind, I do what Mataji tells me and concentrate on the orbit of my breathing. Thoughts fade. Maybe this is what's really meant by— Breathe in, out. In, out. Impatient for the next step. Fill, empty.

Another stew that evening, turnips maybe. Sleeping on the deck. Up at first light. Same routine.

Third day, a word. "Sibatha."

"What does it mean?"

"It means sibatha. Stop talking."

Concentrating on sibatha instead of on breathing. Why a word instead of— Sibatha. Sibatha. Sibatha.

Not sleeping well that night. Tender from the hard deck, mosquitoes. What's Rals doing? Is he all right? Does he feel abandoned?

"Here's your getaway car, man." Rals, the next morning, alongside in a small taxi-boat. Mataji leaping to the rail, watching me rather than Ralston. I stay still, say nothing. Sibatha. Sibatha. Ralston slips away as silently as a stray thought.

Mataji looks at me. "So?"

I try to tell her that without all the camouflage we wrap around our flaws—denial, excuses, blame, explanations, psychoanalysis—they become small, weak, negotiable, fleeting.

Mataji stern. "You think too much. But okay. Now cleansing." I remember yogi tales of knotted string passed through body channels like floss. She touches my head, heart, midsection. "Clean the spirit." She tells me how.

Sitting again. Looking not inward, but at the entirety of the moment. Sounds, smells, a pressure in my gut, a workman's hammer along the bank, my own thoughts and feelings. Fears, hates. Nasty little secrets. Not chasing them, not worrying them like a yappy dog or chewing on them. Why would— Just look at them, whatever bubbles up. A crow caws overhead, my mother's scolding, a pang about Rals.

In flashes, feeling like nothing but a point of consciousness. No self, no inside or outside. Something says I'm breaking ground. Something else says it's an irrelevant accident of brain physiology.

For a week, she only exchanges nods with me at mealtimes. The rest of my waking day is spent meditating—cleansing.

Until one day, it's different. Cleansing doesn't mean keeping things away or forcing them out, it means letting them in and not holding on to them. The boat's rocking, the tingling pain in my butt, a child's cry. Past and present, fact and fantasy. The future teeters on a billion fulcrums of happenstance and decision, infinitely branching. They're all here. No need to fuss with them.

With no focal point—breathing, sibatha—I float free, without tether, without grasping.

I stand up. The world looks different. Of course it has looked different before, too. But that's all right. The boats, the river, the birds, the people, the clouds, the horizon. It's beautiful, not so much for its symmetry as for its wonderfully broken symmetries.

Mataji asks me what happened. I tell her.

She's smiling. "Now go. Try. See."

Wait, what about astral projection, ESP, past lives—hell, what about escaping the wheel of birth and death?

Smiles again, shakes her head. "You don't have the soul of a yogi. You Buddhist. Different. Now, go." Points away from the sun. "Tibet."

Shock. To find and lose a teacher so quickly. I plead. Two of her other students exchange smirks. Mataji gently adamant. I leave her some money, take a taxi-boat back to town, and inevitably run into Ralston amid the hippie houseboat scene, sharing a chillum with a tall Nordic chick. "Hey, man. Meet Lilit. You know Finnish is like Hungarian?"

A week later, telling some gorgeous Jamaican girl about my time with Mataji. The girl's eyes shine. The true lesson hits. The journey to transcend ego is an ego trip. I don't tell the girl about it.

I climbed into Walter's SUV to check my email. Adele had sent a rough first outline of her novel. I closed my eyes for a moment then forged ahead, opened the attachment and started reading. Chapter 1, the three protagonists meet and talk about their plans. Chapter 2, they get together, and Della explains how Leda and Adie need to get their financial acts together. Chapter 3, they take a walk in the country, where nature inspires Leda to tell her secrets about... Chapter 4, Adie gives them tips on disposing of enemies. A lecture series pretending to be a novel. At this point, in New York, I would usually head to Café Lalo for a dose of espresso and college-girl smile, but now I was stuck in a swamp. Cabin fever already.

A tap at the window—Daph, all sweaty and healthy. "What are you doing here?" she asked.

"Just what I was wondering."

She laughed. "No, stupid. In Walter's truck."

"Email." Later, I'd give Adele a lecture of my own. I signed out and climbed down from the cab.

She looked around. "Marco?"

"Went for a walk."

"Marco doesn't do walks." But here he came, out of the woods down near the river. He almost stumbled when he looked up and saw us watching him, then gave us an easy wave and went into the house.

"Daph, what are *you* doing here?" I asked.

She socked my shoulder. "What am I ever doing anywhere?"

I stared at the email logged-out page. I'd more or less logged out of my editing gig too, at least since Rals had come to town. I hadn't edited anything, just batted a few emails back and forth. Nor had I found new clients. Except Walter, maybe. At this rate, wherever we lived, I'd be bringing in little if any income.

Late that afternoon, a light rain saturated the forest's greens, browns, and grays into deep, brooding hues. We all sat out on the porch with cups of tea, plus a beer for Marco, watching the woods develop its colors like a three-dimensional slow-motion Polaroid. Now and then we'd look up at the porch ceiling to check for leaks, and Rals took a couple of trips to the attic. "Dry so far, but this rain is nothing, and no wind."

Marco pulled out his sketches of Ritz, about eight of them—standing, sitting, profile, three-quarter, frontal. With their angularity and unsettling tone, they were definitely Marcos, yet despite the distortions, Ritz looked beautiful. The inner landscape Marco portrayed was different from how I saw her. In the drawings, she came across as bottled up, dangerous, potentially violent. Writers often borrow characters from their lives—friends, lovers, spouses, family—and bend them to their novel's purposes by morphing them into someone completely new yet still recognizable. Do artists do the same thing, changing the model's interior terrain to fit their own moods, or was this how Marco truly saw Ritz?

"Gonna do a painting from one of these." Marco's gaze shifted back and forth between two sketches. "Probably this one." In it, Ritz was sitting down but seemed about to get up, looking in one direction while getting ready to move in another. Her legs looked sinewy and there seemed to be the ghost of a nipple on the flat left side of her chest, though it might have been just a smudge or an inclusion in the paper. Marco handed her the other sketch he'd been considering. "For you. For sitting." In this one, she was standing and seemed in the throes of self-destructive remorse.

"What were you thinking about right then?" Opal asked her.

Ritz frowned. "Well, since you ask." She looked at me, then Daph, then Marco. "I was thinking about the deer fly biting my ass." We laughed.

By some mysterious selection process, Marco picked out three of the other sketches and gave them to Daph to add to his gallery in the Great Hall, tore one up, and stowed the rest in his sketchpad.

Rals leaned in close to Ritz and me, ogled the sketch, and gave us a wink that only we could see. Then he said, loud enough for all to hear, "Hey, Ritz, before you got here, Opal offered Jules a barter for editing. A tantric sex lesson."

"Did you take her up on it?" Ritz asked. I shook my head. "Why on earth not?" There was an edge to her voice, which she softened. "Aren't we here to break out of our set ways, try new things, see what's left for us to discover in our dotage?"

Rals put on his innocent face, Opal smiled at me, and Walter looked away.

Chapter 17

When I knocked on Walter and Opal's door after dinner, she let me in, closed it behind me, and led me to a mat on the floor. At least she didn't take me to their bed. Candles on the floor lit the room. Incense smoldered near the open window, and the smell of an unknown flower colored the night air. She sat down on the mat and motioned for me to do the same. Instead of her usual long loose dress, she wore thin leggings and a T-shirt, which made her look more delicate yet more athletic.

"You know what tantra is all about?" she asked me.

"Enlightenment through sex."

"You know more about it than that. What did Psycho-Metaphysics—what do you call it, PMP?—have to say about tantra?"

"That sex is too much of a distraction and can too easily become obsessive for its own sake to be a reliable path to anywhere else."

"Probably true, for most people. Quick and only lecture: Humans have just two strong basic passions. One is the urge to stay alive, the other is for sex. If you don't get food, water, shelter, and so forth, you get weak and die. Lust you can save up and use for other things. Tantra is about transforming sexual energy into higher forms of physical energy and then into spiritual energy."

She stood up. "We're going to begin by waking up the body." She raised her arms over her head and swayed to her own internal music. "Move your body, dance, shake, jump up and down."

Talk about hokey. I got up and shook my hands and arms, stretched my neck, then bounced on my toes.

"Free-flowing," she said. "Get the whole thing moving. Wake it up." She was dancing now, twirling about. "It's just the two of us, nobody's watching, you might as well get into it."

I started turning now, arms raised to shoulder height, one in front of me and one behind, sort of like I'd seen dervishes do.

"Good, good. But don't fall into a set pattern. Change it around, wake it up." She was prancing now and flapping her arms like a bird.

I twisted back and forth at the waist, up and down, letting my limp arms flail about on their own. Now Opal shifted to a jazz style of dance, sinuous and serpentine. For sure she wasn't wearing a bra under that T-shirt. I kept my eyes elsewhere.

"Do what I'm doing," she said, and when I did for a few seconds, "Now do something completely different." I did a little ballet but realized I was getting physically sarcastic, so instead danced as if I were with Ritz at a party, snapping my fingers and trying for a laidback funky look.

Opal went into a frenzy, twitching all over almost as if having a seizure. I shook like a bear climbing out of a river. She stopped and smiled. "Did it wake up?"

My heart was beating at a good clip, my limbs buzzed as if caffeinated—I felt energized. "Guess so."

She sat down facing away from me. "Sit with your back to mine. No, touching. Push your back against my back.

Gentler. Good. Now we're going to quiet the mind." Fat chance. "We're going to do that by focusing on something." Like Mataji's technique. "Close your eyes. I'm imagining a ball of white energy, like a soft comet, coasting through my mind. Now I'm passing it to you." Not at all like Mataji.

Almost against my will, the comet pushed into my inner field of vision as if from behind. I waited for her next instruction. Why was I being such a jerk about this? Best case, I'd learn something. Medium case, it would be a farce and I'd have a good laugh with Ritz about it. Worst case, what, a little embarrassment?

I retrieved the comet from nonbeing and floated it toward Opal. "Back to you now."

"Got it," she said. "Now make your own ball of energy." I did. "And let's trade." As mine disappeared through the back of my head, hers reappeared. "And again. Again. Again. Again." She sat up away from me and turned around. "Did that quiet your mind?"

"Sort of, sure." I felt quite peaceful. And relieved that this lesson was staying abstract and, well, metaphysical, which was good common ground for forging a friendship between us.

"I'm pushing things along at a fast pace here," she said, "but you're a pretty hip guy, and I want to show you a bit more of the territory than an introductory session would normally cover. That all right with you?"

"Sure, it was interesting, thanks." I started to stand up.

"No, stay right there. Now we'll activate our sexual energy." She got up on her spread knees, her hands on her outthrust hips, her belly less than a foot from my face, her T-shirt riding up to reveal her bellybutton. "You too." I did so, backing away a little to put more space between us.

She touched her lower abdomen for a moment. "You know what your PC muscle is—your pubococcygeus?" I nodded. "What we're going to do is inhale and pull back." She took a breath while moving her hips back until she was almost sitting on her heels. "Then rock forward, exhale, and clench your PC muscle." In one forceful motion, she huffed out her breath and thrust her pelvis forward as if offering it to me. "Now you." I inhaled and moved my ass back, then slid my hips forward as I exhaled and squeezed my PC muscle. "You get the right muscle?" she asked. "Not your anus?"

"Like trying not to piss."

"Perfect. Again." This time she did it with me. "Now let's get a rhythm going." Huff, huff, our crotches almost touching at the top of each thrust. "Can you push it out a little further?" she asked. "Curl your hips under a little more?" I tried, but it seemed the same. "Your pants are too tight."

I stood up. "I'll go get my sweats."

"Then we'd have to start all over. Just take them off." I hesitated. But why not? If I wanted her to trust me, I had to trust her. I turned my back, took off my jeans, and buttoned the fly on my boxers.

"Much better," she said after the first few thrusts. "Keep going." I could smell her musk now. She was looking straight into my eyes. Her lips, slightly open, quivered with each thrust, and her damn nipples were hard. Whoa, nice tits. I tried hard to think of cold, unpleasant things, like icy river water and coiled cottonmouths.

"Breathe harder," she said, "and vocalize. Ah! Ah! Ah! Like this. Ah! Ah! It brings energy to the heart. Ah! Ah! Come on." We grunted in sync as we rocked. "Ah! Ah! Ah!"

Marco's voice wafted up from the porch below. "Hoo-eee, ride 'em cowboy!" Ralston's cackle followed.

She stopped. "You know we're trying to awaken sexual energy."

"Sure, sure."

"That means getting aroused, turned on."

I glanced at the window. "Those clowns down there."

"Don't be embarrassed. I've seen hundreds of woodies. It's as much a part of tantra as dreams are to psychoanalysis. In India, tantric monks parade naked through the streets at their annual festival."

"No problem." Yes, problem. But one discipline I'd tried to instill in myself years ago: not to let bullshit fears scare me away from the new.

"We'll use a different position," she said. "Lie down on your back." She straddled my thighs. "Same routine. Rock up toward me as I rock forward."

She didn't need this extreme method. As soon as I took off the mental brakes, even before we started rocking again, I was getting hard. Now we touched at the apex of each thrust. "Ah! Ah!" Why hadn't I quite seen it before? She was gorgeous. The surface beauty some women have—pretty face, sexy smile, extravagant tits—was fashion-driven window dressing. Opal's whole body was a sex organ.

I strained up as high as I could with each thrust. Sweat had made her T-shirt translucent, her thigh muscles jumped at me through the leggings, and Christ, her pussy outlined itself against the thin material. I had to clench my fists to keep from grabbing her ass.

"How are we doing?" She reached down and put her hand on my hard-on. "Much better."

I gasped. The sudden shock and the bizarre impersonal intimacy of her touch, combined with the slithering orgy of my fantasies, propelled me headlong toward the adolescent humiliation of shooting my wad in my undies. I froze and willed it to stop.

She must have seen it in my eyes. She lifted her hand away. "Take a deep breath. Clench your PC muscle. Now relax that sexual energy so that it flows away from your genitals. Draw it away, spread it out."

I did so, and slowed to teeter on the brink.

"Now pull that energy up your spine. Draw it up. Let out your breath and take another. Draw the energy higher, higher. Send some to your brain but don't pack it in. Let the rest flow out your feet and hands."

My fingers and toes began to flex and spread apart, my arms and legs tingled. My chest got light and airy, my sinuses opened. A feeling of well-being trickled through my body as if I'd just come. But I hadn't. The sexual urgency drifted away, and my dick subsided—not depleted, but just lounging with a confident reserve of ready energy. I slumped back and lay still.

Opal climbed off me. "You're a natural at this." She sat down with her legs crossed and gave me a concerned look. "How come you don't make love to your wife?"

London, mid-'70s. Lena, a big girl. Not a fat woman, a big girl. Six-two, taller than me. Spacious face, firm lips around a wide mouth. Muscular legs, rock-hard ass, triumphant breasts. Late bloomer, wants to try everything. Right-side up, upside down, backward, forward, freestyle contortionist, manual, oral, genital, anal. Goes naked under a raincoat to the supermarket, unbuttoned to mid-chest, leaning down to pick up the tin of dog food the gaping pensioner dropped. Me with a hard-on the whole time but not letting her grope me in the pub on the way back, not with the football yobbos watching. Blowjob on the night train. Al fresco in the back yard listening to the neighbors argue, not stopping when the man comes out for a smoke just the other side of the hedge. I stuff her jeans leg into her mouth when she comes. I'm hopelessly in love—with Ritz, lost and gone forever.

Lena wants to learn, wonders how others do it, would go in for group sex if the PMP community didn't frown upon carnal exuberance. Too much frowning about all kinds of stuff for such an enlightened bunch. She gives me everything, asks nothing in return but my love. Which I can't give. Five years. More sex in the first six months than in the next two and a half years. More sex that first weekend than in our final year. She cries when she leaves, five years' worth.

"Ritz told you?" I asked.

Opal shrugged. "It was obvious. Your dam was about to burst. Not getting along?"

"Just fine."

"Afraid she's going to die?"

"Every day. Always have been. Since way before the cancer. They say she's clean now, but you never know."

"Okay, I give up."

Grief welled up in me as suddenly as my near-ejaculation had. I got up, looked out the window, and struggled to push the sadness down before it turned into tears. Instead, it twisted itself into a confessional urge. "It's weird. It's the scar."

"She's still beautiful, can't you see that?"

"Of course. When I see it, I just feel pain. Then I usually can't do it. I love her and I can't show her, and that hurts her feelings, which makes me feel even worse. I tell her it's just an age thing—my age, not hers—but she doesn't buy it. So I avoid the issue and don't even try."

"Have you tried a pill?"

"It's not physiological—as you've just seen."

"There are other ways to show love."

"Come on, you know what I mean."

"I mean you don't need an erect penis to make love to her."

"So after I hurt her by having a limp dick, I should go down on her?"

"The pain you feel, is it pain for you or for her? Be honest."

"Mine I can handle. Hers I can't."

"But is hers really hers?"

"Look, I'm not one of your—" I took a deep breath and clenched what I imagined was my spleen muscle. "I know it's not literally hers. My pain for her."

"You're not one of my New Age ding-a-lings?" She laughed. "Don't worry, I know my client base. As I'm sure you knew yours in London. And now know your new one."

"Clawing our way up the hierarchy of wannabes."

Her half laugh had a bitter edge to it. "I guess that nails it." She stood and pinched out the burning joss stick with her bare fingers. "This isn't from tantra, but I'll tell you something. You can transmute any emotion into something else. Try that next time you start freaking out about your wife's missing tit."

I stood up and started pulling my pants on. Now I'd made her feel bad. And jeopardized the Monkey Temple mission Rals had sprung on me. I let go of my pants and hobbled over to her Charlie Chaplin style with my jeans around my ankles and kissed her cheek. "Sorry. Thanks." The good laugh came back and she slapped my ass.

Downstairs, I found only Marco, Daph and Walter on the porch. Without a word, Walter got up and headed inside. I grabbed his arm. "Nothing happened, you know. Exercises and stuff."

"I know." Walter kept going. What was their arrangement?

Marco and Daph were smoking a joint.

"Where's Ritz?" I asked. "And Rals?"

Marco offered me the joint. "Pull up a pew, stud."

"Nothing happened, goddamn it. Where's Ritz?"

Daph looked up towards our bedroom.

Marco pushed the joint closer to me. "Right after your rodeo got started."

"And Ralston?"

Marco retracted the joint, shrugged, and toked up.

From the end of the hallway at the top of the stairs, soft light came through the crack under the door of our bedroom. I turned the knob and stepped in. Ritz was under the covers. On top of the sheet, in his underwear, Ralston lay curled up, his head on her chest, his hand on her hip, her arm around his shoulders.

"What the hell is this?"

"Just what it looks like," Ralston said.

"Exactly what it looks like," Ritz said, "and nothing more."

"He's been trying to get into your pants for years."

"Pretending to," she said, "and you know it. You really think he'd try to bed me?"

Ralston turned his head to look up at her. "Why wouldn't I try to bed you? He balled Martine."

"That was the seventies! Both you and Martine asked me to. Burning away your jealousy or whatever bullshit you called it."

Rals snuggled closer to Ritz. "Should try it with yours."

Ritz patted the bed. "Jules. Come. Sit."

I sat and tried to transmute my pointless pique into trust. And trustworthiness.

"This is what it's like," she said, "remember? Sharing a house with a bunch of people who're all going to do whatever the hell they're going to do."

"Just so you know, I wasn't having sex with Opal."

"I didn't think you were."

"I thought you were," Ralston said. "Did Opal think you were?"

I sighed. "Walter thought I was."

How easily I slipped back into the groove with Ralston. I'd found him in bed with my first girlfriend after Ritz, in Spain, the one before Chrissie, and I'd gone after him with a fireplace poker. Not because I cared so much about the girl, but because that's what you had to do, wasn't it? I still wasn't sure if I'd have hit him if I'd caught him. The next day we were again spearing fish together.

There were the other times, though, when I'd had enough and ditched Ralston, sometimes for years. I was getting the feeling again, that I had to get out of here, now. He was leering up at me from my bed, lying next to my wife in a wrecked house he was bulldozing me to buy. Wrinkled and gray, sick and desperate, terminally old, almost friendless.

"So are you and Opal now best friends forever?" he asked.

"That was your master plan, huh?"

"Except for all the sound effects. And your balling Walter's girlfriend, or not, which doesn't exactly help."

"Easy for you to say."

"Easy? You're the one who still has his wife and his damn money, and now the long-overdue sex education."

Ritz clapped her hands to her ears. "Why are you two arguing?"

"Just keeping him honest," we said in unison.

London, mid-'70s. Explaining learning by opposites to Rals on one of his trips over from Paris. "You can learn about something by studying its opposite. Like, who the hell knows how to be happy? So instead, think about what makes you unhappy, and avoid it. If it's hard to figure out the smart thing to do, instead of falling back on what we usually do, we can list the dumb moves, skip them, and try to come up with something better."

"That's just the old Zen crock about how there's no light without darkness, no wisdom without idiocy, no good without evil."

Sufi, Taoist, and implicitly Christian crock too, not to mention physics. "Of course it is. That's what Psycho-Meta-physics is all about, taking abstract philosophical principles and seeing if they can be given practical applications. Instead of just spouting poetic profundities."

"Oh, I see. You have people learn about sex through celibacy? That sounds good. How about learning about life through death?"

"It's not some literalistic dogma, it's a tool. Like, I have this one guy who wants to be braver, so we look at what he's afraid of, then he goes out and does some of the stuff he was too scared to before."

"Jump off a building?"

"Oh, come on. Approaching a woman he likes or being more assertive at work."

"This whole know-thyself trip is horseshit," he says. "Our self-deceiving brains have other plans. That's why everybody needs somebody like me to tell them when they're full of shit."

"Why are you giving me all this crap?"

"Just keeping you honest." His eyes following Lena as she crosses the room, steering clear of the bloodbath. Besides, PMPs consider it unseemly and pointless to argue with detractors. But this is Rals.

"I'm about to try out a new learning by opposites reset," I say. "Has to do with helping people find the truth about themselves by looking at the lies they tell. Want to be a guinea pig?"

"Hey, I'm just trying to learn something about your Pyro-Masturbatics. Why are you giving me shit?"

"Just keeping you honest."

The opposite of buying the Monkey Temple. Staying in New York? Slowly crumpling into nothing?

Ritz crossed her arms over her chest. Ralston sat up with his back against the wall, no longer looking at me. For a brief second his lips moved as if he were going to say something, then he swiped a hand across them, as you do when you catch yourself talking to yourself in public.

I tried to follow Opal's advice and transmute my anxiety into excitement. If I couldn't make up my mind to say yes, how about its opposite—could I say no? If *yes* was a jungle full of dangerous creatures, *no* was a dark pit of cowardice and failure.

Ralston stood up, took a slow, deep breath, kissed the top of Ritz's head then mine, and left without another word.

I went downstairs, crossed the dark porch, empty now, and climbed into Walter's SUV to check my email.

Adele:

> Jules, how do you expect me to bring out my characters without having them think and talk about themselves? That's what this book is all about. Adele

Adele, in literature as in life, people reveal
themselves more vividly and truthfully by what
they do than by what they say, especially in times
of crisis. You need to give your characters some
tough situations and have them work their way
through them. That's how readers will learn who
they are, and have a lot more fun doing so.

She must have been lurking online, for she pounced right
away.

You make me laugh. That's just what I tell my
people at work: don't listen to the bastards, watch
them. Let me see what I can do.

I brushed my teeth, washed my face, and slid into bed
next to Ritz. "This can work out perfectly for all of us," she
whispered into my ear. "You, me, Rals, the birdies. Even
Freddy. And the rest of the gang."

The two or three times over the past year I'd made love
to her, or tried to, I'd kept her nightie on, turned her onto her
side, and lain next to her where I could touch her right breast,
even see it if I pulled the strap down, and pretend the scar on
the left side wasn't there.

Now I kissed her. She kissed me back and snuggled
closer. Then I turned her onto her side to display her breast
and bury her scar in the air mattress. Her breath caught in
her throat and she turned back toward me with tears in her
eyes.

Idiot! Every time I saw the scar, the terror rose up again,
and I couldn't imagine anything less erotic. But my special
lovemaking position only told her I found her ugly.

When I was young and with a new lover, the only anti-dote besides alcohol to penis-numbing performance anxiety wasn't to try to talk myself out of it but to immerse myself so thoroughly in sensation that things took care of themselves. I peeled off the nightie. Her right breast was as beautiful as ever. In fact, the smooth, flat expanse of the rest of her chest and the asymmetrical position set it off like a solitaire diamond. Two such gems would be decadent opulence.

I was so lucky to have her. I kissed her mouth, her nipple, her belly, her pussy, taking my time over each. Down below, Little Jules was doing just fine. Maybe the sexual energy I'd reinvested during the session with Opal was paying dividends. For the first time since Ritz's operation, I made love to my sweet, beautiful, one-breasted, actual wife instead of to my hypothetical two-breasted wife. And I almost wore out my PC muscle trying to hang in there and not come until she did, calling my name and clutching my ass with both hands as in days and nights long ago.

Chapter 18

Thighs burning from the previous night's contortions with Opal, I was the last one down for breakfast, and for a moment I was taken aback, in my morning daze, by the grayish group of geezers on the porch. Then I caught sight of Ritz among them and they came into familiar focus. I kissed her cheek, both because I wanted to and as a sign to the others of marital harmony. She patted my face.

I'd planned to talk to her before I left for town so we could go over our finances in sober detail without Ralston's kibitzing, but she was stuck on Walter's phone with a bird person in New York. "Let him eat until his crop is full and he'll be a happy bird." Ralston was impatiently waving me into the car. I tapped Ritz's arm. She ignored me. "Right, and then when he's in his happy stupor, have the vet-tech give him the shot. He'll get sleepy, right there in your hands, and in about three minutes his heart will stop... Yes, the last meal for the condemned... The posture, the head twisting, I'm sure they're right, avian paramyxovirus... Very little chance, and he might still be a carrier, and it's very contagious... No, no, only bird to bird... Carol, you *have* to take him in."

Someday, when my time comes, maybe she'll do the same for me.

Ralston and I spent much of the day in town at Matt's offices. I put in a formal counteroffer of $280,000 to continue the negotiations that Ralston's down payment had begun. "One little complication," Matt said, no doubt the first of many. "Jules, you're making the offer, but the down payment came from Ralston. How do you want me to word it?"

"Don't worry about it," Ralston said. "Let's keep it simple—my name doesn't need to be in there at all. Jules and I can work out the details between us."

Matt put us in another office with a fax and a phone so I could get busy on all the paperwork involved in putting the New York apartment on the market and arranging a mortgage for the Monkey Temple. When I was put on hold at the bank, I asked Ralston, "Why do you want your name kept out of this?"

He frowned at me for a few moments. "Tax scam."

"Why did I bother asking?"

"I'm flying under the radar. I came back into the country on a fake passport. If the feds find me, I'm toast."

"For tax stuff?"

"Besides, everybody knows we're partners in this, so when push comes to shove and we have to sell it, I can claim half."

"What?" I hung up on the bank.

Rals shook his head, got as far as the door then came back. "How come it's easier for you to believe that I'm some kind of international criminal trying to rip you off than that I told Matt the truth and I just fucking trust you with my money?"

"With all this going on, you decide to pick a stupid fight?"

"You're the one who asked why I wanted my name kept out of it, after I told Matt exactly why."

"Bloody hell, don't get your knickers in a knot. I didn't know what you were going on about. And yes, I can believe the taxman wouldn't mind a gander at your books."

Rals gave me a terse, slit-eyed smile. "When you slip into that Brit lingo, any idiot can tell you're lying. You learn to lie over there with PMP?"

"Look, it's a lot of money, I'm kind of freaked out—for Christ's sakes, moving to the swamp."

Rals's smile had become wide. Not a good sign. "Remember when you found me with Lena, and I was telling you I was having problems with Martine, I was lonely, I needed a woman's point of view and all that shit? Remember what you said?"

"I'm going to kill you?"

"After you said that. You pulled this PMP shit on me. Skip the excuses or something like that."

"Look past the excuses."

"Right, so look past the excuses, find the real reason you're being such an asshole, and try to do something about it." Rals shrugged. "Just saying."

Nobody's ever just saying. People say and do things for a reason, even if they don't know what it is. That was some more PMP shit to pull on Rals—and probably an upcoming lesson for Adele—but not now.

"Sorry, man," I said. "You're right, I was being an asshole."

"Hey, no problem. Takes one to know one." Ralston yanked a chair close to me and sat down. "So what did she say about all that anyway?"

"Who?"

"Lena."

"What was there to say? I got home a day early and walked in on you two."

"No, I mean when you were doing—what's your bullshit word for it? Retard?"

"Reset, asshole."

"Didn't she have some golden shower reset?"

"Cute."

London. Everybody has some version of the golden rule: do unto others as you'd have them do unto you, or don't do to others what you wouldn't want done to you. Ancient and widespread wisdom, and therefore prime territory for PMP. Aside from its stature as a revered but mostly ignored guide to conduct, I help find a practical application for it, a reset. Every time you break it, have a good look at how come, and look past the excuses—past the automatic, ingrained, wrong responses.

The golden rule reset, the beginning of the end.

Not with Lena, whose end began simultaneously with the start. You look at a woman and you think she's interesting or sexy or dangerous or all three. Maybe you think you could fall in love with her. Or, at first sight, whatever else you think, you know you'll never fall in love with her.

Beginning of my end with Psycho-Metaphysics. The international director wants me to give him a golden rule reset on his latest stratagem: hiring salesmen.

"We need the money," he says.

"Look past the excuses."

"No, Jules, we need the goddamn money. Buddhism and Taoism failed because they didn't have the money to record, preserve, and teach what Gautama and Lao Tzu said when they were alive. The most successful religion in the world is Catholicism, and they're rolling in dough."

"You want to model PMP after the Vatican?"

"Just an analogy."

"Look past that excuse. If you, as Director, don't think there's anything wrong with hiring salesmen, then why do you want a golden rule reset about it?"

"To make sure there's nothing wrong with it."

"Look past that. What first gave you the idea there might be something wrong with it?"

"Jules, we're going in circles here. I think we need to refine this reset."

"Maybe, but first let's look past that excuse—"

He stands up and leaves.

A few minutes later, so do I. I wander the London streets and end up on a bench in Mount Street Gardens, cloistered by churches, trees, and quiet brick buildings. PMP offers some brilliant ideas and promises to replace mysticism with a scientific approach. But now results are dwindling, and an orthodoxy seems to be firming up. Marketing becomes necessary, then excuses. What's next, lies? The man who can't find a teacher becomes one. And then markets his services.

The mortgage forms started oozing from the fax machine. Combined income, total assets, total debts. Worse than the IRS. Ralston kept grabbing my glasses so he could read them too. "Lena. She was something, wasn't she? What did she say about me during her re-spazz?"

"That's between her and her guide."

"Come on, you were part of the gang."

The golden rule. Another human universal, like stories? A recessive one if so. Maybe just a late bloomer, like Lena. "I wouldn't tell you even if I knew."

"Remember that total rat-fuck Ollie the Asshole," Ralston said, "who came out from Oregon in his hotted-up Mustang? Snowed us all? Sold us killer dope?"

"I remember giving him money for killer dope, anyway."

"He told me he left the dope with you."

"And he told me he gave it to you," I said.

Ralston held up his point-making finger. "After he split and there was no dope and no money, did you for one second think I'd ripped you off?"

"No."

"And I didn't think you'd ripped me off. Trust. That's what we need to make this thing work."

"Neither of us for one second didn't trust Ollie, either. Until he split with our bread."

"That's the next lesson." Rals looked toward the door and lowered his voice to a whisper. "We shouldn't blindly trust Matt."

"That's why we have contracts. And a lawyer. Just stay away from his wife."

"Opal's another one to watch out for, no matter how buddy-buddy you manage to get with her. She's a career girl. I don't know what career, but she's working. She's not here like the rest of us." Whatever he currently imagined that to be.

"Then what's she doing with Walter?"

Rals pushed the stapler across the desk and parked it in front of me. "Walter's money." The tape dispenser went right next to it. "That harebrained book he's writing—Son of Bible with a numerological twist—the New Age crowd will lap up that shit like fudge ripple at a bong party."

"You should trust her."

"Because she worked her sex magic on you?"

"It felt good to trust Ollie the Asshole. We trusted everyone. I trusted you with Ritz, and Chrissie, and Lena. Trust is a better, cleaner frame of mind. Instead of looking over your shoulder every second. Even if you get screwed now and then."

I made a grab for my glasses but Ralston was too quick. "Let's compromise then. Trust me." He stood up and handed me the glasses. "But don't trust Opal." He hefted Matt's stapler and stuck it in his backpack. "I'm going to go buy some glasses. Like five pairs of those three-dollar drugstore ones, so I can leave them around." He opened the door. "Don't you just hate it when you go into the john, sit down, pick up your magazine, that first turd begins to claw its way out, and damn! You forgot to bring your glasses." Matt's secretary was staring open-mouthed at Ralston's back.

"I keep a pair in the medicine cabinet," I said.

"You would." He pulled the stapler from his pack and set it on the secretary's desk. "I'll leave you to your scutwork, my man."

Scutwork: signing away my comfort and security for a crazy dream. He came back a minute later. "Daph's in town, I'm going to catch a ride back. I'll give Ritz your best. Or my best." He took a few steps then came back and stared at me goofily. "We're on a new plane, man. Ka-thoong ka-thoong."

Ka-thoong. A new plane where our dwindling lives flash before our eyes.

Northern India. Eight-Finger Eddie sitting at the corner table of a steamy Patna teahouse plucking the strings of his air bass with his deformed hand, running his monologue. "Ka-thoong, thoong, thoong, man, I am up there. Ka-thoong, thoong, eight miles up, man. A new plane of existence. Ka-thoong, thoong, thoong."

Eight-Finger Eddie's trip: his swami had a firm rule never to enter his room without knocking. Eddie's curiosity got the better of him one day and he barged in, his teacher flying around the room with no visible means of support. Eddie was banished, he says, has been playing his bass ever since. The fingers? "Oh, man." He lifts his teacup, shakes his head, and stares off into space, as if the incident is too painful to recount, or perhaps temporarily misplaced in his memory.

"Where's this swami?" I ask.

Eight-Finger Eddie squints out the door. "Oh, man."

"India? Nepal? Tibet?"

"Some guys brought me. Some guys took me away."

"How'd you find them?"

"They found me, man."

Rals and I already on our way north to Tibet, but while we're here, a city once visited by the Buddha, why not check it out? Ask around. Small school on the outskirts, a cross between Buddhism and yoga, "Like the lamas, man."

A man in a turban opens the door, steps outside instead of inviting us in. "You say you're a student of the spirit? Then what are you doing?"

"Some of this, some of that."

"This will not do. How do you shed your attachments?"

"What you see right now is all I own." Small bag. Sandals. Shirt. Jeans, held up by a frayed belt. A frayed money belt.

"You're attached to your nonattachment. What teacher do you follow?"

"None right now, that's why we're here."

"No teacher? What do you know of the head body, the heart body, the mind body, the spirit body?"

"I don't know—"

"You know nothing." But doesn't send us away. A test, maybe.

"Can you teach us?"

Ralston says, "Like, teach us how to pull your head body out of your ass body."

The man steps inside, slams the door on us.

I punch Ralston in the chest, turn my back, and walk away.

Ralston, gasping and clutching his heart, catches up. "Hey, man. He was full of shit. You can always tell when they start coming on like how they're better than you 'cause they know all this shit. Like that asshole John Pujutoki."

I'll never find a teacher with Rals around. I can't bring him with me to Tibet. "I got to go see someone about something," I say.

"Let's go."

"Alone."

"Alone?" Stares at me. "With your backpack and shit."

"Right."

Long pause.

Rals turns and walks off. "Adios, amigo."

Awash in sad freedom, I hop the bus for Kathmandu.

It hairpins up the Himalayan foothills, anywhere else called a mountain range, hours from the last town, hours to the next. A vertical landscape, grays, greens, browns. Like an amputee's ghost limb, the empty seat next to me talks to me, a steady line of wisecracks.

A bright spot of red deep in a gorge. A loincloth on a rock, a solitary sadhu bathing in the icy stream far below.

Chapter 19

A bright red spot by the river—Ritz's shirt, the one I'd bought for her in Mexico. A shout, a splash, laughter. All of them, skinny-dipping with my wife while I gave away my life to buy them a playhouse.

I huffed down to the river and found them all in bathing suits or underwear. "Jules! Come on in!"

"What's with the bathing suits? You look like a bunch of old fogeys."

Rals slapped some river water at me. "Strip on down, nature boy. Show the world your jolly jelly belly, your acned ass, your withered worm."

Instead, I sat on the steps. Once again, my eyes told me I was hanging out with a bunch of old folks. I was pushing ahead with the Monkey Temple scheme, staking our entire future in it, without any real passion for it.

Scenario #1: Rals had taken advantage of Ritz's love of birds, our worry about him, and my loose-endedness to rope me into this commune scheme. Scenario #2: I was just tagging along on Ritz's vector because she was the only thing in life I was sure about. Scenario #3: This was one of those Gurdjieffian tangents that life naturally and inevitably takes when you don't make a conscious effort to jar yourself back on track.

Each scenario had its pros and cons. They also all had a common element: I no longer had a track to jar myself back onto. That's what I tried to tell Ritz when we got back to our room late that afternoon.

"My track has no significance," she said. "Chances are, any bird I save will be dead of something else in a few months. No bird is ever going to cure cancer, end world hunger, save the environment, or change the course of history. Neither will I. I just like doing it, I get a sense of satisfaction from it, and I hope in some small way it raises people's awareness of wildlife. It's my way of being creative." She peeled off her bathing suit and frowned for a moment, one hand on her hip, the other hefting the wet bundle. "Psychoanalyze it all you want, but for me, it's as simple as that."

Her stance and the tension in her muscles made her naked body look lean and hard. The conversation could wait. I stood up and took a step toward her. She flung the wet bathing suit at me, catching me full in the face. "Damn you. After all that let's-do-it crap yesterday, now you're telling me you don't want to be here? You're just doing me a favor?"

I followed her into the bathroom. "Baby, it's no big deal. I just need to get used to the idea."

She turned around so abruptly I almost ran into her. She put her face close to mine. "You've been unhappy with your life for years, shuffling along, making enough money to get by, maybe getting a few kicks from being the guru again."

"Guru?"

"And now you plan to tie up our future in this fiasco?"

"I thought you loved this place."

"Don't lay this on me. I just want somewhere I can do my birds as part of whatever our life will be. I never asked for a huge white elephant. That was your idea. Or Ralston's.

I thought you had something in mind, some new direction. 'Cause boy, do you need one."

"Baby, listen—"

"This isn't going to work if you're half-assed about it." She stepped into the bathroom and closed the door. I slouched into the hallway.

Scenario #4. I was just plain too old. My pilot light had flickered out.

Ralston grabbed me in the big room downstairs. "Get the paperwork done?"

"What do you think I was doing all day?"

"I made some calls," he said. "Roland and Boland are out, not even married anymore. She inherited a shitload of money from her father."

"The one whose factory she tried to blow up?"

"She's collecting art now. And Andy's teaching poli-sci at Loyola."

"The Andy-Christ is teaching Papists?"

"Sardis didn't even want to talk to me. Hi, how are ya, gotta go, fuck you."

"What do you expect, after what happened with that girl?"

"He'd already broken up with her. But Kelly might come."

"Right, about five seconds before you put the moves on her. Kelli Kute? Didn't she join an atheist nunnery?"

"Give me a break. Carlos Kelly."

"Didn't he—how do you keep track of all these people?"

"I do my homework, man."

"Before you left Martine and Paris, didn't you? Before you even knew about Ritz's bird house. That just landed in your lap like a, like a—"

"Like a lid of weed somebody tosses out the window 'cause they think the cops are at the door? Serendipity favors the prepared."

"You've been scamming me all along—the moping, the long sighs. Did you really take those pills, or did you set Martine up too?"

The sideways smile disappeared from Ralston's face. "Think whatever you want. The road trip was your idea. The night you laid it out, I went back to my cousin's and hit the Internet and the phone."

I headed for the door. "We need money, not just more—"

"Not more freeloaders like me?"

I dragged myself outside to Walter's SUV, to something I could at least wrap my wits around. Nothing from Adele— she'd said something about a business trip to Kisangani. I answered the mail from other clients, scared and thankful that no new manuscripts were attached.

At dinner and afterwards, Ritz kept away from me, and Ralston clearly noticed. He'd looked back and forth between us few times, but for some reason didn't butt in. Marco was drawing Daph, who wouldn't sit still for it, and he wouldn't let her see what he was doing. She offered the lit joint to Opal, who declined with a smile. I wanted to talk but canned the idea of having another heart-to-heart with the group—we'd already done that, overdone it. Then I looked beyond the excuses.

I caught Opal a few steps away from the others. "Take a walk?" She didn't ask Walter along when I headed down toward the river. I cast a glance back at Ritz; she hadn't moved and wasn't looking at me. Walter stared, mouth ajar. Neither Rals nor Marco attempted a wisecrack, at least not within our hearing, but Ralston's eyes followed us at least as long as I bothered to look back.

"If I were Ralston," I said, "I might ask what you've got against pot."

She laughed. "If I were you, I might be curious but let Rals ask the rude questions."

"Got me."

"This will sound like you expect it to, but I think psychedelics are better used as a sacrament. A kick in the ass, a portal to a new way of looking at things, thinking, and feeling. Then you have to work on what you learned, to try to make those highs natural states. If you just keep passively taking the drug to get stoned…" She shrugged.

We stopped on the bank above the river. The crescent moon reflected a thousand shades of blue, gray, and green off the river. Faking an expansiveness I didn't feel, I swept my arm across the scene. "Enough to make you swallow the Gaia theory whole, isn't it?"

"Gaia theory is a male-dominated reductionist rationalization of Wicca."

I looked at her for a moment, and we both smiled. A woman who could poke fun at herself. In her line of work, probably a lifesaver. "By the way," I said, "thanks for the tantra lesson. Interesting." She smiled as if she knew more than either of us was saying. Professionally, of course, such a smile would be an asset.

A head-on approach to Monkey Temple finances wasn't going to work with her. Her concern was Walter and his book, not the rest of us or our commune. But maybe she needed a friend here. "Who are your tantra clients? Seekers of enlightenment, or of sex?"

Rueful smile. "Mostly sex."

"They say so?"

"Some do. More beat around the bush."

"So to speak. And do they get sex?"

"Why do you ask? Want more lessons?"

I laughed. "Just being nosy."

"Nothing wrong with that."

"In that case, what is it between you and Walter?"

"He loves me. And I love him." A strange sequence in which to order those two statements.

"Why do you love him?"

"What do you love about Ritz?"

"She's beautiful, smart, sane, funny, principled, strong, articulate, brave…and a bunch of other stuff."

"You're lucky the person you love is all that. But haven't you ever fallen for anyone stupid, mean, dishonest, or cowardly?"

"What are you saying?"

"Just that I can't answer your question," she said. "We have no idea why we love the people we love."

"You do what Ritz always accuses me of, taking a perfectly straightforward question and turning it into a philosophical conundrum." An owl hooted nearby.

She looked out over the water. "This should be enough reason to be here. But it never is, is it?" We sat on the steps. I tried to spread myself out into the night, to disembody myself, to disentangle essence from ego. A futile task if in fact everything turns out to boil down to biochemistry, but the attempt calmed me.

"Speaking of nosy," she said, "I've heard some good things about PMP but don't know much about it."

"A group of jaded truth-seekers who used to get together and argue about who knew more, who was wiser."

She laughed. "That doesn't sound very wise."

"They got smarter. Instead of pushing their own beliefs, they began asking questions, devil's advocating each other to shake out the bullshit. They soon realized that personal growth and philosophical insight can gridlock—beliefs limit growth, and, vice versa, personality warps philosophical perception. So they came up with a sort of Socratic dialogue that forced them to think critically about both their behavior and their ideas—"

"And how the two interact, I get it. And so both move forward." She gave me a wry smile that looked well practiced. "So why did you leave?"

"Other people wanted in on it, and it got too commercial."

"Did you boo Dylan at Newport when he pulled out his electric guitar?"

"Manet wasn't bound by the orthodoxy of the Salon," I said, "and Dylan wasn't bound by the orthodoxy of folk. It wasn't about money…or maybe it was, but he was great, so who cares?"

She gazed out over the moonlit river.

"Stepped right into that one, didn't I?" I said. "Okay, the marketing hype pissed me off, but that's not what it was about. It was a terrific idea, taking the so-called wisdom of the ages and moving it from the theoretical to the practical. A lot of people are now a lot better off."

"So how come you're editing instead of PMPing?"

"How conscious are we of the emotions that drive our actions? Perhaps the emotions we're aware of are the equivalent of rationalizations—excuses rather than real reasons."

She laughed. "Now you're teasing me, the thing with twisting a straightforward question. I mean, why aren't you still doing PMP?"

I'd give her the straightforward theoretical rationalization rather than the straightforward sordid one. "It's great to help people be better human beings, but that's not what I really wanted. Even for myself. I was more into the ecstasy of the saints, occult powers, nirvana, astral travel, satori. I always assumed I wouldn't understand what enlightenment was until I attained it."

"That's what they tell you, isn't it? Like heaven."

"Like fairytales."

"Don't be embarrassed," she said, "we all want those. No secret monastery in the mountains?"

An old man with bright eyes. "How'd you know about the secret monastery?"

She laughed. "Everybody wants a secret monastery." Her professional smile again. "It's about the journey, not the destination."

Istanbul. Turkish cat comes up to us on the street, mimes smoking a joint.

Ralston scans the block, looks over his shoulder. "Forget it, man." Turkey's got scary drug penalties.

A strange, almost surreal invitation. The opening of a door, a sign, a test? "Come on," I say.

"You crazy?" But Ralston follows.

The Turk takes us to a lumberyard, early evening, the day's business over, deserted. Neat rows of eight-foot-high, ten-foot-square stacks of cut boards. Leads us to the far corner of the yard and a stack like any other. Pulls some boards away and lifts aside a tarp. The stack is a shell, the outer layers only one or two boards thick, the ground beneath dug out four feet deep. He steps down.

Rugs and cushions cover the dirt floor. Candles burn in the dark. Three other Turks already there waiting. Young men, though older than us, dressed like workers. We nod to them. They gesture for us to sit. Everybody on edge. Handing out tea in small, wasp-waist glasses.

We can't possibly look like we have enough to make a robbery worthwhile. Sex? No such vibe.

One of them pulls six sheets of cigarette paper from a pack and glues them together into a large square. Breaks up four or five cigarettes and heaps the tobacco on the paper. From a small metal box he takes a block of hashish, which he heats over a candle then crumbles onto the tobacco. Pours the mixture from the paper into his left hand and kneads it with his right thumb. Piles the blend in a pyramid on the paper. Carefully rolls it up into a neat, fat, five-inch cone, about a cigarette's diameter at the narrow end and an egg's at the other. Folds two corners down to cover the wide end, takes a fresh piece of paper, wets the glue and wraps it around the whole joint to keep it from unrolling. Finally the mouthpiece: matchbook cover rolled up and inserted into the narrow end.

He licks the joint all over until the whole thing is wet, lets it sit a moment. Then lights up. Takes a deep hit and, as he holds the smoke in, carefully inspects the lit end to see how it's burning. Nods, exhales, passes it to me. When I raise it to my lips, the Turks mutter, shaking their heads and waggling fingers, miming for me to put it down on my tea glass. I do so. Gestures, three or four English words: one must wait to let the ember in the middle cook to catch up with the paper. After five minutes, a raised palm invites me to smoke. I take my toke and pass the joint to Ralston. Like a pro, lets it sit on his glass awhile before smoking. Passes it to the next Turk.

Cat looks the joint over, takes a sheet of cigarette paper and puts a patch on the joint. Licks a finger and wets down a couple of spots of overeager paper. Lets the joint sit before taking his hit.

Next Turk: a major repatching, five or six papers. Guy next to him ignores the bulk of the joint, rebuilds the mouth-piece before taking his toke, then passes it to the original architect, who admits to no need for major renovation but lets it sit a good while before smoking. Elapsed time, maybe an hour; elapsed joint, about a third its length.

Smells of hash, bodies, cut wood mingle and separate. Patterns on carpets and cushions wriggle and crawl under us. Shadows twitch in the corners. The train has left the station. The bird has flown. Dig it.

I don't feel at liberty to remodel the joint, just give it a good rest then take a hit. Rals dabs at a few hot spots with a wet finger under the scrutiny of our hosts.

Back to the Turks. The first one heavily reinforces the mouthpiece, makes a hollow fist, places the joint upright between his little and ring fingers, sucks on the hole made by his thumb and index finger. A hand chillum. Next one follows suit after a small patch-up. Passes it to his friend, who removes the new mouthpiece and constructs a long thin one, like a cigarette holder, elegant. Smokes, and passes it to the master builder.

He sets it aside and fashions a separate long, thin mouthpiece, open at both ends, not attached to the joint. Refills our tea glasses, then picks up his own with a finger across its mouth. Down one side of the finger, he slides the joint's mouthpiece right to the bottom of the tea. On the other side, he slips the new, separate mouthpiece into the air space at the top of the glass. Squeezing his fingers to seal the gaps, he sucks on the new mouthpiece. Ember glows, smoke bubbles up through the tea and into his mouth. We each do the same in turn, sucking the smoke through tea-glass hookahs then drinking the tea.

No more daylight seeps in through chinks in the boards. Dark shadows in the corners of the secret bunker. Joint nearly gone. The Turks give each other nervous, even fearful glances.

They stand up, and so do we. One of them opens the entryway. Black outside. The Turks whisper briefly amongst themselves. Three of them remain in the hut while the one who speaks a few words of English leads us to the entrance of the lumberyard.

He's jittery, almost panicked when we reach the gate. Opens it to let us out and steps back. Outside, nothing moves. Not about to die, I relax, smile, thank the man for his hospitality, his tea, his smoke. "I hope we can do this again one day soon."

The Turk shakes his head. "You must never come back here." Closes the gate.

I turned to Opal. "Bullshit, it's about the destination. The journey's a consolation prize. Or a waste of a life. The smartest dog in the world will never be able to check your phone bill or understand why you would want him to, yet we share ninety-six percent of the same genes. Where do we get off thinking we suddenly have the mental capacity to understand the universe?"

"The universe?" she said. "We should start with ourselves."

"Mysterianism's second law of thermodynamics, cognitive entropy. Any intelligent system is too complex to fully understand itself."

She put her hands on her hips and frowned. "You think looking for enlightenment's a fool's game? Maybe the first law is that faith trumps knowledge."

The evening call to prayer. At least a dozen mosques lie within earshot of this roof. The calls differ but words recur, *Allah, akbar.*

The minarets to the west silhouetted by the setting sun, the ones to the east glow bright gold. You can see the muezzins in some of the closer minarets. One finishes his call, another starts. As the sunset deepens, the roar of Istanbul subsides below, and the singing echoes from building to hill across the city.

"I had too much faith," I said.

"Why don't you write a book about it?"

"I just gave it to you in twenty-five words or less."

"Write what you know, isn't that what they tell writers?"

"That's not what I tell them. You're picking my brain, aren't you?"

She laughed. "My mantra is never to pass up a chance to learn or to teach."

"That makes you happy?"

"It gives me something to do and makes me feel useful. What makes anybody happy? Why does Ralston hate me?"

"He doesn't, just bad vibes or something."

"Whose bad vibes?"

"No one's, it's in the pheromones. A collision of auras."

"You're mocking me."

"I'm mocking myself. I've been thinking about Walter's book. Something that's missing."

She held up both hands. "Tell him, not me. Back to Ralston. Why do you put up with him?"

"He's a smart, perceptive guy. If you get to know him—if he'll let you get to know him—he's quite...wise." She looked incredulous. "He sees below the surface of things," I said. "Of people." Now she looked insulted, and I hurried on. "But wisdom doesn't always prevent him from being an asshole."

"Doesn't *always*? He's constantly on the attack—you, me, Walter. Can you get any peace?"

"I'm not sure peace is what I need. Anyway, he can't be all bad, Ritz likes him."

"Of course she does. She's never his target, and he puts her on a pedestal."

"Don't worry about me and Ralston," I said. "The question is you and Ralston. The worst thing you can do is a direct approach. Don't try to impress him, don't try to tackle the issue head-on."

"Zen it away?"

"Right. Though I'm not sure how to Zen away Walter's resistance to the editing."

"He's getting used to the idea," she said. "It's not that he doesn't want it, but that it's painful. I think you're taking the right approach with him, firm yet not dogmatic. But something else is worrying you."

"This house. The future." I took a breath. "Money."

She looked at me directly while mulling this over. "I can't give you any guarantees."

"I didn't expect you to."

"But one always hopes."

I looked back out over the river. "This seems too good to pass up. Doesn't it? Not just for Ritz and me."

"And Ralston."

"And Walter. He's always needed a safe space."

"Yes, safe. I think he'd buy in. If it works out." She looked at me steadily. "If it's safe for both of us."

"In other words," I said, "Rals. And that's my job."

She hugged me. Only for a second, but spontaneous displays of affection weren't part of her profile. Was that how she sealed a deal?

Back at the house, Ritz, Rals, Marco, and Daph sat in a tight group, knees and shoulders caroming, laughing their asses off, passing a joint around, while Walter nervously paced the perimeter. Opal took Walter's hand and led him inside. I could have gone to bed too but didn't want to look like I was sulking, so I sat on the porch steps.

Ritz hardly ever smoked, even when it was available, said it made her anxious and mean. Now she toked up and held the joint out to Ralston, who, before taking it, kissed the sweet spot on the inside of her wrist. After a while, Rals got up, handed Ritz the joint, and sat down next to me. He twisted a glance up towards Walter and Opal's room. "That looked real cozy, down by the riverside, you and the ice queen."

I waited for him to ask for a progress report. He was probably trying to find his train of thought and the words for his question before they scurried away. I looked around: the clouds on safari across the sky, the warm wind in the trees, the soft darkness of the woods, people I liked and loved. I patted his shoulder.

He stood up, intercepted the joint as Marco tried to pass it to Daph, and handed it to Ritz, who took a quick toke and leaned over to give it to Daph. I walked over and gave Ritz a quick kiss on the cheek, then went inside to bed.

It seemed much later when she came into the bedroom, quickly undressed in the dark, slipped on a nightgown and slid under the covers. Ritz had never worn one when we were young, but suddenly, a couple of years after we got back together, she unearthed several from her closet. When I'd complained, she'd looked surprised. "I've always liked wearing one." Maybe so, but why had she picked that moment to resume the nasty habit? Lena had taken only a few months.

I put a hand on Ritz's hip. "Sweetie? We'll make this work—I'll make this work. I love it here too." After a moment or two of what seemed like hesitation, she sat up, pulled off her nightgown, and snuggled around me. I kissed her and stroked her. So far, Little Jules was being eager and steadfast, and I resolved not to think about it lest I jinx the spirit. On all fours I went down on her, fingers and all, spicy-sweet as always, until she grabbed my ears and pulled me up onto her.

After a few minutes, she stopped moving and drummed her fingers on my ass. "Sorry. Hip hurts."

I got off. "Where do you want me?" She patted the bed next to her. We assumed geezer position number one: she on her back, I on my side, our legs entwined. Neither had to bear the other's weight, yet we were still face-to-face. I kissed her, held her breast—yup, Little Jules still holding up just fine— all the while moving in and out slowly, contemplatively. The joys of geriatric sex. Twice the pleasure for a tenth the effort, each minute of meditative motion worth five of callow, sweaty pounding. Now and then, she or I would shift position slightly, bringing in new hues and timbres. There's a book to write, the *Granma Sutra*.

After a while, a discordant note of discomfort modulated to an ache. I turned onto my back. "My shoulder's being a pain in the ass." She slithered across me but I stopped her on top. "Climb aboard."

I loved her sitting up there, my cowgirl queen. I used to reach up with both hands but now with only one. She took my other hand, brushed the fingers across the flat left side of her chest, and shuddered for a moment. Little Jules kept chugging right along.

It was like the second time with any new lover: the performance anxiety that made the first time an ordeal transmuted to pleasure-enhancing confidence. She moved my hand over her scar and shuddered again. Finally, I got it. I feathered the back of my fingers across the blank area. This time she clutched my hand with a little laugh and pushed into it.

"What?"

"It's so sensitive…sensitive nice."

We may have lost a breast, but we'd gained an erogenous zone.

After a while, she slid off. "Sorry. My damn knee." She lay on her back on the other side of me. I licked, kissed and caressed both sides of her chest until she demanded me inside her again and we mirror-imaged our earlier geezer position.

Without stopping the to-and-fro, I worked with my fingers too until she came to a gasping-on-the-way-up, whimpering-on-the-way-down orgasm. She laughed, kissed me, then twisted a little away from me and pushed her butt harder against me. She reached between her legs, cupped my balls, and ringed my penis with thumb and index finger as I moved in and out of her. With that, I wasn't long for this world.

Afterwards we lay spooned. Maybe the Monkey Temple was working its healing powers upon us. I stayed inside her as long as I could, until Little Jules, now small and slippery, popped from her grasp like a litchi from its shell. I kissed both of her cheeks then her lips.

"Rals is worried about you," she said.

"Is that what you two were laughing about down there?"

With an exasperated sigh, she rolled away from me.

I stroked her shoulder. "Just kidding, sweetie."

She stayed where she was.

Chapter 20

The next morning, I packed for the trip to New York. Papers to sign. The official reason. I could have done it all from North Carolina, but somehow this seemed simpler. More focused. More separate and distinct from the wrangling. This would be something I, on my own, would do. Or not do.

Just before I left, Walter, with Opal shadowing him, cornered me in the French-windowed room at the back of the ground floor—the solarium, as Rals had taken to calling it. "Opal said you had something else to say to me about my writing." Walter threw it down like a gauntlet.

"Look, forget it, you're doing fine." I started go.

Opal stopped me with a hand on my shoulder. When Walter's eyes flicked over to the touch, she let go and took Walter's hand instead. "We said we'd ask his help, so we should at least listen to what he has to say."

"I'm all ears."

"All testosterone," she said. "Now just listen."

Walter stared at me and waited with an uncharacteristic expression of almost boyish stubbornness on his face. A spritz of sadness misted my eyes when I caught myself not looking at an old friend, or even a client, but a prospective investor who needed to be kept happy.

"Walter, I'm sorry for butting in. Occupational hazard. I'll wait until you have some questions for me."

Whatever went on behind my back in the two silent seconds it took me to walk out, Walter called after me. "Sorry, I'm just not used to having to listen to someone smarter than me."

I laughed. "Smarter than you?"

"In this subject. More experienced."

I led them upstairs to their room, past the mat where Opal had instructed me in California tantra, and over to Walter's worktable. "You've got the history. You've got the prophetic, charismatic characters. You're doing pretty well with the language, and I'm sure you've nailed the numbers thing. But listen." I opened Walter's dog-eared old King James at random and read aloud.

> The sword without, and terror within, shall destroy both the young man and the virgin, the suckling also with the man of gray hairs.
>
> I said, I would scatter them into corners, I would make the remembrance of them to cease from among men.

I flipped a few more pages.

> And after a time he returned to take her, and he turned aside to see the carcase of the lion: and, behold, there was a swarm of bees and honey in the carcase of the lion.
>
> And he took thereof in his hands, and went on eating, and came to his father and mother, and he gave them, and they did eat: but he told not them

that he had taken the honey out of the carcase of
the lion.

"Forget the content for a minute," I said. "What's the
feeling?"

"You picked pretty dramatic passages. A lot of the Bible is
fairly humdrum." Walter grabbed it and found his own passage.

> And Cain went out from the presence of the Lord,
> and dwelt in the land of Nod, on the east of Eden.
>
> And Cain knew his wife; and she conceived, and
> bare Enoch: and he builded a city, and called the
> name of the city, after the name of his son, Enoch.
>
> And unto Enoch was born Irad—

"Point taken," I said. "But still, what's the feeling?"

"Honestly? Weird and hyper. Overwrought, manic, fren-
zied. In a word? Well, I don't want to say crazy. And I don't
want to sound crazy."

"Can you put a positive spin on it?"

"Evangelical. No, that's negative too. Intense, driven. Ecstatic."

"Bingo."

"That's what Rals said when I first told you guys what I
was doing." It was? "So I should hyperventilate as I write?"

Opal stroked Walter's back and looked pleadingly at me.

I took a slow breath. This is my friend. My rich friend.
"Why are you writing this?"

"It clearly needs to be done."

"I don't see you knocking yourself out to cure malaria or
end child abuse."

"This is something I can do."

"You think it's easier to write the Bible than cure a disease? Maybe that's the problem."

"I know the history. I know the characters. I've figured out the numerical patterns. I've got you as an editor. What else do I need?" Opal edged back into the shadows near the door. To remove herself from the dispute, or block an abrupt exit?

"Why this project?" I said. "Why you?"

"You're saying I lack passion?"

"I'm saying the writing lacks passion. It's well-reasoned, well-organized, and stylistically fairly clean. The Bible is il-logical, haphazardly organized, and a stylistic yard sale, full of repetition, purple prose, and just plain bad grammar. The writing in the Bible doesn't suggest that it was written by com-petent and qualified authors. It says it was written by inspired madmen. And there's no narrator or character more riveting and scary than an inspired madman."

"So I'm an uninspired madman."

My friend was slipping away. With his money. Just—be straight. "Walter. I'm saying you need to tap into whatever purpose or impulse got you going on this project."

"Maybe it's time for the Bible to be written by a reasoned voice."

"Then it's just a history book, not a religious text. You said you had a calling. Whatever you ascribe it to, what's a calling but an intense, driving passion for something not completely rational? I've seen you ecstatic—over numbers. That's not ex-actly reasonable. You may have fallen over the edge back then, but you don't have to now. You know what I'm talking about. Motor on that juice. Burn on it."

Walter stared at me, eyes wide, panic rippling his lips and brow. He gasped a quick, deep breath, took a moment to composed himself, and only then exhaled slowly and looked over at Opal, who still said nothing, as if this transaction concerned only Walter and me.

Then he nodded. "I get it. I don't like it yet, but I get it. Thanks."

I flew back to New York, alone. Alone is bad. Alone is good. Alone is like a cold shower—painful, bracing, clarifying. When we landed at LaGuardia, I unhooked my seatbelt and held my hands out, palms down, in front of me. They were shaking a little.

My first stop was Zabar's for an antidote to all the camp food I'd been eating. Olives, a tub of gazpacho, triple-cream Pierre Robert cheese, truffle mousse, an oversized Eli's baguette, marinated beet salad to balance the grease a little—and to hell with it, an apricot strudel. A bottle of wine would be nice, but I didn't drink alone. To hell with that, too. Who knew what was going to happen? I wasn't going to teetotal for the rest of my life. I picked up a ballsy Malbec and uncorked it as soon as I got home.

The phone rang. Damn. But maybe it was Ritz. It was Freddy, inviting me to dinner with him and Charmaine at their place. I was touched. Freddy had never been a chronically difficult child, yet once he'd started college, he'd fledged eagerly and never returned home to live, even for summers. I pleaded travel fatigue. I needed to be alone.

"And Dad? The loan and cosigning stuff?"

"I'll be there tomorrow."

Alone in my New York apartment, I drank too much before eating, then gobbled my food—half the baguette, the whole strudel—and so instead of the pleasure of satisfaction, felt bloated and foggy. What juice was I going to motor on?

Pwee! Pwee! Pwee! Dawn, and the damn cardinal was up early trawling for avian nookie or whatever they're after with that insistent call. I looked out the bedroom window. A light mist floated among the leaves of the birch and ailanthus trees. A mourning dove fluffed itself up on a branch and another cooed its sad song. A squirrel had second thoughts about climbing all the way up the tree, stopped in the crotch where the trunk split, and scratched his ear. Two weeks ago, I would have asked myself why we needed to move to the swamp when we had all this right outside our Manhattan bedroom window. Now the view cloyed, as had the old favorite meal last night.

I had to get out of here.

I got up. Things to do, money to kiss goodbye.

Freddy wanted to buy me a coffee after the cosigning. He was in a good mood—why the hell shouldn't he be?

"I still think you're too young to be settling down," I said. "Young guy like you should be on the prowl for new experience."

Freddy laughed. "And old guys like you are supposed to be well into the I-know-what-I-like years and rant against all things newfangled."

"Newness for its own sake," I said. "Adventure."

"Why?"

"As Louis Armstrong said, Man, if you have to ask…" He looked blank. "It should be self-evident."

Again with the laugh. "It's self-evident that old farts are supposed to be cautious. There's nothing wrong with law per se, or with home ownership and parenthood. Some people would even say that civilization runs on them."

"You're supposed to reject conventional wisdom," I said.

"And you're supposed to prefer it to sophomoric whippersnapper bullshit."

"There's no third alternative?"

Freddy toasted me with his latte. "Hey, pilgrim, you tell me."

The next morning, despite her travels, Adele had sent me a new outline. Christ, she moved fast, no screwing around, just get to work and see what pops out, no excuses, no embarrassment. She had passion—an unadorned, unromantic, businesslike, no-frills passion, but still a passion—for her book, for life. I opened it and read.

The Adelian trinity combines forces against a cabal of corporations and politicians bent on regulating and commercializing philanthropy toward financial and ideological ends. It read like a thriller but was clearly a roman à clef. A tremor of excitement and apprehension passed through me. She learned so fast and jumped so far ahead of my lessons, she was like a horror-movie monster. "Professor, it's growing and evolving a thousand times faster than science ever thought possible!" But at the triumphant end of the story, the characters, from what I could tell from the summary, were essentially unchanged.

After I congratulated her on her storyline, I said:

> Characters don't only reveal themselves through action, they also change, develop, evolve, move on from their past failures or successes by struggling with a challenge—not by sitting around and agonizing, but in the real world, through action, which tests their strengths, attacks their beliefs, ridicules their weaknesses, tempts their evil impulses, and forces them to push past their self-imposed limits. That's what any story is really about.

She got back to me quickly with what might have been a wisecrack:

Dr. J, do you practice what you preach?

One PMP salesman used a particular line on wealthier clients who were hesitant to fork over: your money is a millstone around your neck on the path to enlightenment. Buddha and Jesus had similar lines, but history doesn't record any instances of either of them doing their disciples the favor of taking the cash off their hands for them. And who was this salesman to promise enlightenment, what with his three divorces, an ulcer, a supercilious attitude toward his colleagues, and all those fat commissions he didn't seem to mind dangling in gold around his own neck?

By the end of the day, after signing away most of my money, my millstone only seemed heavier. On my way back to the apartment, I called Ritz from the park. Her phone wasn't getting my signal so I called Walter, who put her on.

"Looks like we own the Monkey Temple."

"You didn't have much choice, did you?" she said.

"You think I couldn't have said no?"

"I mean yes or no isn't much of a choice when you don't see where either leads. You chose yes. That was positive and brave."

"Big deal." But it made me feel better, if for no other reason than she saw strength in my action rather than weakness in my acquiescence.

As I walked out of the park, a freshly squashed pigeon lay in the street, and another fussed around it, now and then pecking at it or tugging a tail feather.

"Look, Mom," a little girl said. "The pigeon is eating a dead pigeon."

Her mother made a face and pulled her daughter away. "Disgusting creatures."

"Excuse me," I said. "It's not eating the dead bird. That's her mate. She probably has eggs or babies in the nest and wonders why he isn't home helping her." The child watched stricken as the pigeon, with a quietly desperate air, gently groomed her dead mate around his flattened eyes and beak. The little girl burst into tears.

"Thanks a lot, jerk." Mom led the weeping child away.

The next morning, not a sound from the back garden. The window was open, the sun hadn't come up yet, but the sky was light. I closed my eyes again. The remnants of my dreams brought forth the memory they were based on.

Kathmandu. First perception each morning: the sound of drums, bells, and flutes. A ragtag daybreak religious procession passes under the window. Freezing cold. Rushing shivering down to the bathroom, a cement cube with a hole in the floor at one end. I've never seen my piss so dark, beyond yellow to brown. I hope it's just the change in diet.

Singh, the landlord, runs a tailor shop on the ground floor next to his family quarters. The two upper floors are the hotel. The street-side wall of my room is one long open window. Woven mats cover the uneven floor. In one corner sits an old foot-pedal harmonium. One pedal is broken, but if you pump hard on the other, it will wheeze out its notes. Behind the harmonium, a dead bat with a three-foot wingspan, mummified in the dry air. Outside, a lovably cute baby goat cavorts acrobatically, its tiny hoofs clattering on the stone wall.

The day of Kathmandu's annual sacrifice. Ten huge buffalo lined up in the main square and beheaded, each with a single blow of a sword. Singh performs his household sacrifice, the baby goat. His wife holds its torso, his eight-year-old son stretches its wooly head forward with a rope, Singh chops it off with a Gurkha knife, one stroke, a good omen. Blood spurts in two streams from its neck. His wife cooks a goat stew, gives some to me. Not hungry but unable to refuse, I eat alone sitting on the stone wall.

Across the valley, the Monkey Temple squats on a hill. From each of the four sides of the square cupola atop its golden dome, a huge pair of eyes gazes out across the farms, the valley, the mountains, the city. Stares straight at me as I chew baby goat.

My eyes flashed open. No birdsong? No sign of the usual gang of pigeons, no squirrels, who often took advantage of these hungry early hours to raid the flowerboxes and bird feeders on the terraces and roof gardens across the way.

As usual in New York these past few years, first thoughts turned to disaster. A biological attack? Poison gas? Which only made gut sense, for I was still alive and heard no sirens. I padded naked to the window and had a good look around. Suddenly, there was the terrorist, sitting in a tree, nearly two feet long by the look of the son of a bitch, calmly preening its breast feathers. The red-tailed hawk leaned forward slightly, half spread its wings, gave them one slow flap like two oars in a slow stream, and drifted off among the trees. By the time I finished my shower, the usual crowd was back as if the killer had never been there.

"Somebody's good karma brought you in here," the sleek young agent said. "Not mine, I assure you." His name was Nealy—first name. "I have two couples ready to rape and pillage for a brownstone floor-through on your block. If one hasn't already murdered the other, we'll get a bidding war."

"We're in a hurry," I said. "Can you show it to them today and start the auction?"

"I'm falling in love with you already."

"I'll be in all day, just send them over and I'll show them around."

"Are you kidding? Then we won't be able to gossip about you behind your back. Look at that tacky sofa, who *are* these people? No, seriously, they're too polite if the owner's there. I have to hear what they think. So you go feed the ducks or something. After you show the place to me and give me the keys. Shall we?"

By the end of the next day, I was ready to accept an offer for about $100,000 more than I'd expected, enough to buy the Monkey Temple and do a lot of repair and renovation, but leaving little to live on, much less a nest egg. I tried to talk to Ritz about it. The first two times I called, no one answered Walter's phone. When I finally got Ritz, reception crackling, she was in the middle of freeing a duck who'd gotten tangled in fishing line.

"The numbers don't...out of context...long as Freddy... You know what you're doing...take care of it just fine. I love... you're doing this for me."

Nealy warned me the oral acceptance amounted to a contract and we couldn't back out without risking a lawsuit. I dithered for a moment, then told him to go ahead and accept the offer.

"We'll send you the written contract as soon as they can drag their lawyer back from the Hamptons," Nealy said.

"Within a week." I gave him the address of our real estate lawyer in North Carolina. I didn't want the package coming straight to the Monkey Temple for just anyone to open.

It was done. With it came a pleasant release of pressure. Like the one following a wisdom tooth extraction as the Percocet kicks in before the Novocain wears off.

Chapter 21

When I walked into the Monkey Temple, Rals was arguing with Opal over something stupid that he couldn't possibly have given a damn about, the amulets and talismans she'd hung in the Great Hall across from Marco's sketches—and a painting now, a nude of Ritz. Opal looked relieved to see me. At least Walter wasn't watching the carnage. Rals slapped my back. "Hey! We own the Monkey Temple yet?"

"Getting there."

"Good man. You brought presents?" I handed him the bag of leftover cheese and pâté plus a loaf of bread and a fresh strudel. He pawed through it. "Damn, I miss this shit." He stuffed a hunk of cheese in his mouth. "Why the hell did you drag us to the swamps?"

I pulled Ralston outside. "Hey, remember? Lay off Opal. We need Walter."

He clicked his heels together. "Jawohl, mein führer."

"Jesus, man. Do you want this place or not?"

"I mean it, sorry."

"If Opal's happy, Walter's in. It's as simple as that."

He glanced at the house and spat on the ground. "She has him wrapped around her finger so tight—"

"Lay off or we might as well go back to New York right now. You want the Monkey Temple or not?"

He took a breath and let it out. "Hey, you always need one imperfection to remind you how good you got everything else."

"There you go. Where's Ritz?"

"Doing the deed with Marco in the shed."

She was alone in the shed. Not quite alone: the duck lay on its back on a board with a cloth over its head to keep it calm. Ritz held it down with one hand and with the other gently pulled its legs this way and that. "Left leg okay. Left hip. Right. You're fine." To me it looked like forced physiotherapy; to the duck it must have been an alien abduction and probing.

Ritz twisted her head for a quick kiss. "The fishing line only caused some chafing, it wasn't on long enough to dig into the skin and cut off circulation." She took away the cloth and set the bird right-side up. It bit at her fingers. "Oh, nice and feisty." Ritz extended each wing and let the duck pull it back into position. "Keep her away from the window, would you?" I stood in front of it. She set the duck down on the floor and it scuttled away from her. "Good, she walks fine." When Ritz faked trying to grab the duck, it flew up and headed for me. "And she flies." I waved my arms and it reversed course and landed in a corner, where Ritz quickly trapped it. She tucked it under her arm, opened the door, and strolled down toward the river.

"Rals said Marco was here," I said.

"He went off into the woods with a hoe, looking for truffles or something. Mission accomplished?"

"In the pipeline. Looks like the apartment will net us—"

"Hang on a sec." Atop the riverbank, Ritz set the duck on its feet and let go. It waddled a few steps, eying us with suspicion, then took wing out over the river, banked left, and made a water-ski landing close to the opposite bank near a few other ducks. "Life back to normal," she said.

"Well done, babe." We walked back to the shed. "How've you been?"

"Busy." A tiny robin huddled in the corner of a small pet carrier. "He's acting neuro—trouble with balance, and sight I think. Must have fallen out of a nest, but his parents weren't feeding him on the ground, either."

"Injury?"

"Nothing I can see." She offered it a small blunt syringe full of yellow mush. "Could be internal. Concussion maybe. Or something congenital." The bird didn't seem to notice the food, even when Ritz gently tapped its beak with the syringe. She made a peep-cheep sound through her lips and teeth, and suddenly the tiny bird chirped, took the syringe into its mouth and with a series of desperate little spasms, worked it halfway down its throat. "Good baby." Ritz slowly pushed the plunger down until the bird threw itself off the syringe's shaft and swallowed.

I looked around. "No cages yet?"

"I made some sketches, but I'm not going to put any money into building until we're sure this is going to work. I don't want a dozen birds here and then suddenly have to move out."

"Move out?" I said. "You sound a little different from a few days ago. What's been going on?"

"It hasn't been all peaches and cream here in paradise. Rals needles Opal every chance he gets. He promises to back off but then can't help himself, and when she gets fed up with it, she gives as good as she gets, which just eggs him on. If this little group is supposed to be his salvation, he sure is working hard to screw it up. Marco must be bored, he keeps saying we should buy a TV. Walter, he just works."

"At least somebody's doing something."

"But he doesn't mix much with us at meals. Marco's always sort of treated him like a dork, he doesn't like what's going on with Opal and Rals but doesn't know what to do about it. Daph seems fine, but you know her, kind of in her own world." I didn't want to get into an argument with her, especially since this was the first time we'd been together for the better part of a week.

At bedtime, the conversation forced itself out again. "Today went well, didn't it?" I said. "Easy living, good company?"

"I guess so. I stayed pretty much to myself."

"Come on, Ritz."

"By the time we get a serious offer on the apartment, we'll have a better idea of how things will work out. When will he start to show it?"

"Babe, I told you, he already did, and we—"

"I could hardly hear you over that damn phone. But don't worry, we don't have to commit ourselves yet."

"Commit ourselves? Ritz, we already have."

"In spirit, I know. Now let's see if reality catches up."

"No, I mean for real."

Ritz started for the door. "I should feed that baby one more time."

Did she just not want to hear it? She seemed a little brittle tonight. Had she always been, and I just hadn't seen it before? New setting, new phase of life, new light. I wouldn't force it, at least not yet.

"At this time of night?" I said. "It's dark, its parents would be asleep if it were in the nest, they wouldn't be feeding it."

She shrugged but stayed. When birds and I competed for her attention, birds usually won—"It's in pain," or "It's in bad shape"—but not always. When she went into the bathroom to brush her teeth before bed, I sniffed the pillows and sheets for an alien scent. Just to prevent any stupid niggling nighttime brainmares from keeping me awake. But the fresh smell proved nothing, did it?

The next morning, Ritz found the baby robin dead. We were on the porch when she told me. I took her in my arms. "I'm sorry, sweetie."

Ritz accepted the hug then slipped out of it. "I expected it. When they're that young and have something so wrong with them."

"I shouldn't have given you crap about feeding it last night."

"Wouldn't have made any difference, probably."

While I was wondering if I should delay any further talk about the apartment sale, a jeep pulled into the driveway. A tall thin black man with short gray hair and a neat beard climbed out in worn jeans and work boots. He looked familiar. I scrambled to peel away the years and place him.

Ralston jumped off the porch, a smile of vindication on his face. "Carlos! Hey, man, I knew you'd come." They traded handshakes and backslaps.

"Hey, Daph, looking good. Jules, suave as ever." He eyed the sketchpads propped up on the porch. "Marco, still drawing, good for you, man."

Daph pirouetted a rather expert two-second balletic parody. Carlos kissed her, shook hands with Marco and me, then looked around. "Got yourselves a fixer-upper here."

"Great, isn't she?" Ralston said. "We're getting her for a song. Come on, show you around." We all headed for the outbuildings. When Carlos ducked into the stable for a moment, Ralston whispered into my ear. "He's looking for a place to put some money. A lot of money."

"You legal now?" I asked Carlos.

"Why wouldn't I be?"

"The draft-dodging thing. Where'd you go, Sweden? Was there an amnesty or something?"

Carlos laughed. "I dodged the draft, all right. By enlisting."

"What? You were so into the whole antiwar thing."

"You can talk about back to Africa, groovy European chicks, and all the rest of that crap, but there's only one place for an American black man to live—and it ain't in jail. Anyway, it was time to face the beast I was yelling my head off about. So I joined up."

Daph pushed his shoulder with both hands. "You shit, you never told us, we were so worried."

"Hey, if I'd told you, I'd have lost all my friends. When I just disappeared, I became a legend in my own time."

"Some legend." She shoved him again. "Glad you're alive anyway. I guess."

"You went to Vietnam?" I asked.

Carlos looked around the stable. "Big. Empty. They sent me so fast, if you didn't know better, you'd think they wanted to get rid of me."

"What were you...what do you call it? Assigned to do there?"

"Oh, man. People are shit. But you got to love them."

"A regular Jesus of Nazareth," Rals said.

"There's some bullshit for you."

"You used to go to church, too."

"Facing the beast."

"And majored in philosophy."

"The beast of bullshit."

"So you can harness it," Ralston said. Carlos laughed long and hard and put an arm around Ralston's neck.

We bumped into Ritz at the shed. She and Carlos shook hands—they'd never been close—and she stayed behind when we headed back to the house.

"What do you think?" Rals asked Carlos. "Want to get in on the deal?"

"Nice spot."

Rals was going for the money too quickly. I asked Carlos, "What do you do now?"

Carlos's expression took on a grim edge. "Whatever they pay me to do."

Daph and I nodded knowingly, but Rals squinted at him with a sneer on his lips. "And just what is it they pay you to do?"

Carlos laughed again, but this time not so long or hard. "Mostly their tax returns." He put his hands on his hips and looked around again. "Speaking of bullshit, Rals painted a picture of endless dope and broads. Looks more like an old folks' boot camp."

Ralston spread his arms. "Once we get it all set up—"

"Then you be sure to give me another call." Carlos looked at his watch. "I got people to see, but I could probably squeeze in some lunch."

At lunch, Rals seemed miffed, so after we ate, I walked Carlos out to the ghat to groove on the river. I'd noticed his fork hand trembling when he ate, and now, when he turned to face me, his head and shoulders had the faint side-to-side jitter that old men get when they try too hard to stand up straight.

I looked out over the water. "Beautiful, huh?"

"Jules, this ain't going to work."

"Got to give it a shot."

"You mean Ralston does. A Jesuit priest once told me that a man with a low sex drive makes the best decisions about who to marry. A person who isn't greedy is the smartest businessman. Someone without much ambition plans the best political moves. Problem is, none of them makes a good leader because they don't have the balls it takes."

"Sure, coming from a priest. So then does an atheist make the best religious choices?"

Carlos laughed. "Oh, man. Great minds. That's just what I asked him. He said maybe they already have." He stopped laughing. "Ralston wants it too bad."

"He's not the only one here. Look, give it a try, a couple of weeks, who knows?"

He patted my shoulder and shook his head. "Sorry, man, living rough's not my bag."

"But what about—" He laughed off my further attempts to continue the conversation.

After Carlos had driven his full belly and fat bank account back off into the sands of time, Ralston and I headed to town. "Carlos is probably right," was all Ralston said. He'd started a pissing contest with Carlos even faster than he'd grabbed for the man's cash, but I saw no point in ragging on him about it, probing for hidden motives, or trying to reform him. Push ahead.

We caught up with Matt at his offices. He handed me the seller's contract. "Your lawyer already has a copy. Read it over when you get a chance. It's pretty standard, no surprises." He came around the desk, but instead of ushering us out, shut the door. "Take a seat. Let's have a little talk." When we were all settled, he offered coffee then beer but got no takers.

"I like you boys. You've been straight with me and did what you said you were going to do. Can't ask for more in this business. Course there's some city folk come down here, buy a little place, take up gardening."

"Hard to resist," I said. "My wife's thinking of putting in some vegetables."

Matt's smile dropped to a scowl. "Look. I'm trying to do you a favor here, save you some trouble. And keep our deal alive. I don't only sell real estate, I'm also a deputy sheriff. Personally, I couldn't give a good crap if someone smokes a little weed once in a while. But after the state boys do one of their infrared flyovers and find a field, they sometimes call us in on the bust. Happens real quick, too."

"We're not—"

"I'm not saying you're doing anything." Matt stood up. "A word to the wise and all that."

Once we were back in the car, Ralston said, "What the fuck was that all about? Think he gives that little speech to everybody?"

I waited until we were out of town and checked the rearview mirror before speaking. "It was a specific, direct warning."

"Of what?"

"You ever known Marco to be a nature lover, a woodsman, a husbander of natural wonders?"

"Shit." Rals slapped his forehead. "Those fucking walks in the woods. But we haven't been here long enough."

"Rich river soil, warm sunny weather, occasional rain, the new fast-growing strains—they could be six inches high by now."

"You can't smoke that."

"You can sure as hell get busted for it." I'd taken us up to 75 on the country road. "They grab your whole damn property these days, throw everybody in jail."

I left ten-foot skid marks coming to a stop in the drive, and when I stepped out of the car, a thick dust cloud was resolutely advancing on the group gathered on the porch for their afternoon snacks.

Marco tented his hands over his sandwich. "What are you doing, man?"

Rals laughed. "What are *we* doing?"

Ritz stood up. "Jules, what's wrong?"

"We just got told the cops are going to bust this place," I said. "They spotted pot growing from their helicopters."

All eyes turned to Marco. "Bullshit," he said. "Who told you that?"

"A cop," Ralston said. "Good enough for you?"

"Those helicopters are a scam," Marco said, "they can't find shit. The cops do an illegal search or they want to protect a snitch, but they need a warrant before they can bust, so they tell some dumb judge they've done aerial surveillance."

"Either way, they know there's dope," Ritz said.

"Bullshit," Marco said. "You heard any helicopters? We're here all the time, so we would have seen them snooping. We know anyone at all here who would rat us out?" Ralston glanced at Opal but had the sense to keep his mouth shut. "Somebody just don't like Yankees, that's all," Marco said. "Or wants to buy the house out from under us."

"You saying there's no dope here?"

"You know there's dope here, we smoke it every night, but we could flush my little baggie before they could get out of their damn cars."

"What about what you're growing?" I said. "The hoe. The muddy shoes."

Marco picked up his sandwich, looked at it, then set it back down on his plate. "It's not on the property."

Rals paced, hands on hips, jaw muscles working, chin high, sinews standing out on his neck, giving him the air of a scrawny, over-the-hill rooster. "And you know where the property line is?" He turned to me. "Do you know exactly where the property line is?" He whirled back toward Marco. "*I* don't even know where the fucking property line is!"

"I don't need a surveyor to tell me you don't own a quarter mile of riverfront. I never go there the same way, so I'm not beating a path to the house." Marco stood up. "Now listen." He glared at Ralston. "You, too."

Then he took a deep breath and brought back the smile. "Our whole scheme here, what's the big problem? Money. This is the answer. The shit never has to come onto the property, it can go straight up to the road through the woods or out by boat." Marco's smile was in full bloom now, and his speech slowed to his usual drawl. "Enough money to live like we want to and not have to scuffle, weed when we want it without having to risk a buy. Friends coming in and out, maybe a little boat on the river."

Ralston seemed to be mulling it over. The idea was seductive. Plenty of money, free dope, good times, all in bright soft shapes and gracefully shifting perspectives. The Yellow Submarine comes ashore.

"I don't know about the rest of you," I said, "but I don't want to be looking over my shoulder all the time."

Marco spread his hands. "Guys, cool it, nothing's going to happen."

Ritz put her plate down and stood up. "Let's get rid of it right now." Daph jumped up. Walter looked questioningly at Opal but when she set down her apple, he put his plate aside.

"Forget it," Marco said. "No one's going anywhere near my shit."

"You gonna stop us?" Ralston stepped up onto the porch. "Like you really did this for all of us. You never gave a fuck about anybody but you." With both hands, he pushed Marco's chest, hard.

"Whoa, man." Marco stepped back—stepped, not flinched or staggered, which should have reminded Rals.

"This is our place, and you start growing dope on it without asking us?" Ralston pushed him again. "Shit, without even telling us?" A third shove.

Marco feinted a punch at Ralston's face. Ralston got an arm up to block it but by then Marco had thrown the real punch, a controlled, almost gentle fist to the midsection.

Rals stumbled back, and Daph leapt at him and shoved him further away from Marco.

Ralston looked confused, stung for a moment, then rushed past her at Marco.

As if he had all the time in the world, Marco reached out and grabbed Ralston's fist, pulled it toward then past him, and gave Ralston's back a gentle shove as he lurched by. Rals spun around, hit the rail, and with the sound of splitting wood, fell backwards off the porch, taking a section of the balustrade with him. He landed face down and lay still.

Ritz ran to him. "You all right?" I knelt next to him. Rals was breathing, and a few moments later he pushed himself to his elbows, coughed, and spat out a mouthful of blood-laced dust.

"Just lie there," I said. "Take it easy."

Gasping for breath, Ralston struggled to his feet but stayed hunched over, his hands on his knees. Ritz held his arm, and I stood between him and Marco.

"Relax," Marco said. "Nothing's going to happen."

I took Ralston's other arm. "Come on, sit down. Walter, could you bring him some water?"

Hands still on his knees, Ralston turned around, away from the others, and spat some more. No teeth came out, and only a little blood. With one hand he wiped his mouth, but I could see that his fingers also brushed over his eyes and came away wet.

Walter brought the water. Ralston rinsed out his mouth then splashed some over his face. He still hadn't said a word. At last he let Ritz lead him to the edge of the porch, where he sat down and fingered the broken end of the rail. "Fuck, look at this."

I faced Marco. "Where is it?"

Marco started a staring match with me, then spat on the ground. "Hell with it. This is all fucked up now anyway." He walked toward the woods.

I patted Ralston's shoulder. "You stay here, we'll take care of it. Need anything?" Rals shook his head.

We stopped at the shed to pick up a shovel, a trowel, and the hoe, then followed Marco. I glanced back at Ralston. He was hurrying to catch up with us and, although clearly trying to hide it, limping. I waited for him.

"We can do this," I said. "You stay." He hobbled past me.

At the edge of the woods, we all looked up to watch a small airplane fly over—not very low, not slowly, and in a straight line.

"Fuckin' paranoid," Marco said. "See any police markings on it?" But we all started walking faster.

We came to an irregularly shaped clearing maybe fifty feet across. Neat rows of plants, anywhere from two to six inches high and a foot or two apart, marched over it in straight lines. "Everybody pick a row and start digging them up," I said. "Make sure you get the roots, don't just break them off."

Ritz made fast work of them with the spade, and Opal was stitching right down her row with the pointed hoe. Daph, bent over at the waist with her knees locked straight, worked the trowel. We men used our hands—Marco slowly, with frequent mutters, and Walter awkwardly, like a person not used to being on his hands and knees. Ralston had always been spry, but now winced as he squatted.

I spoke quietly. "You okay, man?"

"Fuckin' Marco."

Opal came over, seemed about to offer the hoe to Ralston, then handed it to me instead. "I do better with my hands in the dirt." At least Rals had the grace to refrain from a wisecrack. Once Opal went back to work, he accepted the hoe from me without comment and started digging.

When we'd dug up maybe a fifth of the plants and thrown them into a pile at one end of the clearing, Ralston hoed it together and pulled out some matches.

"Too wet," I said.

"I'll get some charcoal starter fluid."

I shook my head. "Too much smoke. We can chuck it in the river, it'll float away."

"Stone the fish." We each took an armload of little cannabis corpses and headed toward the river. At the edge of the clearing, Ralston suddenly dropped to his knees. "Hold up! Get down!" We all crouched and looked through the trees to the river. Not far from the bank, two boats bobbed in the current.

"Jeez," Marco said. "Couple of dudes fishing." He didn't sound very certain.

"We'll come back tonight and finish," I said. Half running, we scuttled across the clearing toward the woods. "Grab the tools."

We slowed once we were well into the trees. "Cops wouldn't spy on us in boats," Marco said. "They'll either bust or not bust. This is Podunk PD, not the CIA."

"How do you know so much about this stuff?" Ritz asked him.

"Friend of mine in Maryland grew his own. Sold some. I went in on it with him, but it was his property. Lost it all. What we've been smoking, that's the last of his crop."

"How'd he get busted?"

"Wasn't helicopters, that's for sure. Maybe an illegal search, but I don't see how, it was well hidden. He must have told someone. I don't know who, I was the only guy he ever talked to, far's I know."

"You didn't tell anyone?" Ralston's voice sounded strained, as if it hurt to speak.

"Course not."

"Not even Elaine?" After a long silence, Rals asked, "How'd she feel about you being in the pot business?"

"Fuck you, man."

"About you making your own money?"

"Fuck you."

"About you being down here with us? She know Daph's here? Probably doesn't know for sure about the pot farm, but she knows you pretty well. Rich girl like that must have lots of contacts in high places."

When Marco spun around to face Ralston, Ritz held up her hand like a traffic cop. "Rals." We walked the rest of the way back to the house in silence.

I was the first to step up onto the porch, and I turned to face them. "We've got to get a hundred percent clean. Marco, your stash. Anyone else have anything? Anything at all, even a pill bottle that's not yours."

Opal headed inside. "I have a couple of hits of E." She was back less than a minute later with a baggie.

"Anyone else? All right. The E we can flush but not the grass, because who knows, maybe they'll check the septic. We'll burn the grass. Marco?" While the rest of us scoured the porch and the yard next to it for roaches, Marco went inside and didn't come out for a long five minutes. When he did, he had his pot in one hand, his suitcase in another, and the sketches and painting he'd hung on the walls under his arm.

"You're not burning my stash. I'll take it with me. You guys are running this place like a fucking junior high school. No dope, no TV. Grow the fuck up. You want to burn something? Here." He crumpled his art into a loose ball and put a lighter to it. "Daph, you coming?"

She looked at him long and hard but didn't move. Marco waited in his van while we stood watching the fire. The minerals in the paint added red, blue, and green highlights to the flames. Daph still didn't budge, and Marco took off in a shower of gravel from spinning tires.

Daph took less time than Marco did to pack. She came out of the house with tears running down her face and started walking down the driveway.

Ritz stood up. "Daph, come back." Daph waved over her shoulder but didn't look back.

Rals called out, "I'll give you a ride!"

Daph swung an arm around behind her with the thumb in hitchhike position.

The charred paper smoldered until it could no longer hold its shape and collapsed into ashes.

Lights flittered eerily among the trees and bushes. A whip-poor-will's cry brought a moment's stutter to the sound of footfalls. A pair of yellow-green eyes peered from behind a fallen log.

We took turns holding the flashlights while the others dug. It was slower work in the dark, but cooler, and the nighttime adventure, with its staccato images, made the chore vivid and memorable if not exactly fun. We carried handfuls of limp pot to the river and threw it in where the current came close to shore. When the last clump started to move off and we were sure that, after all, the SWAT team wasn't biding its time in the forest, we trained our flashlights on the green convoy, which had already started to subside into the water and spread.

We walked in a close group back toward the house, Opal in front, holding the only flashlight with any battery left.

"Physics says that sunlight is something," I said, "and darkness is nothing. But ever notice how you can swim through darkness? I guess because it's opaque, the dark seems something like water. Light is like air, darkness like water."

Ritz laughed softly and ruffled my hair.

"It's coming right through our skin, man," Rals said. "Marco was growing some righteous shit."

I sniffed my arms. "Better go to the laundromat tomorrow, wash the smell off these clothes."

The house came into view through the trees. "A gingerbread cottage for children lost in the forest," Ritz said.

"Children," I said. "Boy, if we get busted, we'll be in deep trouble with Freddy." Ritz clutched my arm and laughed.

"Gingerbread." Walter picked up the pace. "I think I have some cookies."

"We'll find more people," Opal said. "Marco was never really happy here." Ralston's eyes snapped up to stare at the back of her head and he seemed to be sharpening his words. I put a hand on his shoulder. He looked back at me, and I shook my head. With his face turned away from the flashlight, his expression was lost to the darkness. He continued his silent march to the Monkey Temple.

Kathmandu, city of temples and shrines. Some tiny, with space for only a bell or statue. Full-sized temples, well-tended or neglected. Figures of the Buddha carved on the same column or painted on the same wall as Hindu gods and goddesses. A tiny corner storefront not more than six feet square with two sides open to the street, its two inside walls covered with religious posters, holds three musicians, one playing a hand-pumped harmonium and singing, another drumming, the third bowing a stringed drone. A huge demon head dominates the market square. One shrine has just enough room to shelter a sleeping sadhu.

Rising three stories tall, a large temple, the edges of its peaked, overhanging roof supported every few feet by large wooden struts, scores of them, each intricately carved and painted. Stopping in the street below to look up. Each strut is unique, depicting two or more figures engaged in complicated and sometimes contortionist sex, an architectural *Kama Sutra*.

Ganja Man claims to be a sadhu, looks like a sadhu, dresses like a sadhu, perhaps is a sadhu, but also sells homemade hashish. Collects ganja resin from hemp plants growing wild in the countryside, adds opium, loco weed, morphine, plus powdered deer antler and rhinoceros horn for sexual potency, all bound together with some kind of tree sap. One pipeful paralyses a whole room.

I don't smoke any. Looking for a guide to sneak me across the border into Tibet then to Lhasa and the Potala Palace, said to be the last place on earth where true Buddhism is practiced. Ganja Man says his home village is near the border, he can take me. Weak and shaky, wondering if I can make the trip.

Meeting a cat who's done it, an Australian, then two others, a Cambodian and a Canadian. All three say it's dangerous.

And pointless. The spirit and knowledge have fled, maybe with the Dalai Lama, maybe before. Nothing left but forms, rituals.

Rumors in Tibet, they tell me, say that a few good teachers came to Kathmandu. To the Monkey Temple. But the abbot, the old man of the secret monastery, has to accept you.

"Looks fine to me." The next morning, the real estate lawyer handed the Monkey Temple contract across the desk for me to sign. Offhand, as if the decision had been made long ago and this was just paperwork. Ralston, eyebrows raised, picked up the pen and poked it into the middle of my hesitation.

I took the pen and set it down. "Maybe Ritz should read it first."

"Of course," the lawyer said.

"What for?" Rals said. "She wants the place, she knows the terms, she left it up to you."

I scanned the print without reading it then let my eyes roam around the room. I caught sight of my name on a FedEx envelope on the lawyer's desk. Wouldn't that be a tour de force, for me to sell the New York apartment out from under us but fail to buy the Monkey Temple?

Ralston picked up the pen again and held it close to my hand. "Don't be a Carlos, man. Don't Marco out on me."

I was sick of babysitting Ralston, catering to his schemes and mood swings, and trying to keep him from attacking Opal. I'd also had enough of my New York life, of waiting for nothing to happen. Karma was forcing me to a Zen epiphany: neither the past nor future is real. The lawyer was looking at me strangely. Ralston threatened me with the pen again.

In high school biology lab, way back when such things were not only conceivable but standard, the teacher had passed out tiny medical blades to the students so we could prick our own fingers to test for blood type and clotting time. I had gingerly pricked at my finger without drawing blood until a few of my neighbors started to snicker. I could do this. In a rush of willed courage, I stabbed my finger deeply—that wasn't so bad, what was I so chicken about?—and then again, and again. Lots of blood.

I grabbed the pen from Ralston and signed the contract.

Instead of the dread I'd expected, a rush of pleasure ran through me. Something had broken—broken through, broken out, broken away. That was what I missed from those old days. Despite the bullshit and pain and self-delusion, life was open-ended, anything could happen, the boundary of the possible hadn't yet closed its circle around my world. The answer was always yes. The essential ingredient wasn't the philosophical worldview, but throwing yourself into the world. Look before you leap, sure, but leap, for Christ's sake. Leap!

I tore open the FedEx package and signed those contracts too, three copies. I pocketed one and tossed the others across the desk to the lawyer. "FedEx them back to New York."

On the way out the door, Ralston slapped my back. "Good man."

We avoided Matt's office and picked up Opal at the laundry. The clothes now smelled of Tide rather than felony quantities of a controlled substance. Opal sat quietly in the back seat and looked out the window. Rals neither needled her nor pointedly ignored her.

I wanted to talk to her. Of all of them, she was the one who might understand. I laughed to myself and pretended not to notice Ralston's questioning glance. No, I wouldn't say anything to Opal, this was something I had to digest on my own rather than turn into words. I needed to not need an understanding ear.

Buddha had it right. You have to give up what's precious to you—what you think you can't live without, what panics you to imagine gone, everything whose loss fuels your nightmares—not simply forego what you don't really give a damn about. Back then, in New York, in Spain, on the road, in Asia, I hadn't given a damn about creature comforts, good food, nice clothes, social status, personal success, or recognition, and so giving them up was false abstinence, an empty gesture. My innermost desire was for enlightenment. That was where my ego held court, that was who I was—a man on a shining quest. It glued everything together and sanctified my existence.

Back then, I'd ditched Ralston to reach the Monkey Temple, and I'd go this one alone too. I quickly made a mental list of what, in addition to all my money, I needed to ditch. A short, painful list. I tuned out my passengers and watched the scenery rush at me as the car bumped up against the line that separated the present from the future.

First stop once we got back, Walter's SUV.

> Adele, we've been going about this the wrong way,
> as if you were just anyone and we had to create
> a book that will sell. In your case, the opposite
> approach makes far more sense. You get hold of
> someone who badly wants to sell the hell out of
> any book you write, and then find out what he
> or she wants that book to be. In other words, I'm
> an unnecessary middleman. Call Lucius LeClerc,
> the super-agent, he'll get you a huge advance and

shepherd your book all the way through. Best of luck, J

I wrote less hopeful farewells to the others then logged off.

After lunch, the five survivors lingered. Slowly, stiffly, we pulled our chairs off the porch and sat with mugs of tea by the dead live oak under heavy clouds. Yesterday's bending and pulling in the pot field had taken its toll on us, although I wondered if Opal, in the best shape of all of us, was faking it for solidarity. The need for a postmortem loomed. The silence on its own was doing a fine job of the dirty work, but Ralston stepped in to give it a hand. "Marco did the same thing last time we saw him. Freaked out and split."

"It was probably meant to be," Opal said.

Ralston jerked upright in his chair, then looked at me and subsided back down. "You believe that shit?" He said it casually, as if genuinely curious rather than as a stab to the neck. "Everything happens for a reason?"

She closed her eyes for a moment before answering. "I was just agreeing with you. If he's done it before, sooner or later he'd probably do it again."

Ralston shrugged and settled further down into the chair. "It's going to happen. People will come and go. It's part of the growth cycle with these things."

"George and Pam thought it was a great idea when I talked to them," Ritz said. "I can call them. You ever meet them, Rals?"

"Why do we need more people?" Walter said. "What's wrong with just us?"

Ralston rubbed his thumb against his fingertips.

"Money's not the reason," Ritz said. "We're here because we want to be with our friends."

Walter took Opal's hand. "I'm with my friends. And we're all doing all right in the money department, aren't we?"

So Opal hadn't talked to Walter about Monkey Temple finances. I looked over at her. She steadfastly kept her eyes on Walter.

"Not like you," Ralston said. "Know what Marco's problem was?"

Although Rals clearly meant it as a rhetorical question, Opal answered. "Vanity."

Ralston gave her a long stare. Of their own accord, my hands spread out like oil on stormy waters. I pulled them back and watched.

"I have nothing against vanity," Ralston said. "It promotes personal hygiene, professional accomplishment, even moral fiber. Too bad it also breeds assholes."

"Vanity of vanities." Walter spoke without looking at any of us. "When the first multicellular creature appeared in the unicellular world, it must have been like Godzilla emerging from the ocean. Now it's just a tiny rudimentary fossil. Likewise the first to grow teeth, the first to fly. These days, the first primitive creature that can consciously plan and build for the future thinks its tiny intelligence is capable of anything, that it's the end point of evolution, God's favorite child. Vanity of vanities. Maybe that's what it means in Ecclesiastes. If that's a correct translation of the original word." He scribbled something in his notebook.

"On earth as in heaven," Opal said. "Whatever human beings become, we get more godlike. Evolution is God's reproductive system."

"Who the fuck let God butt into this conversation?" Rals looked at me. "Hey, I'm trying."

I smiled at Ralston and Opal, which seemed to make them both uncomfortable.

In college, Ralston and I used to sneak into the pool at night. He liked to swim slowly, mostly underwater, "grooving on weightlessness." I would climb the ladder to the high board, take a running start, jump on the far end of the board as hard as I could and, twisting and spinning at random, head for the ceiling. Not until at the apex of my trajectory would I begin to plan my descent. Reentry usually hurt like hell.

Now, sitting on the porch in the ascent of another jump, I ran my tongue over the capped front tooth I'd broken in that pool. Walter used numbers to slow time, and I used a diving board. Little matched the high of those few long seconds of freestyle freefall. Of course, back then, I'd had a somewhat forgiving cushion of water beneath me. I hadn't yet reached the apex of the current leap, it was too early to start planning the descent, and so I leaned back to watch Ralston's feud with Opal follow its own trajectory.

"You don't believe in a creator?" Opal asked Ralston.

Ralston looked down at his lap for a few moments, at me, at Opal, then waved an arm through the four points of the compass. "It's the simplest explanation for all this crap. But you don't have to make a damn religion out of it. Oh, shit."

Two vehicles were slowly making their way down the drive, an SUV with state police markings and a sheriff's department car.

Chapter 22

Both had racks of lights on their roofs but they weren't flashing. About half a dozen men stepped out, and a dog. Matt, who was among them, hung back. No guns were drawn, but they parked blocking anyone from getting in or out the driveway.

"Afternoon ladies, gentlemen," the officer in charge said. "We're here to execute a search warrant on the house and property. Y'all can relax right where you are."

"Can we see the warrant?" Rals asked. He took a quick look and handed it back. "Never could read that legal stuff. Hey, Matt, what's going on?"

"Howdy, Ralston."

The officer looked back at the dog handler and pointed at Marco's small pile of ashes, now soggy from the rainstorm that had passed over us in the early hours of the morning. The dog sniffed around it but quickly got bored. Two policemen took off with the dog in the general direction of the river but certainly weren't bee-lining it for Marco's field of dreams. The rest went into the house, Matt taking up the rear. "Boys, don't forget this is one of my listings. Don't trash it too hard." He turned to wink at Ralston and me, then disappeared into the house.

After a whispered round of questions and assurances about any remaining drug traces and the effect of the rain on Marco's field, we suspects sat mostly silently under the big tree. The cops worked quietly; at least no sounds of smashing, ripping, or prying came from inside. Nevertheless, Walter kept glancing up at his window. The dog team returned deadpan after a good hour, gave the dog some water, and led it toward the house. Just before it reached the porch it swerved to Marco's favorite nighttime sitting spot, sniffed intently, scratched at the earth a few times, then lost interest. The K9 team stalked into the house.

After a half-hour, Walter suddenly stood up. "They're in our room." Opal tugged at his hand and he sat back down. "What if they wreck my machine?"

"You do backups twice a day," Opal said.

"What if they confiscate everything?"

"They won't."

"We should have been sending backups to a remote site."

"We can start doing that."

Fifteen minutes later, two cops came out onto the porch and leaned against a roof post. Matt sauntered out and chatted quietly with them.

"Why don't they get the fuck out of here?" Ralston muttered under his breath.

The dog handler emerged and put his animal back into the SUV. The two last cops came out of the house and had a brief conversation with the three on the porch, then all five walked toward our group under the tree, a little too officially for comfort. One of them held out a plastic bag with a sneaker in it. "Whose is this?"

Walter took a closer look at it. "Mine."

"Stand up, turn around, put your hands behind your back."

Opal pushed to the front. "Why? What's wrong?"

"Please stay back, ma'am." Another officer cuffed Walter, who'd begun to tremble.

"What did he do?" Opal said.

I turned to Matt. "He won't run, do you need the handcuffs? Confinement kind of freaks him out."

"He better get used to it," the lead cop said. "He had marijuana hidden in his shoe."

Walter looked close to panic. "No, I didn't."

"Cultivation to sell is a felony," the cop said.

"Nothing's going on here, you checked it out yourself," Ralston said. "You plant it on him?"

"Please step back, sir."

"Where are you taking him?" Opal asked. The officer didn't answer.

"To Williamston," Matt said. "You can follow us if you want. Just stay a good ways back. Don't worry, we'll take good care of him."

Ralston got behind the wheel. "Take good care of him, what the fuck's that mean?" He started the car.

I opened the driver-side door. "Rals, you're too pissed off to drive."

"And you're not?"

"Why did they bust us?" Opal asked once we were underway with Ritz behind the wheel. "I've heard the same thing Marco said—they hardly ever do aerial surveillance. Matt had no reason to call it in. Could Marco have?"

Ralston shook his head. "Marco's an asshole but not an evil asshole."

"Maybe a local noticed his little garden," Ritz said.

"Only a smoker would recognize it," Rals said, "and they might steal, but call the cops? I still vote for that wife of his."

First thing, once we got to the lockup, Rals managed a shouted message. "Ask for a lawyer and say nothing else!" Walter shot a desperate glance to Opal, who pointed to Ralston and nodded to Walter as he was led out of sight.

It was now after five and all the lawyers' offices had emptied for the evening. With some help from Matt—who was "just hanging around to protect his fucking commission," Rals said—I reached the real estate lawyer at home, who referred us to a criminal-law colleague, who told us he'd be right down. Once there, his first question was what the charges were.

Matt crinkled his brow. "The prosecutor's guy'll be here first thing in the morning and figure that out."

"His questioning can wait until then too," the lawyer said, "and not without me. Right now I'm needed elsewhere." Home for dinner, probably.

Opal wouldn't abandon Walter, so we all spent the night at the jail. We drank vending-machine coffee, except for Ralston, who sucked on the festively colored hard candies, probably leftover from Christmases past, displayed in a bowl on the counter.

The suited, slicked-back kid from the prosecutor's office showed up bright and early well after lunch the next day. Half an hour later, Walter stepped unsteadily from the back, picked up his possessions, and was let go.

Ralston spat his hard candy into a metal wastebasket with a clang, put both hands on the desk, and leaned over toward the cop on duty. "What the hell's going on?"

There's a time to let things roll as they will, and a time to act. I pulled Ralston away. "Let's go. Thank you, officer."

Walter was silent and shaky. "Why'd they let you go?" I asked him. He shook his head. From the car, I reached Matt in his office.

"I'm not the one telling you this," he said. "They found one leaf stuck to the bottom of his sneaker, and he has no record. There's no case, never was. The state guys are under pressure, could be they had to make a bust so's the unit's stats don't look too bad. Just a crazy guess, don't quote me. Hope there's no hard feelings, whole thing wasn't my idea, y'understand, but I don't have the clout to call off something like that."

"Don't sweat it." The call was breaking up anyway the farther we got from town. I flipped the phone shut.

Ritz glanced over at me. "Don't sweat it? You might have thanked him. His warning saved our butts."

Walter put a finger to his lips then pointed around the car. Rals laughed. "You think they bugged our car?" Walter shrank back. "A thank-you would have amounted to a confession," Rals said.

By the time we got home, a fine rain had begun to fall again, and a gusty breeze carried it onto the porch. Walter rushed upstairs. Opal and Ritz brought chairs inside and wiped them dry. Rals grabbed the first one ready. Ritz looked around at the gloom then peered at the taped light switch. "Can we turn on the chandelier yet?"

Rals shook his head. "Haven't finished rewiring."

Opal took a couple of deep breaths. "I like it like this. Crepuscular. The rain sounds peaceful." After a few minutes, Walter came back down, nodded once to Opal, sat in a chair, and stared off into space. Opal slid her chair next to his and held his hand. When Ralston stepped out onto the porch, Opal glanced at Walter and spoke softly to me. "We just have to calm everything down."

Ralston came back inside. "Nasty." The room was getting darker. Ritz turned on a camp lamp, but it served only to throw harsh shadows on the walls and highlight the dents and stains. She turned it off. A sudden violent gust made the whole room thud like a flaccid drum. A moment later, from above, came the faint sound of glass shattering. Rals hopped to his feet. "What the fuck was that?" I grabbed the camp lamp and went upstairs, Ralston following.

At the end of the right-hand corridor, we found the fragments of a pane of glass the wind had blown from the window. Rain already streaked the wall and soaked a crescent of floor. "Look at this piece of crap." Ralston rattled the window. "Doesn't even fit, somebody jury-rigged this chingadero and never came back." He took a closer look. "Not even the original window. Whole damn thing could blow out. We got a shitload of work to do on this place."

Rals and I covered the empty pane with a plastic bag and duct tape, then shimmed the whole window with wood scraps from the basement to steady it in its frame. When we'd finished, he clapped me on the back. "Good job."

"What makes you think that's the only bad window?"

"Shit. Come on." We examined every window in the house, duct-taping loose glass back into the grids and shimming several frames. By the time we finished, it was dark outside. Ritz and Opal had thrown together a stew on the camp stove. We all sat down to eat. "Looks like windows might be a higher priority than the roof," Ralston said. "But what we did should hold us tonight."

Walter let out a deep breath and looked at each of us as if finally emerging from shock. "Tropical storm."

Rals gobbled a spoonful of stew. "Too early for them. We got a month before they start up."

"I heard it on the radio," Walter said. "They've been following it for a few days. Say hello to global warming."

Ritz squinted out the window. "And this is it? Big deal."

"Just the outer fringes," Walter said.

Rals stopped with a spoonful halfway to his mouth. "It's headed this way?"

"They think it'll veer north and peter out. But they've been saying that for two days."

"So which way's it going now?"

Walter pointed straight down at the floor.

Rals set down his bowl and spoon with a clatter and stood up. "How long were you going to sit on this?" He tried to make a call on his phone, threw it onto his chair, grabbed Walter's off his belt, and called 411 for Home Depot. No answer, and he did the same for local hardware stores and lumberyards.

"All closed. Jesus, Walter, if you'd bothered to tell someone a little earlier." He looked at me. "We'll go first thing in the morning, get plywood to board up the windows and hope to hell the roof holds." He shook his head and tossed the phone back to Walter, who bobbled it onto the floor then got down on his knees to retrieve it. Rals grabbed the duct tape and headed for the stairs.

"Leave him alone," Opal said. "It's not his fault."

Ralston slowed, took a deep breath, and almost looked like he'd keep going. But he turned. "You're absolutely right. The weather's not his fault. The house isn't his fault. But he could have fucking told us. And so could've you, you're with him all the time."

"You think he spends all day checking the weather?"

I tuned them out. I was still flailing upward from the diving board. The bust had only added a twist and a given me a higher line of flight. Now a storm. From the vantage of a leap's arc, it was easy to separate everything into what didn't matter at all and what might just possibly matter. I stood. "Everybody shut up." They did, even Ralston. "Rals, worst case, what are we looking at? Total destruction?"

"It's not a hurricane. We could lose the roof, but there's nothing we can do about that at this point. I'm worried it'll blow a lot of windows in, along with a few inches of rain. Water damage could be a disaster."

"Shouldn't the owners be doing something about it?" Ritz said.

I grabbed Walter's phone from him and called Matt. "They ain't gonna do squat," Matt said. "I'd come over except I've got two properties right on the damn river and if we get a storm surge or flooding—you know insurance don't cover flooding."

"Flooding. Is that what they'll call rain damage?"

"No, but the insurer asked for some roof repairs before they'd cover any storm damage."

I hung up and filled them in. "We could just leave. We'd be safe, and if the house blows away, tough luck for the owners, they'll have to give us back our down payment. Any takers?"

None. I laughed. "Down with the ship it is."

Chapter 23

Over the next couple of hours, all five of us worked with what we had to stormproof the house. We taped windows until the tape ran out, nailed others until nails ran out, and shimmed what we could.

Walter and Opal went to their room as soon as the work was done but came back downstairs just as Ritz and I were about to go up to bed. "I'm sorry," Walter said. "I wasn't thinking."

Ralston pursed his lips and nodded, nothing more.

"You've been working hard," Ritz said, "and spent the night in jail. Don't worry about it." Opal took Walter's arm to trot him back upstairs.

"No." Walter moved his eyes around as if rearranging his mental furniture. "Mystics all say, be here now. But the guys who wrote the Bible had a bigger here and now, they saw stuff we can't—I can't. I see a bunch of meteorological equations and miss the damn storm. Do we ever see the bigger here and now? I don't."

Opal took his arm again. "But we keep trying, honey. Let's go to bed."

Walter's sudden laugh quickly trailed off. "A biblical flood."

This time he let Opal drag him to the stairs.

"Then why are you writing more Bible?" Rals said.

"Because it needs to be written," Opal said.

Ralston ignored her and waited. Walter turned to face him. "Because it needs to be written."

"That's not what I asked."

"I said I'm sorry." He turned and climbed the stairs. Opal followed.

Ralston stared in mock amazement at Ritz and me. "He's pussy-whipped black and blue. You know what she's up to? She's got listings of literary agents and books on marketing your own writing."

"You snooped on them?" Ritz said in a shouted whisper. "We're supposed to be wooing them as investors. We need them."

"I was checking the windows in their room. This is a business for her—*he's* a business for her. Liquid assets, no debts, production capability."

"You didn't like her from the start," Ritz said. "You never gave her a chance."

"Sure I did. I'm going to bed. Home Depot opens at seven."

The rainy wind continued into the night and the gusts hit harder and more suddenly. Ritz went to bed to read. I prowled the house listening to the storm, went out on the porch to sniff it. I climbed the stairs and listened—to the storm, and then for any human activity. Ralston was snoring. Ritz was silent. So were Opal and Walter, but candlelight flickered under their door. I paused for a moment, cleared my throat while walking past their room, descended the pitch-black back staircase, and ended up in the solarium, where I lay down on the floor and watched the wet shadows lash the glass.

Opal soon materialized from the darkness and sat beside me. "Thank you for being nice to Walter. He knows he screwed up."

"Nice—that'll be my epitaph." It was also near the top of my to-undo list.

"No, really."

"No, really, yourself." I sat up. "I always had that to fall back on. I was the nice one, the reasonable one, the sensible one, the reliable one, the responsible one, the one you could trust, the one you could talk to without getting your head bitten off."

"What's wrong with all that?"

"It's a pose. A safe, acceptable way to be. An excuse to look down on others, if you're in the mood. A consolation when you've screwed up everything else—well, at least I'm a nice guy. Virtue as a last refuge."

"Relationships and society run on people being nice even when they don't feel like it. We have to—"

"No, we don't." Nor did we have to talk about it. Niceness—tiptoeing around the frailties of the human psyche and relationships, calling it civility but really just a cement that binds you to the attachments you're afraid to let go of. Friendships, marriage.

The buzz I always felt with her was as strong as ever. When I was with Ritz, I'd never acted on that buzz with any other woman. It just wouldn't be nice, would it? Now it wouldn't be nice to Walter and therefore not nice to Opal. Not civilized, moral, just, or upstanding. And if Ritz found out?

You never know your innermost attachment, your core self-definition, the illusion that imprisons you and *is* you, because you're too close to it to see it. Maybe all you can do is break every attachment you *do* see until only one remains, or maybe none.

I reached out and ran a hand down Opal's arm—slowly, feeling the shape, gently squeezing to test the muscle tone. She neither shied away nor melted into it. I touched her calf the same way, with the same lack of response. It was a game to her, and she was calling my bluff.

I reached under her long, loose skirt and slid my hand up her leg to her hip. No panties—but then, she'd probably been in bed. I ran my hand across her belly and onto her other thigh. She leaned back onto her elbows, uncrossed her legs, and put her feet flat on the floor, knees apart. See you and raise.

I flipped the skirt up over her legs, exposing her from the waist down.

She moved her feet farther apart.

I got down on my belly and dove right in. She was almost hairless, maybe de rigueur for her profession, smelled slightly of sandalwood—freshly washed with scented soap?—and tasted of cumin. I wanted her to moan and cry out but all she did was thrust against my tongue and teeth, more in competition than in passion. I put a finger in as I licked and sucked, then two, and wiggled them come-hither until I was sure I felt some involuntary spasms, even if silent ones. Mouth still working, I wrapped both hands around her ass and deep into her crack. She was so soaking wet that my fingers, almost of their own accord—one, two, three—slipped inside.

She pushed me away. "Take off your pants." To hesitate would be to give ground. Without standing up, I pulled off my shoes, jeans, and underwear then got up on my knees in front of her, my erection, faintly luminous in the near blackness, waving in a tight circle.

"What if Walter finds out?" I said. I wiped my mouth with the back of my hand. My fingers smelled faintly of shit.

"Why should he?"

"Secrets have a way of getting out."

"People have a way of getting hit by buses, but I still cross the street." Oh, Walter. She reached into her skirt pocket, took out a condom—so she *had* come prepared, but maybe she always carried one—and rolled it down over my penis.

I climbed between her legs, and my dick, as if guided by radar, unerringly found its way inside her. I explored, teased, pried, churned, and pounded—there was no kissing. Using the technique she'd taught me in the lesson, I kept myself just this side of the edge until she let out a series of sharp gasps. Barely in time not to come, I pulled out.

I took several seconds to taste the moment—her juice on my face, her smell, the sounds of the storm, the warmth and pressure of her thighs around my waist, the shifting shadows, the presence of Ritz and Walter upstairs, the energy of my upward momentum.

It felt like a strange victory, but that was just another illusion. I turned her over, pulled her up onto her knees, eased myself back in, and slowly, exquisitely, holding her ass in both hands, brought myself to climax.

She crawled off my penis and lay down. "I knew it."

I said nothing.

Opal sat up close to me. "I'd better get back to Walter." When she leaned in to kiss me, I turned away, stood up, and walked to the tall windows and looked out. After a brittle moment, as silently as she'd arrived, Opal faded back into the house.

I stripped off the condom, tied it in a knot, and threw it into the kitchen garbage. I also washed my hands and face, rinsed out my mouth, and wiped my crotch with a wet paper towel then dried everything off.

All that was left to do now was to tell Walter about it. That could wait until morning.

I put on my pants and went back upstairs to Ritz to attend to the next task on my hit list.

"Oh, man," I said. "I've just been with Rals. He's in bad shape."

She put down her book. "What's up?"

"It's all coming to a head with this storm. He thinks he can't do anything right, that he's a failure in life."

She grabbed my arm. "He's not thinking of killing himself again, is he?"

"I don't think so... He hates to admit it, but he's so desperately lonely without Martine. He's worried he'll never be able perform again. Sexually. And the longer he waits..."

She pushed me toward the door. "Go. Don't let him be alone."

I'd always prided myself in my abstinence from manipulating people. "You remember the other night," I said, "when he was curled up on the bed with you, just holding you? That's the best he's felt since leaving Martine. Since long before he left her."

"You want to bring him in to curl up with us? Okay, I guess."

I stayed silent awhile, as if thinking it over, but in fact slowing things down in this day and night of change, testing the air, checking my angle of flight and, before the roiling mass of anxiety and regret caught up with me, twisting midair and rushing on ahead of it. "I was thinking more like you could go in to him." She looked at me quizzically. "Spend the night with him," I said.

"Spend the night with him?" She bolted upright. "Wait a minute. You want me to sleep with him? Have sex with him?"

"The idea of it tears me up." True. "It might be the only way to pull him out of this funk." Plausible, but dangerous.

"It wouldn't be like cheating, because…because it's my idea."
Cheap, laughable.

"You froth at the mouth every time he looks in my direction."

"That's my hang-up. I can live with it. I couldn't live with doing nothing."

"We're not talking about *you* doing anything. God almighty, you're asking me to sleep with Ralston, your best friend, a guy who's always claimed to have a crush on me."

"He'll say that to any woman."

"But in this case, we both believe him. You certainly do."

I needed to clinch the deal fast. "I'm not afraid of losing you—if you wanted to go, you'd have gone. I'm afraid of losing him."

She clutched at her missing breast.

"He saw you posing for Marco," I said. "He thinks you're beautiful."

"Goddamn it. Why do you lay this on me?"

"I'm sorry, you're right, forget it." I got up and headed for the door.

"Right, forget it." She pulled the covers aside. "How am I supposed to feel if you lose your best friend because I'm a prude?" She got out of bed and looked in the mirror. "I just showered. I better brush my teeth again. Do I look all right?"

A sharp spike of dread—good. "Never more beautiful."

She went into the bathroom and started brushing her teeth. So for her, this wasn't a sacrifice, a charity fuck, but something she wanted to do. *Prod it.* Has always wanted to do. I couldn't con her into this if she didn't want to, and she jumped at the chance. Maybe Rals will turn out to be a better lover, spectacularly better. They'll run off together—no, they'll stay here at the Monkey Temple and drive me away.

She rinsed and came back out. "I'm ready, I guess. Wait, I don't know."

"You don't have to," I said. "I just don't know what else we could do."

"You're absolutely sure?" I nodded. She grabbed me for a quick, nervous kiss. "I love you. I'm doing this for you." The toothpaste must have hidden Opal's taste and scent.

"For Rals," I said.

"For you."

"Wait, he doesn't know. This wasn't his idea and I didn't say anything. I have to tell him it's okay."

I knocked on Ralston's door and went in without waiting for an answer. In his underwear, he was on his knees on the mattress, peering out the window. "Fucking storm. Fucking Walter. Fucking Opal."

"Hey. Don't ask any questions."

"About what?"

I slapped him, not hard. "What'd I just say?"

He slowly nodded, and I went back to send Ritz in.

I concentrated on the cries and moans of the wind to tranquilize my raging imagination and quiet the panicky voices from whatever it was I'd broken and discarded—my persona, my self, my stand-in. Maybe, over the last couple of days, I'd finally gone insane, but that was just a word—an empty, nondescript label of no help in dealing with the situation. Slowly I turned in my arc, not yet ready to plan my descent.

I finally fell into a deep sleep but woke up, alone, shortly before dawn, when a particularly nasty gust shook the bedroom window and forced a few drops through the gaps and onto my face. For a minute I tried to get back to sleep but sensed the rest of the house was astir. I was sitting on the pot when Ritz burst into the bedroom. "If this place is going to blow away, we'd better be able to get out of buying it. Where's that contract you signed?"

"On the floor next to the bed. Both of them." She grabbed one, sat down to read, then jumped up, strode into the bathroom, and started the shower. At least she wasn't floating on a pink, post-coital cloud.

When I went downstairs, a row of suitcases stood at attention on the porch. Walter and Opal came down the stairs with more. "Why?" I asked him.

Without looking at me, Opal said, "We can't work in a hostile environment."

Ralston stood on the landing in a raincoat that doubled as a bathrobe. "Then why don't you leave and let Walter stay?"

Opal staggered to the door with her suitcases. Walter followed with his, then backed his SUV to the porch and started loading it, engine running. Opal plucked her amulets from the walls, squeezed past Ralston, and headed back upstairs.

Ralston, also without looking at me, marched out to Walter on the porch. "At least you can give us the latest weather report."

"It's headed right this way," Walter said. "Landfall this afternoon. Sustained winds forty to fifty, gusts up to seventy. Rainfall up to three inches, but we've probably had an inch already." After carefully packing the last bag into the geometrically precise space he'd left for it, Walter looked at me with the same trust in his eyes, and then at Ralston. "I'm sorry, guys."

"Not your fault," Ralston said.

"Not the storm, I mean about leaving. That it didn't work out."

"It's working out fine." Ralston pulled Walter's phone from his raincoat pocket and handed it to him. "I talked to

Jerry, he's thinking of coming in with us. Fergus wants to come down. And Georgie—German Georgie, not Jumpin' Georgie." He threw a dirty look in the direction Opal had disappeared, then turned to Walter. "She's what's not working out."

"That's what I meant," Walter said.

Opal came out of the house with her last bag, flashed me a look full of resentment and scorn, climbed into the passenger seat, and closed the door. Rals leaned in close to Walter. "What about that here and now? Fuck the rest of the bullshit."

Walter glanced over his shoulder at the SUV's cab, closed the rear hatch, then spoke in a low voice. "Remember Diane? My first girlfriend?"

"Mousy Diane?" Ralston said. "Sure."

Walter jerked a thumb toward the front of the SUV. "She's my second. Believe me, I am fucking the rest of the bullshit. At this age, Opal's my here and now." He shrugged, gave us half a wave, and stepped toward the driver's door.

I took a deep breath and put a hand on Walter's shoulder. "I have to tell you something."

Walter turned around and looked at me with guileless eyes.

"Last night," I said, "I…" This wouldn't be a crazy dive into a pool, this would be drowning babies in it. "Look, Rals is right, it isn't your fault, forget about it. Good luck, man. With all of it."

Walter shook my hand. "Thanks. Same to you. You've been a big help." He got into the SUV and drove off.

Rals took a few steps out into the rain. "Walter! Goddamn it!" He scrambled back up onto the porch and stood next to me as we watched the truck disappear down the driveway. "What was that stink-eye she gave you? What were you going to tell him?" Rals still hadn't looked at me. "You better keep an eye on things here." He got dressed and drove off to town alone.

Just as I sat down on the porch to watch the wind and rain and try not to think about Ritz and Ralston, she stormed out, contract in hand. "The escape clause is vague, no mention of weather disasters. I should have read this before you signed."

"You said you loved the place. You wanted me to be more take-charge about this retirement thing."

"You're scaring me, Jules. Like you did all those years ago in the East Village. You started shooting speed without telling me. You dropped acid without telling me. You went into that Subud thing without telling me. You smuggled drugs without telling me."

"You'd already dumped me by then."

"I thought you'd wised up after you left the PMPs and became an editor instead of a career hippie."

"You un-dumped me because I became a solid citizen?"

"You've gone off the deep end again."

"Did you read both contracts?" I asked.

"They're not just copies?"

"The other's the apartment sale."

"Oh, the contract with the broker, it can wait—"

"No, the sale."

With a spark of real fear in her eyes, she ran back into the house.

The wind and rain let up for a moment; maybe the storm was turning. But the leaves on the trees started quivering again as if anticipating their own demise, and then a drenching gust slammed into me.

I would spend the rest of the day soaking wet anyway. At a leisurely pace, I set off for the shed and garage to collect ladders, hammers, crowbars, work gloves, anything that looked useful. When I finished, Ralston still wasn't back. I didn't feel like going into the house and so went to the shed again, hung my wet shirt up to dry—fat chance in this humidity—and sat down against a hay bale with my arms crossed over my chest for warmth.

Kathmandu, mid-'60s. *An old man with bright eyes approaches, radiating warm wisdom. Spiritual kinship recognized, acknowledged. An invitation to follow him over the mountains to the secret monastery, to enlightenment.* But not yet.

My piss is nearly black. I'm feverish, weak, my legs jumping with electrical spasms. My skin and eyes are turning yellow. But first, the Monkey Temple.

Trees cover the hill, home to thousands of monkeys. To reach the temple, you climb the hill through the forest on a long stone stairway of two parallel sets of steps, each bounded by iron railings. The two inner rails run in tandem about a foot apart. At the top of the hill, monkeys jump up onto the twin rails, one hand and one foot on each side, and slide down between the flights of stairs at breakneck speed. Screeching and laughing, they rollercoaster past you as you labor up towards the temple. Some suddenly leap off the rails and over the stairway, barely missing you, and scream up into the trees. Several times, I have to stop on these monkey steps to catch my breath and regain my balance.

From the terrace courtyard that surrounds the temple, you can see the valley below, the city to the east, and the snow-capped Himalayas to the north. Monkeys loiter. The dome's enormous eyes gaze out over your head like apocalyptic beacons.

From within the temple, the sound of chanting, Tibetan Lamaist chanting that sounds almost like only one low note, an ever-changing note that shakes body and soul with sonic interference patterns created by tiny differences in pitch. Listening expectantly, hopefully, fearfully.

Ever so respectfully, I knock on the abbot's door. An old man with a shaven head and bright eyes opens it. "You're Jules."

Something close to ecstasy fills my chest, rises to my head and makes me sway. The abbot recognizes me! For a moment I see the entire Monkey Temple at once as if from above, then settle back in. My first out-of-body experience? All that's missing is the abbot's smile.

"I know all about you," the abbot says. "Go away."

A test. "I'm here to learn."

"You're here to sell drugs to my monks. I've been warned about you. If you ever come back, I'll tell the police and you'll go to jail."

I scramble for an answer to the test. "How can I sell anything to people who have nothing to offer but wisdom?"

"Go. Now!" The abbot grabs a staff from inside the door and brandishes it like a weapon.

Staggering back, nearly falling. Sitting for a moment in the courtyard, waiting for the abbot to come smile at me, tell me I passed the test.

The chanting ceases. Whatever has been going on inside the temple—the sought-after mystery—is over. The rustle of moving bodies and robes, the scrape of sandal on stone. The monks come out, trailing saffron. Some young, younger than me, some older. I stare at their faces for whatever information or wisdom they might impart.

But I've seen these expressions before, the all-too-familiar, boredom-relieved, class-is-over look of kids all over the world.

The abbot reappears in the courtyard, sees me among the monks, shouts in rage. The monks stop and look at me, close ranks, and step toward me. I bolt for the stairs, trip, start to fall.

And am caught. "Man, you look like shit—okay, more like piss." Ralston staring at my face. "Jesus, you've fucking got hepatitis. What did you think would happen if you jumped into the Ganges? Enlightenment through sewage?"

"What are you doing here?"

"Still mad at me? Come on, let's get you to the hospital." He supports half my weight as I stand.

"You bastard. *You* told the abbot I was a dealer."

"Just saving you from yourself. You can die of this shit, you know."

"How could you do that?" Pushing Ralston away, stumbling down the first few stairs, losing my balance, sliding down three or four steps on my knees and almost pitching headlong until Ralston grabs the back of my shirt. A blur of tears, struggling to my feet and clutching the rail. "Get away from me!" Ralston holding me up. A roar of effort. I swing at Ralston. A jolt as my fist connects. Ralston stands silent, blood flowing from nose and mouth. The abbot and his squad of monks glare down at us.

Amid the monkeys' screeches, bathed in the putrescent yellow-red of the setting sun, I slowly start back down the stairway to the city, Ralston's footsteps following.

A honk. I grabbed my shirt and walked out of the shed. Ralston was back, followed by a pickup full of plywood. We helped the kid unload the wood and other supplies onto the porch. Ralston nodded toward the teenager. "I promised him twenty-five for delivery." I found some damp bills in my pants.

Ritz barged out onto the porch with an overnight bag and pounded a fist on my chest. "You sold our apartment. Our home! Without consulting me!" I'd never seen her so angry. She didn't deserve this. Or maybe she did. Still, her pain splashed over me like acid.

I tried to hug her. "I bought you a new home. I tried to tell you—"

She pushed me away and backed off the porch into the rain. "You sure didn't try very hard! You didn't buy this for me, you bought it for Rals! You sold our apartment for Rals!" Her face twisted in a spasm of terrible contempt. "You even gave him *me*!"

I lurched back. "Holy shit. Holy shit."

She dashed to the pickup and said something to the kid, who nodded. She ran around to the other side and hopped in.

Ralston shoved me. "Go get her!"

"Holy shit."

Ralston rushed off the porch. "Ritz! Where are you going?" The truck started moving, and he chased after it. "Wait! Ritz! Wait! For Christ's sakes! WAIT!" He spun around and finally faced me. "You're just going to let her go?"

The brake lights flashed, but only for a moment, and then the truck shot forward even faster.

"Holy shit."

Chapter 24

Ralston stood limply in the rain. "Maybe we should just let the damn thing blow down and wash away."

"No! Come on." I grabbed a ladder and threw it up against the northeast side of the house. "Upper windows first. It's only going to get harder later."

"You're the boss." Ralston propped the other ladder next to mine. "This is going to take both of us." Between us we slid a sheet of plywood up the ladders to the second floor and tried to wrestle it up against the window. "Keep it close to the house," he said. "Close to the house!"

Too late. A gust got under it and blew it outwards. I tried to fend it off but it slammed into me and knocked my ladder to the side and ripped my face with a jagged edge before pinwheeling to the ground. I slapped one gloved hand to my cheek to make sure my eye was still there and held on to the ladder with the other as it slowly canted sideways. I was about to break every bone in my body—unless the top of the ladder caught the eave.

It did. Hand over hand, I worked my way to the ground. The cheek was bloody but the eye intact. Not bad.

"Impressive," Ralston said. "Can I see that again?"

We changed our tactic, working the plywood up the side of the house rather than along the ladders. It was slower and harder, but it worked. Pounding in the nails was almost fun. A job well done. I didn't try to count the number of times we'd have to do it again.

We saved the southwest side of the house for last. The wind was so strong by the time we started on it that if we hadn't been in the lee of the house, it would have been suicidal even to try. Not that that would have stopped us.

The first-floor windows should have been a cinch compared with what we'd already done, but we were both close to dropping. My back was so sore I could hardly stand up straight, and Ralston was limping. He lost a fingernail even through his gloves, and I had a three-inch splinter stuck deep in my forearm I didn't have time to remove.

It looked like dusk and felt like midnight when we finally finished, but it was only mid-afternoon. We collapsed on the floor in the Great Hall, gulped water by the cupful—"Who'd have thought you could be so wet and so thirsty at the same time?"—and ate whatever our foraging hands found: flaccid potato chips, brown bananas, dry cereal straight from the box.

I yanked the splinter from my arm, howled in pain, then forgot about it when I found half of one of Marco's candy bars, which I split with Rals. My rubbery fingers could barely tear off the wrapper.

"Better look around inside," he said, "see if it's holding." The lights didn't work. He tore the tape off the chandelier switch and joggled it up and down to no result. "Storm probably knocked down a line somewhere."

The rain had become intermittent but the wind stronger and steadier. Walter had taken his camp lantern so we did our inspection of the house with a dim flashlight. Trickles of water showed around some of the windows, there was a steady drip into the attic from one place on the roof—we shoved an old washtub under the spot—and a couple of small puddles had formed in the basement under an old coal chute. Rals slapped me on the back as we climbed the cellar steps. "Our baby's holding."

We sat in the Great Hall listening to the wind and the house. He tore the top off a bottle of beer Marco had left behind. "She'll be back."

I didn't say anything.

"Sure she will," he said. "Listen, I've stayed in touch—gotten back in touch—with some old friends who know how to keep off the grid, untraceable. Don't look at me like that, not the crazy ones. So we go to Plan B, kamikaze geezers, a final selfless act to make the world a better place. With the Monkey Temple, as a nonprofit animal-rescue center, written into their wills."

A loud crack punctuated a particularly vicious gust. "Porch roof." Ralston hobbled for the door.

We inspected the roof and its posts but found no breaks. He risked the stepladder to search for cracked rafters or struts but found none. I got on my aching knees in the mud to peer at the supports underneath the porch, but they all looked and felt solid.

Another, louder crack came from behind us and we spun around. "Fuck!" Rals stepped to the edge of the porch, stared out, then dashed into the rain to embrace the dead live oak. "Fuck! FUCK!"

We eyeballed the situation from all directions. The lopsided tree's weight would topple it right onto the house even if the wind weren't already pushing it that way.

Ralston slumped onto the edge of the porch. "We're fucked."

I stagger-ran to the shed and brought back several lengths of clothesline.

He scoffed and dropped them on the ground. "Rope. Lots of it!" The stables yielded nothing thicker than hay-baling twine. In the garage, I found two coils of thick rope, filthy but apparently sound.

Ralston pulled a ladder off the porch, almost beheading me when the wind caught it, and managed to lean it up against the tree. He put his arm through a coil of rope and, as I held the ladder, started to climb. When he got close to the top, the wind was too strong for me to keep the ladder from tipping. He scrambled down just before it blew over.

"Just tie the rope at that height," I said.

"It has to be higher, for leverage." He wrangled the ladder back onto the tree.

I grabbed the clothesline. "Hold the ladder."

"That's not strong enough or long enough!"

"Just hold the ladder!" I climbed as Rals gripped the ladder. When I reached the point where Rals could barely keep the ladder upright, I tried to pass the clothesline around the tree, but my arms weren't long enough. I went up one more rung, clawed the bark with one hand for stability, and tried again. Inches too far.

"Let the wind do it!" Rals shouted from below. Blow the tree down? "The rope!" Of course. I held one end of the clothesline and threw the rest to the wind. It whipped frantically then snapped around the tree to slap my face. I grabbed for it but missed. A few seconds later, ready for it this time, I caught it and lashed the top of the ladder to the tree. Then I climbed back down. "Give me the rope."

"No way." Rals slung it over his shoulder and started up the ladder. With me holding it below, he climbed to the top and then worked his way onto a branch.

"High enough!" I shouted.

Rals clambered to a higher branch, almost lost his balance, then hugged the trunk for a few seconds. With one hand, he worked the rope around the tree above a stout branch. He tossed the rest down to me. "Hold the ladder! I'm coming down for the other rope!"

"No! Stay there!" Leaning on the ladder, my arms between rungs, I tied the end of Rals's rope around the beginning of the second coil, then flashed a thumbs up. He hauled up the second rope, tied it to the tree, then worked his way back to the ladder amid the writhing ropes. After untying the clothesline, he half scrambled, half fell the rest of the way down. He threw the ladder to the ground, shoved the end of one rope at me, and pointed away from the house.

"Tie it to that tree over there!" Rals picked up the other rope and lashed it around another tree. "Now pull! See if we can pull it over backwards! Run like hell if it starts to go!"

We both pulled for a minute with no visible results. We staggered back to the porch. The wind hit our faces even harder, the tree let out a groan, and the two ropes gave up what little slack they had.

"Think they'll hold it up?" I asked.

"Fat fucking chance." Rals looked around. "We need more rope."

"Wait." I staggered to the shed, frantically felt into the dark corners, and finally found what I'd dimly recollected: a rusty axe. I ran back to the tree and started chopping.

"Not there, moron." He grabbed the axe from me and started chopping, low on the trunk on the side away from the house. "Go pull!" Chop! "On the rope!" Chop! "Hard!"

For several minutes, I pulled while Ralston frantically chopped. When he couldn't lift the axe again and instead propped himself up on it, I grabbed it from him and started chopping in the same place.

He was panting heavily. "Can't figure—just want to make sure—it falls this way." He staggered over and draped his body across one of the guy ropes.

I chopped as fast as I could for as long as I could, and then there was Rals, ready to take over from me. We made a wide groove in the trunk, hardly the half-V on a horizontal base the Boy Scouts of America favored, especially with my wild swings, but a start. My hands were already blistered. I stumbled to the porch to get both pairs of work gloves, but Rals wouldn't stop to put his on. I pulled on the rope until he could no longer raise the axe, and we again switched places.

The further we got into the tree, the harder the wood became, and the more precise the swing had to be to produce any useful effect. Half of my strokes merely chipped the edges of the groove rather than deepening it. Now and again the tree would give off another crack or groan but never listed in the right direction. I risked a quick sortie to bring us both water, but otherwise we just chopped and pulled.

Then, while I was chopping, an explosive gust hit the tree, and it lurched. I ran out of the way, only to see that it had settled into a cant slightly closer to the house with a couple of branches now ripping into the siding and roof. Ralston grabbed the axe from me and started flailing away at the tree. When he was exhausted he dropped the axe and sat down hard. I ran to him. "You okay?"

"Out of gas. We're fucked." He flopped a hand toward the car. "Let's grab our shit and get the hell out of here while we can."

I stared off at the driveway. "Holy…" I started ransacking Ralston's pockets. "Car keys!" He handed them over. I geezer-ran halfway to the car then back. "You're too beat to chop." I slapped the keys into his hand. "Go! Get it over here!" I picked up the axe and hacked at the tree again.

He staggered to the car, started it, and with tires spinning, fishtailed it across the yard, narrowly missing me. He skidded to a stop, fell out of the car, scrambled to tie the end of one rope to something under the rear bumper, then crawled back in. He waved me away through the open door. "Run!"

I kept chopping. The car roared, dirt and gravel flew, the other rope slackened a little, but then settled back to where it was. The tree moaned as it leaned farther toward the house. I chopped harder than ever and somehow more accurately.

"Rev it up!" I shouted. "Don't stop!"

Ralston managed to get better control of the car as a tractor. There was less flying debris, a higher note to the wind strumming the towrope, more slack in the other rope. I thought I could see the tree slowly heaving upright.

Then, a deep, final crack. The tree was turning and tipping at the same time. I stumbled away as fast as I could, away from the tree, away from the car, away from the house. The car revved to shrieking RPM, and then came the sustained popping crash of a falling tree.

At that moment, the wind paused. The car was silent. I turned and limped back the way I'd come. The tree was down all right, and nowhere near the house. It had landed right on top of the car. "Rals! Rals!"

A big limb lay across the roof, its stump piercing the car's rear window into the back seat. But other than for the dented roof and broken window, the cab seemed intact. I yanked on the passenger-side door, which opened with a groan of protest. He was in the driver's seat, his eyes closed. "Rals! You all right?"

He opened his eyes. "The house?"

"Missed it completely."

"Fuckin' A, bro'."

"You okay?"

284

He twisted his head from side to side, flexed his hands and feet, wiggled his butt. "Guess it missed me, too."

The wind slammed into us again and it began to rain even harder. I stepped out of the car. "Let's get inside." He fumbled with the door handle but couldn't get it open. "Come out this way," I said.

He looked at me across the center console and passenger seat as if I were miles away. "I think I'll stay here awhile."

I got back in and managed to pull the door nearly shut. "You hurt somewhere?"

He took a deep breath and seemed to have some trouble letting it back out. He patted his chest. "Fucker's pissed with me."

"Fucker?"

"Heart."

"How do you know? Maybe you're just tired."

"Not the first time."

"Jesus Christ!" I jumped out of the car. "I'll call nine-one-one." I dashed off then turned around and came back. "You have medicine here?" Rals shook his head.

In the house, I grabbed my cell phone and dialed. Even if I got New York's 911 instead of the local one, maybe they'd patch me through. Call failed. "Damn!" Same outcome with Ritz's number. I found Ralston's phone, but couldn't get through on it, either.

I hobbled back to the car with both phones. "What will help?"

"Whole bottle of aspirin, shitload of water."

I got the water and aspirin. I squinted to read the label but couldn't. "Glove compartment," he said.

I opened it and found three pairs of glasses with the price tags still attached. I jammed one onto my face. "It says one to two tablets." I handed him four, which he swallowed with water. "That's all you get. How are you doing now?"

"Just feel weak." He rolled his left shoulder. "Kind of aches. Not from the chopping. Inside."

I tried the calls again: nothing. I felt his wrist for a pulse. It seemed fast, weak, and a little irregular, but how would I know? "You never told me you had a heart attack."

"All those cream sauces, foie gras, and rich French pussy, goes with the territory. I tried the red wine cure, believe me."

"Why didn't you tell me? Why didn't you tell Martine?"

"Why didn't you tell me you were sending Ritz in?"

Finally, out in the open. "I wanted to surprise you."

Ralston tapped his chest. "Back at you."

"Drink some more water." He did, then coughed with the last mouthful. "Take it easy," I said.

He flexed his shoulders and winced. "That look Opal gave you. You ball her?"

Why lie? For Walter's sake? Or why not? "No."

"Me neither." I had to laugh. "I never balled Ritz either," he said.

My heart lunged at the sudden bright hope, which surprised and disappointed me. I'd jumped off that cliff and wanted to stay off it. "Until last night, you mean."

"Until last night. Thanks, man."

"I didn't do it for you."

"Of course not. You did it for Ritz."

I laughed again, and then once more at the fact I could laugh about it.

"I never balled any girl who meant shit to you," Rals said. "Lena."

"Only fooled around a little, just for the company of it. And because she needed a little loving. She would have balled me, but I didn't. You're the one who fucked Lena, remember? When she was the girlfriend of the guy who got you into PMP. Took her off to London with you."

The young man with bright eyes in the 96th Street subway station, spiritual kinship recognized, the invitation to follow him across Central Park for the free introductory PMP seminar, which he led, with his impressive assistant Lena. It began with a betrayal, and ended with one—or two, or three.

London. Lena saying little the night before, not unusual these days. At work, PMP's international director storms in, throws a magazine at me. Another hatchet job by the press in smirking prose. This one has the inside scoop, the techniques, the organization, the money. All too obvious who the informant must be. I'm given ten minutes to pack up my stuff and get out forever. An excuse for the international board to finally get rid of the troublemaker.

Back at home I ask her, "How could you do that?"

"Easy." Eyes red and face wet with tears, Lena already packed. "Blame me all you want, it was Ralston's idea, he even had the reporter's name and number."

Ralston answers the phone in Paris. I scream at him until my throat is so raw I have a coughing fit. "Still mad at me?" he says. "Hey, just saving you from yourself."

I've got to get out of here.

Ralston had his fingers on his wrist, checking his pulse. "And I'll tell you something else. I didn't ball that girl in Spain, what was her name, Chrissie."

I nodded at his wrist. "Everything okay?"

"Still ticking away."

"Bullshit, I found you in the sack with her."

"You see me fuck her?"

"I saw hickeys all over her neck and tits and thighs. She reeked of sex."

"You've seen dozens of my women, you ever see a mark on any of them? That's macho bullshit. I didn't say she didn't get fucked, I said I didn't fuck her."

"The second gunman theory."

"Why would I lie to you now?"

"What do you mean, now? Why are you telling me all this?"

"Who else would I tell?" He lifted a hand an inch or two toward the storm. "There's nothing fucking else to do."

"Hang in there, mate, someone's bound to pitch up soon."

"I say there, old bean, you're into that lying limey lingo again. No one's coming."

I tried the phones; still no luck. "Here, drink some more water."

Ralston took a sip. "John Pujutoki was fucking her."

"No kidding? Figures. So that's why she said it wasn't your fault."

"What wasn't my fault?"

I leaned in for a closer look. "Rals, you okay? Do you remember what we were just talking about?"

"Hey, man." He slowly shook his head. "It's you who don't know what we're talking about. What else did Chrissie say about all that?"

"Something like it wasn't her fault either. Which I always wondered about, it was such a dumb thing to say... There's something I don't know, isn't there?"

"That's the story of your life." Ralston shifted in his seat and settled back in. "But you're getting smarter in your old age." He wrinkled up his face and voice in imitation of an old Chinese sage. "The wise man knows when he doesn't know. One day after swimming? I called out John Pujutoki about fucking Chrissie while you were off on his wild-goose chases. Up on the high rocks above the cove? He tried one of those pujutoki moves on me and slipped and fell off. Low tide. More smash than splash."

"Fell off—down into the cove? Killed? I thought he just— why didn't you tell me?"

"You wouldn't listen."

"I mean about his going off the rocks, the whole story."

"No one could know Chrissie was balling him, including you."

"Why not?"

He raised an eyebrow. "Think about it."

What would I have done? "Because if his body ever washed up, the cops would start looking for someone who might have wanted to kill him. And in Franco's Spain, they would have stopped at the first foreign hippie who vaguely fit the profile."

"Smarter and smarter."

"But how did Chrissie know he fell off the cliff?"

"One more time, Sherlock."

"You three were swimming together, she was up there with him. And no one could find out about that, either."

"I didn't have time to sweet-talk my way into her bed, and with those hickeys, you'd know she was fucking somebody."

"So you and Chrissie…?"

"Ganged up on you to save your ass."

"And made yourself the number-one suspect because everyone knew you hated him."

"Hey, still mad at me?"

"I'll tell you, I am a little, even after all these years."

He winced and rolled his left shoulder.

"Be right back." I geezer-trotted out to the road, strained to see headlights anywhere, tried the phones again, and stumbled back against the wind. "You could have told me as soon as we left the island."

"And let you blame me for killing your precious guru?"

I held the water bottle to his lips. "He just...fell off?"

He grabbed the bottle with a shaky hand and took a gulp. "You think I pushed him?" His brow wrinkled into an innocent look. "Why would I do that?" He drank some more without taking his eyes off mine. "You still think you're the moral one."

"I always felt like the sneaky one."

"Guess that does make you the moral one," he said. "That's all morality is, the feeling that Big Brother or Big Daddy is watching you. Doesn't mean you're better, just means you're chickenshit." He feebly backhanded my shoulder. "Hey, we can check off number two."

"You need to get to the toilet?"

"You're fucking hopeless. Becoming a man, number two on the list, go one-on-one with the elements."

"Hey, and we won. Sort of."

"Number eight, too. We chased them pussies off. The cops, too."

"Eight?"

"Face down a hostile group. You coming down with Alzheimer's or something?"

"Drink some more water."

Ralston drank. "I told you my father died."

"Let's change this subject."

"I took care of him his last couple of months."

"You didn't tell me that."

"I didn't want to talk about it, it was a mess." And yet he was bringing it up now. "He hated me," he said.

"He didn't hate you, you were just a wiseass punk kid."

"He hated me. I hated him. We both hated my having to change his stinking diapers and wipe his bloody ass. Point is, my father was my number nine."

"How do you figure?" I said. "Number nine is about facing the death of a loved one."

"A loved one can be someone you hate." I helped him drink some more water. "Jesus, I can do it myself. When they start being kind to you, you know you're on your last legs. My father had saved up these pills. I was going to just let him take them."

"You stopped him?"

He was checking his pulse again. "He'd hidden them in the attic years before and he couldn't get up there any longer. I had to go find them, bring them to him, and hand them to him one by one as he took them."

"Why did you take care of him?"

He turned away and closed his eyes. "What's it matter?"

"I want to know. Why? Why you?"

He opened his eyes. "Somebody had to, he had no one else, my stepmother had died, I wasn't going to ask Martine—who would have if I had. I don't know. Some things you just have to do. Like saving this shit-hole of a house. So if I croak—"

"Shut up, you're not going to croak."

"If I croak, I win. This'll be your number nine, but I've already done one through nine and this is my number ten."

"Cut the drama, you're not dying."

"Don't fuck up your number nine. You have to face my death, not pretend it isn't happening."

"Have it your way if it makes you feel better. You're on your deathbed."

"My death bucket seat." He looked around the car. "Not too bad. Comfortable, warm, I'm not lying in shit or choking on my own puke, no one's ripping my nuts off with a rusty pair of pliers."

"Far too cushy to count as a real number ten," I said. "Better hold out for something spectacularly messed up. Drink some more water." He managed another sip.

"Shit-hole of a house?" I said. "You put heart and soul into it, it must have meant something."

"I don't know from meaning. It just beckoned. Like your runty little monastery dude. Does that make my life a story?" His eyes closed. "Think I'll take a nap now."

"I'm not sure that's a good idea."

"Where'd you go to medical school? Staying awake's for concussions. Heart patients need their sleep."

"Right now, I'm your cardiologist, so do me a favor and stay awake."

I didn't want to leave him alone, but if I was feeling chilly in my damp clothes, he was sure to be. I hobbled to the house for sleeping bags. When I got back, Rals seemed asleep. I spread the sleeping bag over him and tucked it in around him.

He opened his eyes. "Sorry to have fucked up your life with this house."

"You had the right idea but the wrong bunch of people."

"It was a shitty idea. Was then, is now. Like your monastery and your psycho-meta-fizzle. Your Monkey Temple, my Monkey Temple. This ain't no world of ideas, it's a world of people, everybody messing with and being messed with by everybody we run into. Speaking of which…" He twisted slightly to look me in the eye. "What the hell are you doing? You conned Ritz into balling me."

"You balled her anyway."

"Fuck, yes. Far be it from me to stand in the way of whatever the fuck it is you're doing. But what the fuck is it you're doing?"

A lifetime of possessions, relationships, habits, comforts, prides, fears, hamster-wheel patterns of perception, thought, and feeling, compressing you from light to flesh to bone to stone to dust. When they're shattered, they leave you not in nirvana but naked, alone, and alive. And acutely aware of your worst defects. "A little re-landscaping."

"Slash-and-burn terrorist Buddhist rampage." He pulled his arms out from under the sleeping bag and tapped a gentle fist on my knee. "Sorry, man."

"Not your fault."

"All my bullshit. In Kathmandu, in London. In Spain."

"Hey, you were just saving me from myself."

"No, I wasn't."

Had he just said that, a genuine confession? He steadily met my gaze. The dread that had been pooling in my belly now filled my arms and legs. I looked out the window. No one was coming. I had to go find help. "Seems to be letting up a little."

"Bullshit."

I stumbled out to the road again. Still no lights. I shouted for help but had no hope of anyone hearing me. I tried both phones again but the calls didn't get through. One last check on Rals before heading out, maybe make him swallow another aspirin and more water.

When I got back to the car, he'd fallen asleep again, his fingers wrapped around his wrist over his pulse. I looked at him carefully. His chest seemed to be moving. I should probably just let him sleep—even without the heart attack he'd be exhausted. I closed the door as far as I could and set out at a trot. Gusts knocked me from side to side, driving rain forced my eyes to slits, and my wet clothes clumped together in my crotch and armpits.

A hundred yards down the road, I suddenly stopped. Was Ralston's chest moving because he was breathing or because the storm was rocking the car? I ran back.

He looked the same, eyes closed, fingers on his wrist. I put my ear to his chest but the damn wind was too loud. I couldn't find a pulse in the wrist or the carotid. I shook him. "Rals! Rals!"

That CPR course I'd taken after Freddy was born—how much could I remember? Check the airways: clear. Give him a lungful: lips-to-lips was weird, but the chest did inflate then deflate—but didn't continue to. Another lungful. I ripped the sleeping bag from his chest, kneeled on the passenger seat, positioned my hands as best I could remember, then realized he should be on a flat surface. I couldn't drag him out into the rain so I reached over him, reclined the driver's seat as far as it would go, repositioned my hands, and started pumping.

"One and two and three and four. Goddamn it, breathe! Six and seven."

After fifteen, two more lungfuls, then back to pumping.

"Come on." Pump. "You bastard." Pump. "Say something!" Pump. "One of your snide snappy…" Pump. "Come on, goddamn it!" Was I pumping too hard? Maybe not hard enough. "Damn it, Rals! Breathe, you bastard! Breathe!"

I suddenly remembered Walter's special antenna. While maintaining compressions with one hand, I grabbed my phone and dialed Walter's number. Two more lungsful for Rals. Mysterious icons appeared on the display, and then it rang: once, twice—a crackling "Hello?"

"Opal? Jules!" A hot silence came back. "Ralston had a heart attack! Call nine-one-one! The local one, not Walter's! We're at the house! I gave him aspirin!" Nothing but static, but the phone said we were still connected. "Opal! Did you hear me?"

"Where…"

"At the house! We're at the house! The Monkey Temple! I'm sorry, I was a shit! Please!"

The connection ended. I went back to work on Rals.

I was drenched in sweat and close to dropping when I realized I'd been doing CPR on him for at least half an hour. I stopped and checked for a pulse or any signs of breathing. None. Even if I could get the heart going again, by now his brain had turned to boloney.

I collapsed across my arms on his chest for a few moments. Then I wiped the tears and snot from my face, unfolded my legs, and slumped back onto the passenger seat.

Why hadn't I remembered Walter's antenna earlier, before I was pretty sure Rals was already dead? Was my brain, my heart, or whatever system that passes for free will ridding me of my final attachment?

Flashing red lights woke me up. Rals's head had turned a bit toward me. His eyes were half-open, his mouth agape. His arms and legs had stretched out and stiffened a little; it almost looked as if his fingers were reaching for his wrist again.

Had he felt his heart stop beating? How many seconds would he have had between the final beat and unconsciousness? Five, ten, thirty? Did he panic? No, because then his fingers wouldn't have still been on his wrist when I found him. He'd felt his heart stop and then calmly waited for death, thinking…what?

I pushed his mouth shut—he wouldn't want strangers to see him that way—and opened the car door. "Over here."

The paramedics didn't take long to examine Rals before putting him onto a stretcher and carrying him to their truck. One of them said something about a tree down across the road and a lot of calls that night. They asked me if I'd injured myself or needed any help. No. They didn't offer to let me ride along with them, nor did I ask to. I would stay with Rals's house one more night rather than follow his corpse away from it.

For a long time, I sat in the Great Hall's boarded-up blackness. Then I pushed myself to my feet and wandered through the house. I could find my way around in the dark quite well now. Though the wind was dying down, the Monkey Temple still moaned in the storm. Upstairs, I howled along with it until it brought me to tears. I could pull the banister down, kick holes in the drywall, smash the chandelier, take revenge on the house that had killed my best friend, driven away my wife, shoved me to the brink of bankruptcy, and turned me into a snake. But that wasn't at all what had happened.

In our bedroom—my bedroom—I sat down on the limp air mattress, then toppled backward and stared up at the ceiling. I tried harmonizing with the wind's whimpers, almost as if to comfort the house for the loss of its fallen champion, but the tears started again.

Chapter 25

I woke up. The wind and rain had stopped. A trickle of light worked its way into the bedroom, not around the boards on the windows but from inside, down the corridor.

My body felt as if a boulder had pounded it flat. I could move—a hand, a foot, then a leg—but each deviation from inertia brought pain. I sat up, bringing on more pain. With the light and the pain came a strange but familiar odor that reminded me of Rals. Of course, right then, in that house, everything reminded me of Rals. But this association quickly established its basis in fact: the tang of burning insulation. The power was back on, and so was the big chandelier.

I limped to the top of the stairs. The chandelier filled the Great Hall with a garishly triumphant glare and a thin but acrid bluish haze. From where I stood, I could see the switch, which Rals must have left in the ON position yesterday afternoon when he'd jiggled it. I hobbled stiff-legged down the stairs. The house might not be insured against the storm, but it was for fire. Had he deliberately left the switch on, in case he didn't survive the storm, to give me an out? Insulation fumes stung my eyes and throat. Did the Monkey Temple belong on my hit list?

The house might be Rals's attachment, but whatever happened, its destruction wouldn't be his decision. I flipped the chandelier off again, waited for the flames to appear or the smell to abate, and when I got the boring result, I went back to bed, where I curled up in my emptiness and fell asleep again.

When I came downstairs later that morning, I paused by the light switch and decided not to turn it back on, at least not yet.

This new morning, the first question I had to answer, now that the storm had passed and left me amid the ruins steaming in the sunshine, was whether I had simply gone nuts.

My inner landscape opened uncluttered before me with austere clarity, which was a bad sign, since true wackos most likely never feel nuts. More objectively, I probably hadn't completely flipped, because instead of sitting around gibbering, going catatonic, donning robes and setting out in search of disciples, or buying a rifle and scope, I tried to figure out how to deal with the catastrophe I'd brought on.

A vague unease set in. Did I need to do anything? I couldn't bring Rals back, and anyway, he'd seemed rather pleased with his exit. Might Ritz be better off without me? Neither Walter nor Opal needed me. Nor did Freddie. Nor did my clients.

What did I want? What did it matter? Besides, that's a treacherous question whose answer can never be trusted.

Matt came by to check the damage—some siding and a corner of the roof had been torn off in addition to water damage—and offered his condolences. He seemed more concerned about me than the threatened loss of the sale. I bummed a ride back to town with him, and he refused to accept reimbursement for the overseas call I had to make.

Martine wept uncontrollably and, based on Rals's account of their breakup, far longer than I expected. She didn't inquire about money or possessions but only asked me to send the ashes to her. I arranged the details with a local undertaker Matt recommended.

"Sorry to bring this up now," Matt said, "but Ralston's check cleared."

"Better send the money to his wife."

"Ex-wife. Your name is on the papers. I can refund you your check. He was pretty clear about the money, no strings attached."

A gift from beyond the grave? In the wrecked car yesterday, Rals hadn't brought it up. On the other hand, do you think about such details when you know you're dying? He might have but hadn't said anything about it one way or the other. Except he had, right here in Matt's office the day he signed the papers: whatever happened, the money belonged to the house.

"Send it to her," I said, and gave him the address.

The next morning, I heard a faint whirring cry from the edge of the woods near the shed. I crept close enough to see a baby bird, probably a starling, huddled at the base of a tree. I knew enough to back away—the bird had just fledged, and its parents would come by regularly to feed it. But when I checked on it an hour later, it was still there and its rasp had gotten fainter and more desperate. I sat down against the shed to wait.

After half an hour, still no parents. Maybe the storm had killed them or blown them too far away to find their way back. I knelt to look at the baby. It stared back at me.

Although I appreciated Ritz's love for birds and her passion to help them, I took a more philosophical view, nature's endless interweaving of life and death and all that poetic horseshit. But this little guy wasn't letting me off the hook so easily. Help me or I die.

I reached out a hand to pick him up, but before I could, the starling flittered its wings, hopped up on my wrist and walked-flew up my arm, rasping and gaping for food with last-ditch vigor.

"Hey, buddy, what do you eat?" Starlings? Insectivores. The bird tried to reach my shoulder, fell to the ground, and stood up screaming for food. I picked him up, went into the shed for a trowel, and came out into the woods to look for a dead log.

Dead log? I headed back toward the house. The dead live oak still lay where it fell. I jabbed the trowel into the rotten-est part and pried away a chunk of bark and spongy wood. Jackpot. I scooped some small creepy-crawlies onto the trowel and offered it to the bird, who just looked at me, beak vertical and wide open, and screeched louder.

I sat down on the ground, put the bird on my knee, picked up a grub and dropped it into the gaping maw. The beak seemed to close for the tiniest fraction of a second, the grub disappeared, and the bird continued its cry. Had I dropped it? I tried again, with the same result.

When I ran out of grubs, I tried a tiny beetle, which the starling spat out with a quick shake of its head. All right, more grubs. I dug out some more, and after a dozen or so, it stopped gaping, stood unsteadily for a few moments, then dropped to its belly and closed its eyes. Had I killed it? When I cradled it in my hand, it opened its eyes, murmured a tiny peep, and nodded off again. Poor little guy must be exhausted.

I made it a nest from a box and some paper towels, which I set back under the tree where I'd found it, but still no parents, even when it woke up an hour later and screamed for its next meal. I brought it into the Great Hall for the night.

Its cries, worse than Freddy's, woke me up at dawn the next day, and when I went downstairs, it had already flown out of its nest and now dogged me, with wing-assisted hops along the floor, until I sat down to feed it.

Matt sent over a couple of guys to remove the plywood from the windows, at the owner's expense. It took them less than an hour. Once it was all down on the ground, I helped them pull the remaining nails and stack the wood in the shed. Sunlight again flowed through the Monkey Temple.

A couple of days later, Matt stopped by again. The Monkey Temple floated in limbo. The owners refused to give up the deal and authorize the return of my down payment, but after the storm damage, nor could they press ahead with the original contract. While they assessed the situation and reconsidered their options, he'd heard no objections to my staying there.

Stay here. I had unspooled my life. I could be ready to die—why not? There was nothing left. But here I was, in an unwelcome rebirth. Yet, something had happened.

I caught a ride with Matt and called Ritz to tell her about Ralston.

"Oh no! The newspaper didn't say anything about anybody dying. That's awful! Oh, god." She started to weep. "Was he in a lot of pain?"

"No."

"He didn't do it himself, did he?"

"Not exactly. The storm didn't kill him, fighting it did. His heart."

"Are you all right?"

"Remember that story in *National Geographic* about the old Indian who spoke only his tribe's language? The children all learned and spoke English, and one by one the older ones died, leaving him with no one on earth he could talk to. There are whole parts of my life now I have no other witness to."

301

"I meant physically."

"Oh. I'm fine."

This was where we'd either hang up or press further into recrimination or peacemaking.

"So, was Rals better than me in bed?"

Silence on the other end. Then a laugh that ended in a snuffle of tears. "He only wanted to talk," she said. "Just curl up and hold me and talk. And that's what we did, for hours."

"That's not what he told me before he died."

"You think he'd tell you something like that?"

Again, a stab of disappointment. I'd gotten over my pain about the thought of Ritz making love with another man, especially Ralston, and now I felt I'd somehow cheated Rals, let him die without fulfilling one last decades-long desire.

"But you sent me in there on a mission," she said. "God knows why, I never will. And I didn't fail."

"So you...?"

"And by the dawn's early light, a second time too."

A residual pang. And a rush of satisfaction. Bon voyage, old buddy.

"If you must know," she said, "he was tender and sweet." She was rubbing it in. "No macho stuff, just gentle. Loving." You could hardly blame her.

I took a deep breath. "What you said when you left. You were right. I did do it for Rals. All of it. Right down to boarding up the windows and chopping down the tree. The whole trip. The Monkey Temple. And it felt good."

She didn't say anything.

"I don't know if he deserved it," I said, "and I don't know if that matters. But the thing is, it was always Jules and Ralston, and he was always the asshole."

"So you suddenly had some karmic need to become him?" Her gibe smacked me as a serious question. I'd think about it later.

"When you got so mad at me and left," I said, "it hit me. All the things he would get into, no matter how badly he screwed up, he always thought he was trying to make the world better, trying to help someone. He might have been the asshole in the family, but I was the selfish jerk. Always have been, even if I cloaked it in some kind of introverted spiritual miasma."

"I'm selfish too, we all are, we have to be."

"Being a teacher may earn you a living, but you also do it to help the kids. You help birds for free. I've never done anything just for the sake of helping someone. Except, in these past few weeks, Ralston."

"Is that your new big answer? Other people?"

"I'm not even sure anymore if there's a big question."

She paused for a few moments then came back in a softer tone. "For a crash course in putting up with someone long enough to help them, you couldn't have had a better coach."

Ritz had hired a lawyer to block the apartment sale, which as well as bringing on the threat of a countersuit, elicited a carrot. The prospective buyers harbored no hope that the feuding couple would ever agree to anything, but they'd also learned through their own portfolios of divorces never to underestimate the power of spousal spite. They offered Ritz another twenty thousand under the table to let the existing contract stand. She accepted. She didn't have to tell me about it, but she did. I laughed.

I asked her advice about the baby bird. After she gave it, I told her I missed her.

"Good luck with the starling," she said.

I checked my email at Matt's office. Adele had sent me a reply.

> Jules, lover, don't be silly. Louche LeClerc is an old friend and he's been bugging me for years for a book. I refuse to give him some piece of shit. Now sober up or pull your pants up or whatever you have to do and get back to work. See attachment.

That all seemed so long ago now.

The following day, the little starling learned to pick up and eat the grubs I scattered at its feet, and a couple of mornings later, out in the yard, it tracked down and ate its first solo kill, a caterpillar. That afternoon, it fluttered up to the jagged stump of the broken porch rail and let out a harsh, defiant yell.

Little on this earth is more helplessly ignorant than an orphaned baby bird. Yet this one flew into the world with such gusto, such naked, demanding courage, such a rage for life. Opal would probably have said this little guy might be Rals reincarnated.

Up in Ralston's room, there wasn't much sign he'd ever lived there. A few clothes scattered around, and his limp, tired backpack with a few more clothes. No books, no photos, no mementoes, no sentimental trinkets like a wedding ring.

The pack's front pouch held the only possession that still seemed to have some life left in it, his swollen address book. First, I looked up myself, a three-page life history in crossed-out addresses and phone numbers of progressively diminishing sizes crammed together and then surrounded by more of the same wedged in every which way between the older ones and the frayed edges of the paper.

Then I started again at the beginning of the book. Some names I'd never heard before, parts of Ralston's life I wasn't connected to. Others I recognized, and faces would murkily emerge, or pop out suddenly, from the haze of memory. People I'd once thought of as friends and then forgot. A world of people. Ralston hadn't forgotten, or at least made an effort not to. People I could imagine again as friends. People who, like me, might need a friend or two, or at least wanted to end life with a bang, not a whimper.

I climbed down into the basement and unscrewed the fuse to the chandelier.

It really wasn't such a bad idea.

Acknowledgements

I worked at this novel off and on for many years, and it charged, burrowed, and staggered through a number of drafts. I would like to thank those who read the various versions and offered comments and encouragement. In as close to chronological order as I can piece together, they include Trevor Meldal-Johnsen, Renni Browne, Patrick Cooperman, Ross Browne, Rita McMahon, Amy Tipton, Jocelyn Giannini, Andrea Somberg, Nathan Gonzalez, Andy Hilleman, Jack Hoyer, Julie Miller, Kate Johnson, Jane Ryder, and Tony Cohan. My apologies to anyone I forgot. I also thank Stevan Nikolic and Adelaide Books for taking a chance on publishing it.

About the Author

Peter Gelfan was born in New York City, grew up in New Haven and the New York City suburbs, and attended Haverford College until he turned on, tuned in, and dropped out. He has traveled widely and lived in Spain, England, Florida, and Vermont. *Found Objects*, his debut novel, was published in 2013. He co-wrote the screenplay for *Cargo, les Hommes Perdus*, which was produced and released in France in 2010. He lives with his wife, Rita McMahon, in New York City, where he continues to write, work as a freelance book editor, and tutor writing in a public high school as part of PEN's Writers in the Schools program.